Gone Where the Goblins Go

a novel

Matt Betts

Print Edition ISBN: 978-1-958370-11-7
E-book edition ISBN: 978-1-958370-10-0

Manta Press, Ltd.
www.mantapress.com

Cover Design by Creative Paramita

First Edition

Dedication

Dedicated to all the writers who give their time freely to other writers. Thanks for your willingness to answer questions, offer advice, mentor new writers, and field quick phone calls to talk newbies off the WIP ledge. You make the publishing world a little better every day.

Welcome to Hōfuna Asia Conservancy. We are happy to have you join us on our journey of preservation and love for all creatures throughout Asia. Established in 1997, Hōfuna, or HAC, is a non-profit, wildlife conservation organization. The mission of Hōfuna is to save endangered and on-the-brink creatures of all genus and species. A large part of our quest focuses on legal and physical efforts to end the destruction of habitat, intervention to stop slaughter of wildlife due to poaching and overhunting, and efforts to increase corporate responsibility throughout the region. A second effort by Hōfuna is to ensure the survival of endangered creatures by collecting a sampling of those animals to house in zoos and private sanctuaries for the express purpose of breeding and repopulation. When a physical specimen is not possible, Hōfuna collects tissue or blood samples, remains, or any other matter our researchers believe might potentially assist in cloning or repopulation efforts in the future. Hōfuna uses innovative methods to investigate and document illegal activities concerning the Asian animal populations, and provide local governments with legal aid, private security, and investigation services, whenever needed. By championing these amazing creatures, their ecosystems, and our own environment, Hōfuna believes future generations will reap the benefits of a diverse Asia.

Your support makes it happen.

Hōfuna.

Giving Life A Fighting Chance.

CHAPTER ONE

Across the table, Mister Harrison clicked a button and a soft blue light projected onto Tilly's face. She shielded her eyes until she grew used to it.

"This is a simple version of the Montpelier/Foxfield Lie Detector and Situational Reaction Analyzer," Harrison said. "There's no right or wrong answer here. So, relax."

In Tilly's experience, no test with the words 'lie detector' in it was just for funsies. "Of course."

"You're aware you need to pass a drug test and background check pursuant to any hiring decision we make, yes?" one woman asked.

Tilly nodded. Her employment record was spotless, and she knew people who could help her pass any sort of drug test they threw at her.

"Are you now, or have you ever been, a robot?" Harrison flipped a page on his pad and then looked up at Tilly. "This includes droids, androids, automatons, windup constructs, ummm… murderbots, deathbots, war wagons, tin men."

"What?" This was a new one to Tilly. "Are there androids out there that look like people?"

Harrison looked puzzled. "I don't know. This is only a baseline question we ask. To see how you react."

Tilly laughed. "That's weird."

"So?"

"Oh, you want an answer anyway? Okay." Tilly thought about the nonsensical question in earnest to make sure she wasn't caught in some kind of lie. "I had surgery on my leg and had to have a pin put in a long time ago, but it's not mechanical in any way. So, no. I'm not a robot of any kind."

"That's your answer, then? *No?*"

Tilly nodded. "Correct." Harrison looked back at his pad. Tilly assumed he was looking for the next question, or assessing her response to the first. The smell of lilacs and fresh fruit filled the room, though neither of those things was anywhere in sight. Was the smell coming from a perfume one member of the interview panel was wearing? It was a little overpowering for her taste, but then she never wore any herself.

"Miss Coleman?"

"I'm so sorry. Could you repeat your question? I didn't catch it."

"Not at all. Happy to repeat it. Out of curiosity, what brought you to Japan originally?" Harrison asked.

"My father moved near a city called Shimabara some years ago," Tilly said. "I never understood why. I guess he liked the view of Mount Unzen. He didn't really explain."

"Moved from the United States?"

"Yes."

"I see." From his accent, Tilly guessed Harrison to be British. His mannerisms were reserved and proper, which also equated to British from her experience. The assumption made sense, as Hōfuna was partly owned by a company from the United Kingdom, Telford Biotech. According to Tilly's job research, the Brits created Hōfuna with a Japanese conservation firm.

One woman in the room broke the silence that followed. "I think he's trying to be delicate in asking about your employment gap." This woman was Japanese, but kind enough to speak English for Tilly.

Harrison nodded. "Yes. Please, don't get us wrong. Your qualifications are impeccable, but there is a matter of this unexplained period." He trailed off again, polite, and soft spoken.

"I understand. I was given a discharge from the military to take care of my father. *Cancer*. A family dependency discharge, they call it. His health was failing, and I was told there weren't many people who would handle him with his particular ailments, and he wasn't wealthy enough to afford a full-time nurse or home care attendant. So, I came to Japan to do what I could."

Harrison nodded. “I see. And when was this?”

“About six years ago.”

“I am sorry to hear his illness was prolonged so much.”

Tilly thanked him. “I appreciate it. He’d been battling the illness for some time.”

“It must have been a trying experience for you to have to care for him like that so unexpectedly. I’m sorry for your loss.”

With a shrug, Tilly said, “It was tough. I didn’t mind watching out for him, but he could be… opinionated. The man could start an argument in an empty house, if you know what I mean.” She laughed, but she could see they clearly didn’t understand what she meant. “He liked to talk, I guess.”

The woman on the other side of the table spoke again. “I see. So, *if I may*, what have you been doing since then?” She didn’t look up, instead she stared at a paper copy of Tilly’s CV. They all had paper copies, except Harrison, who used an old tablet.

The light from the machine flickered a different color and Tilly couldn’t help but flinch. “Do we still need this thing?”

“Yes, only a few more responses we need to record with it,” Harrison said. “Now, what have you been doing since your father died?”

“He had a business he ran with a friend. I had to help keep it going for a time and then, after he died, I had to close up his affairs, sell off his portion of the company. Things of that nature.”

The woman conferred with the men around her and they all checked their copies of Tilly’s resume. “What sort of business was it, if we may inquire?”

“Kites. He made kites. Big ones. Small ones. All kinds of kites.” She shrugged, embarrassed. She had the urge to explain she didn’t play with kites, like a child, rather she helped manufacture and sell kites. As she was debating the distinction in her head, the thought died and she decided to just stop talking.

While she waited for their next question, she gazed around the room, taking in the tacky dark wood paneling that looked like something from 1970s America. The few framed pictures on the wall were of buildings Telford Biotech owned—A factory in Hong

Kong, an office building in the UK.

Near the woman at the other side of the room, a small cart held a lovely silver tea set which seemed out of place compared to the rest of the decor; something nice among the cheap. At the end of the tables, six people—two women and four men—sat as far away from her as the room would allow. Harrison was next to her, pen in hand, notecards with neatly printed questions on them and his black tablet alongside them. A round, white clock above the door ticked away in the silence.

"You speak Japanese." It was the same woman again.

Tilly paused, not sure if it was a question or a statement. "Yes. I'm not entirely sure you'd call me fluent, but I get by. I picked up much of it from customers and coworkers at my father's shop."

"But not Chinese? This job would require travel to China." It sounded like an accusation from the woman. "They speak Chinese in China."

"Yes. *I've been there.* But I was told there would be a translator along to help with the language. The job posting mention it, I believe."

Harrison smiled. "Yes, you're correct. It's absolutely not a problem. None whatsoever. We'd love it if our hire could speak Mandarin or another dialect, but it isn't a requirement. To be honest, there are now so many English-speaking parties set up along the Huang He it may not even come into play." He smiled and looked at the others for further questions or guidance. "The Chinese people are actually fairly rare along the route we're taking."

China was once a place of nearly two billion people, and the possibility they may not see many as they progressed up the Huang He was startling to Tilly. Her time in the country during the war brought her face-to-face with Chinese soldiers and civilians on a daily, even hourly basis, some working for the rebels, others defending their country, and still more working in advisory positions for the various governments scrapping for their piece of the crumbling empire and their hunk of land from the spoils of war.

"Ever kill anyone?"

Tilly sat up straighter, almost sure she'd heard wrong. "Pardon?"

"Did you kill anyone during your military service?"

Tilly wasn't sure if it was an appropriate question to ask anyone, let alone a job candidate, but she was positive she didn't feel like answering it. "I flew a lot of missions like supply runs, troop allocation, things of that nature." Tilly nodded slightly. "But yes, I did have to support the soldiers on the ground with suppression fire, bombing campaigns, the like."

"And people died?"

"I'm sure." There was silence in the room, and Tilly anticipated the woman would follow up for clarification, might ask for details, numbers. These would be things she'd politely decline to discuss. She flew a transport, she flew. She wasn't a gun monkey cutting notches on her belt.

Harrison carefully clicked a button on the panel next to him and the light flickered off. He cleared his throat and shuffled her resume pages. "You are aware of Hōfuna's purpose and our company's programs?"

Tilly smiled. "I have a good idea of the basics." She'd waited in the reception area for nearly an hour with nothing to do but watch the company's three-minute promotional video on a loop. She was interested at first, but after the fourth time, she was done with it. "Conservation, mostly? A focus on legal and real-world efforts to save Asian animals and protect them for the future." It was almost burned in her brain after listening to the video a few times. "So... saving endangered species?"

"Yes. Spot on. We actually have a terrific short video we could show you to explain it."

Her hand shot up faster than she meant it to. "No. No need. I think it was playing out in the lobby."

"Oh, right. That saves a bit of time, then," Harrison said. "If you recall from the video, a big part of our efforts is getting out in the rivers, forests, and mountains to find endangered animals, collect them and their DNA. In the film you may have seen a large structure that looks a bit like a, I don't know, like a huge Yo-Yo on its side." He produced a picture and slid it to Tilly. "It's called a Waterway Explorer and Laboratory, but we call it a WHEEL, so it's not such a mouthful. We use these floating labs all over the world. They can search about any waterway under their own power, anchor on nearly about any shore, and be self-sufficient for months, even years."

After staring at the photo for what she felt was a sufficient time, Tilly listened to Harrison's description dutifully before asking what she hoped wasn't too blunt of a manner. "Interesting. I assume this makes things easier for your group to do their studies and aid in their conservation efforts. But… What does this have to do with me? I'm no scientist and really know nothing about this type of science. I could barely keep a goldfish alive when I was a kid, I'm sad to say. So, I'm not sure where I fit in here. Your employment post mentioned needing a pilot. I mean, I assumed you needed someone to fly something."

"Yes, yes. You see, one of our WHEELs is missing," Harrison said. "In China. I suppose it would have been smarter to tell you up front."

It all came together for her then. Certainly, she'd put her combat time in China on her resume, as was the rest of her military career. There really wasn't much else on her C.V. "I see."

"Would you be averse to going back?"

She shook her head. "Back to China? No. I understand it's wildly different from when I was there. Things have settled down over there, for the most part. It's not the wild west it once was. So, what would you need a combat pilot for?"

"We're taking a pilot and a few soldiers, maybe a half a dozen of them, to search for our missing laboratory. You're correct, things have gotten better over there, but some parts of the country are not as settled as we'd like, so we thought it prudent to bring some escorts familiar with the area. We pursued your resume because we haven't found our pilot yet. The fact you have air and ground combat experience is a lucky bonus for us. The others in the team would be foot soldiers."

She wasn't sure if it was actually an intriguing proposition, or if she was only desperate to get out of civilian life. Tilly missed everything about the military-the discipline, the orderly nature, the day-to-day certainty of life, and flying was something she craved, like an addiction. As soon as she'd turned eighteen, Tilly blindly joined the army looking for adventure, and a way to ease her constant boredom back home. The Army gave her that and more, and when she transferred to the air cavalry, she felt something click for her. It would be more than okay with her to get a surge like that again.

"I'm terribly sorry. I haven't asked if you have questions for us. Is there anything you'd like to know from us? Concerns?" Harrison and the rest of the panel looked at her expectantly.

It was dizzying for Tilly. The return to the air was a thrill, but the concept of going back to China with a group of soldiers never entered her thoughts until he said it. She assumed when the message mentioned China, they'd be flying some sort of cargo runs to what was still officially the country of China, not some search and rescue mission in the still-unofficial areas taken by all the other countries. There was still free trade, though it was heavily monitored. Lumber, minerals, and other material came to Japan from Chinese and free providences with regularity. Japan returned the favor with electronics, manufactured goods and weapons to the high bidders.

"*If.*" The word lingered after she spoke it, as though it had come from someone else. In her mind, she'd already done all the deliberation she was going to do. "If you select me for this position, do you have an idea what kind of transport I'll be flying for you? I'm good with just about anything, but better with some aircraft than others."

"Sorry, we are still making transport decisions. We'd hoped it would be one of the new VTOLs from ExIne the United States has been using, but it's hard to know," Harrison said. "So, at this point, that's up in the air." He laughed, realizing he'd unintentionally made some sort of avionics joke. "*Up in the air*. Undecided."

Tilly chuckled for a moment at the humor in his reply.

"Any final questions for our candidate?" Hearing nothing from the dour group, Harrison clicked off the light, stood and thrust his hand toward Tilly. "Brilliant. Thank you so much for your time. We have truly enjoyed hearing your qualifications from you firsthand." He bowed as he shook her hand. "You will hear from us soon as to our selection process and our final decisions. Did you leave your hotel information with the front secretary?"

"Yes, and thank you. I enjoyed our discussion." Stilly wanted to ask some more questions of her own, something to show she was interested in the job, but it had been so long since she'd applied for a position, let alone interviewed for one, her mind drew a blank. She didn't get clarification on salary, or any benefits, though the term 'independent contractor' was thrown about a bit. "Thank you." Before she realized it, she was outside the dark conference room and standing on the pale red carpet in the hall. She felt a little of the tension subside from her shoulders, but her stomach suddenly rumbled, and she felt nauseous.

Have you ever killed anyone?

Tilly tried to shake the thought out of her consciousness.

"I can show you the way out," the receptionist startled Tilly from her thoughts. The woman smiled and stood ready to walk the twenty steps to the front door.

"Not necessary." Tilly walked down the hall with her small bag and turned at the corner, pushing open the glass doors there.

Once on the street, she walked two blocks from the building before allowing herself to take a deep breath and lean against the rough stone wall there. The ache in her gut had gotten worse in the few scant minutes since she left the building. She put her hands on her knees and inhaled again. She was afraid Telford Biotech might have cameras set up for security or surveillance of their employees and might even use them to watch her leave. She didn't want to risk anyone seeing how desperate she was to get the job. After some rapid breaths, she stood up straight.

Across the street, the sparkling lights of a convenience store twinkled in the afternoon shadows, and she followed their siren call.

She took the stairs up to her floor, remembering to avoid the elevator as it smelled like burnt chicken and pine cleaner since the day she arrived. Luckily, the building was only three stories, and her bags weren't heavy.

The *North Route* was more of a hostel than a hotel, offering inexpensive group rooms for travelers keeping their expenses down.

Tilly opted for a private room, which still included group lavatories and showers, but she was used to that after her time in the Army Air Corp. At least the private room allowed her the ability to prepare for the interview without competing for an area to get dressed, though she still had to wait for sink space when the time came to brush her teeth and wash her face.

The common area between the rooms was nearly empty. So late in the day, Tilly figured it was likely the other occupants were either out sightseeing or off to their next destination. It was fine by her, less noise, and more privacy in the toilets. She unlocked her door and pushed in.

Placing the liquor on the dresser next to the grapes and bread she'd been living off for the last few days, she dropped herself on the bed. Tilly watched the slowly rotating ceiling fan and listened to the traffic of the street and the harbor, not sure what else to do with herself. There was no way to know how the interview had gone; she was sure she was qualified to be their "pilot/soldier/military liaison," whatever it actually meant. And she knew damn well she needed to do something to make money and soon.

She spent three days in the room, hindered by a lack of funds and sudden rains that made it miserable to go out for even a simple walk to clear her mind. She drank, ate grapes and chunks of baguette, and slept. She charged her scratched and ragged NaNi, leaving it plugged in twenty-four/seven to make sure it was ready in case someone from Hōfuna called.

When her device finally buzzed one morning, Tilly dug around for a few seconds before discovering the NaNi beneath a pile of dirty clothes. It was the only device she'd ever owned, issued to her by the military and so woefully out of date they'd let her keep it when she left. It was scratched and dinged from combat, crashes, and brawls, but it still worked, for the most part.

She swept it to her ear and said, "Hello?" She sat up too quickly, and her head immediately ached like someone had punched her in the temple with brass knuckles.

"Good morning, this is Mister Harrison from Hōfuna. I was calling to follow up on our interview." His voice got quieter, and concern immediately came through. "Is now not a good time?"

She coughed a couple times, holding the device away from her mouth. "Yes. No. It is absolutely a good time. Now is good. I just… I just have a bit of a sore throat." She coughed again, trying to clear her voice.

"Are you ill? Are you still healthy and available for the position we discussed?"

"No, no. No big deal. The rain always does this to me," Tilly said. "I'm fine, really."

Mister Harrison paused a moment before simply saying they'd like to extend an offer to her. "If you would like," he said, "We could speak on Monday about the details like schedules, expectations and such. If it's convenient, we could meet here at the office again."

Warm relief washed over Tilly. "I would be happy to, Mister Harrison; I can come by first thing Monday morning." She didn't care so much what the expectations were, or anything else, only that it was money, and it was for flying. The thought of those things made her spine tingle.

"Brilliant. You're aware we would like to leave on the twenty-first. Monday of the following week, yes? Remind me again, you don't have to give anyone notice at a current job, do you?"

She inhaled, realizing how badly she reeked of pot and cheap wine. "No, sir, not a problem. Not at all."

When they were done talking, Tilly let herself relax and felt the strain of the last few weeks melt away. As she stared at the water stains on the ceiling, her NaNi buzzed on her arm. *"Would you like me to add your… appointment… to your social calendar?"*

It was only a few days away, but Tilly knew her track record of sleeping through about anything. "Sure, NaNi. Go for it." Her mouth tasted like the floor of a bar bathroom and she swallowed hard to rid herself of it.

"Appointment recorded. Would you like a reminder about your appointment?"

"No. Not necessary."

The sounds of the city drifted through the open window, and Tilly contemplated her few belongings strewn about the room, already mentally packing the things she needed, discarding what she didn't. There was a much shorter list of items to keep than there were to toss.

"Would you like to know the current time and air temperature in Nagasaki?" NaNi asked.

"No."

CHAPTER TWO

When she'd finished the paperwork in the office, they instructed Tilly to be ready for pickup outside her hotel at seven in the morning the next Monday. The salary was slightly better than she expected. It included bonuses for completing their objectives within various timelines, and an ominous clause for hazard pay, which included monetary compensation based on the level of injury and oddly specific dollar amounts for loss of certain body parts. Tilly skimmed the documents and signed them as quickly as she could. For some reason, she couldn't get her eyes to focus on the words on the tablet, and the more she stared at the lightly glowing pages, the more they seemed to melt into one big dark blob on the screen.

A human resource person sent a copy of the document to her NaNi and shook her hand. "Welcome aboard." The young lady said in Japanese. She was far too cheery for the time of day.

"*Domo arigato*," Tilly said. Mister Harrison wasn't around, so Tilly met instead with a team of six people who took turns peppering her with information and forms for everything from background checks to family history. Since they considered her an independent contractor, she needed to sign medical, dental, and mental health waivers. She didn't bother remembering anyone's name from the HR group. It was a onetime job, and she figured she wouldn't see any of them again.

When she was done, she returned to the same convenience store she had the last time, buying more expensive alcohol—bourbon, vodka, and some soda to mix it with. This time she got some proper food to make up for the weeks of green grapes and bread. Tofu, crisps and chocolate flew into her basket one after another, and then, on a whim, she bought a disposable razor and shaving gel. The items nearly wiped out her savings, but it felt good to celebrate.

Back in her room, she missed the girls who'd breezed through the hostel the previous week. She wanted to share her good fortune with someone, anyone, and the girls were sadly the closest thing she had to friends. Tilly looked at the NaNi on her wrist and thought of calling them. They'd giddily left their details and assured Tilly they'd stay in touch. They were long gone, though. The next day, they were scheduled to leave for their next stop, then the next, and so on, for at least another week.

It was barely past eleven in the morning, but Tilly poured a drink anyway. She drank and shoved her bare necessities into her battered duffle bag, and piled the rest into a box she found in the alley. It took all of ten minutes. After three more drinks and a handful of crisps, Tilly pulled out the gleaming razor and the cold can of shaving cream, shaking the latter absently in one hand. The plan was to shave her head back to the way it was back in the army - bare skin. But as she stared at herself in the mirror, another thought came to her and she sprayed some cream in her palm. She rubbed her hands together until the blue foam felt smooth and light, and then she spread it over the right side of her head. Her hair wasn't that long anyway, barely enough to pull it into a ponytail if she felt the need or the urge. The feel of the cream was soothing and calming on its own. Tilly laughed at herself and took another drink of warm bourbon. On her nightstand was a metal cup half-full of water, which she grabbed and spun the razor in. After a few passes, the sides of her head were bare. In the middle, the hair remained untouched. Tilly ran her hands over the smooth parts, feeling the soft skin there. She stared at it in the mirror and smiled as she bit a chunk off the chocolate bar.

When seven in the morning rolled around on the designated day, she was sitting on a bench, eating breakfast, and drinking orange juice.

"You Tilly Coleman?" A young Japanese man asked in fairly decent English.

She shoved the rest of her breakfast roll into her mouth, swallowed, and nodded. "Yes?"

"I'm here with Mister Harrison. Are you ready?" The man looked more like a college student than an employee for Hōfuna. He wore a torn denim jacket with hand-drawn anime characters down the sleeves, a white dress shirt under it, and tight black jeans with hiking boots. His hair was styled and gelled to the side like he was headed out on a date. He looked young enough to have been a recent graduate of a local high school, but she couldn't pin down an exact age.

"Sure. Yes, I'm ready to go." She wadded up her trash and tossed it in a public trash can nearby. When she went to grab her bag and backpack, she realized powdered sugar covered her hands. She quickly wiped them off on her pant legs, only to find her shirt and pants covered in it as well. She shook her shirt and patted her pants until she thought most of the offending substance was off, and grabbed her stuff.

She followed him around to the side street and he opened the back of a dark, slightly damaged SUV. Like its driver, it seemed a step or two down from what she'd expected her new employer would send. She tossed her bags in the back and moved to sit in the front seat before she noticed Harrison in the second row.

"Miss Coleman?" Harrison said. "You've changed your look a bit."

A deep breath, and Tilly replied, "Yeah. I thought if I was doing a military-style op, I'd shave my head again. But somewhere along the line, I decided I needed to hold on to a bit of my civilian freedom."

"So, you went with a mohawk, or I guess that's really a fucking *murder* hawk? Whatever it is, that shit is *hot*, and I feel you." The kid opened the door, climbed behind the wheel, and nodded for Tilly to sit in the passenger seat.

She could see Harrison shaking his head in the back as she got in. He looked amused as he laughed, and Tilly was thankful there wasn't some sort of dress code for this job. After all, she was an independent contractor.

"I'm Rei, by the way. I'll be your driver for the next few hours. My NaNi says it's about a three-hour drive. So let me know if there's any way I can make the trip more comfortable for you."

"Hey Rei, nice to meet you. Is that a J-model NaNi? I didn't know they were out yet."

"Yeah. It's great. Got it a couple of weeks ago. Light, flexible. Tell time, even. What do you have, an 'I'? Or an 'H' model?

"It's a little older. It's NaNi-C."

"Wow. I did not know those things still functioned. Didn't the manufacturer cut off support and updates for those years ago? Just... wow."

Tilly shrugged.

In the back seat, Harrison was already impatient. "Let's go. We have a lot of time on the road ahead of us."

"Well. Okay, well, let me know if either of you need a break, or you get hungry or something. I'm happy to stop," Rei said. "Happy to."

"Stellar." Harrison waved Rei on. "We'll pick up some more of the new hires along the way. I have to get two people as we get closer to Oshima Island."

Without meaning to, Tilly fell asleep before they even got out of Nagasaki proper. She vaguely remembered stopping once or twice along the way, but otherwise, the trip was a blank to her. She only opened her eyes and paid attention when Rei nudged her and called her name.

"What? What's going on?"

"We're here," Rei said. "Gate is right over there."

Pulling herself out of her slumber, Tilly looked around, surprised to see two more people in the far back seat, a man and a woman, both appeared to be as groggy as she felt. She followed Rei's gaze to find a gate at the end of a long row of rusty chain-link fence. Two men emerged from a small building as the beat-up vehicle approached. Behind those men, huge stacks of metal shipping containers rose to meet the sky, occasionally dwarfed by cranes and lifts. Beyond those, a couple of cargo ships blotted everything else out.

Rei pulled his sleeve back, revealing his shiny new social device. Tilly didn't care about her own, didn't need the latest tech. Lord knows she couldn't pay for it if she did, but she never understood the younger generation and their need for the latest toys. It usually applied to NaNis, cars, tablets, and anything else with a screen on it. She hadn't owned any entertainment larger than her NaNi in years, but many of her fellow soldiers in the war had bragged about their wall-length screens for movies and video games. Some even smuggled their roll-up screens into the barracks to play the latest Worldwide Role-Playing Interface in their off-hours.

Rei's fingers slid across the device, and the gate in front of them buzzed and then rattled open. As they drove in, the guards nodded and waved him on. The young man guided the car into a vast storage area along the fence line until they came to a maze of enormous shipping containers stacked three and four high. They were alternating shades of orange and blue, rusty and flaking. Rei turned and drove between the rows, seeming to move from memory until they'd been at it for what seemed like ten minutes. Soon after, Tilly discovered the smell of fresh salt air. "Come on, we have to be close to this thing, right? Otherwise, you're going to drive right into the ocean."

Rei laughed. "I wouldn't even try something like that. I can barely swim." He slowed down and turned to take them out of the containers, bringing them into an open area surrounded by the containers and a tall fence.

The empty lot ended at the ocean, bordered on the east by three large warehouses. And set off to the side was an enormous gray helicopter, so old Tilly had only read about the particular model in a textbook. The body was a modified and stitched up Sikorsky from decades past. She was sure it had to be there for scrap, or maybe it crashed there, and someone just left it.

"Holy shit." The others in the vehicle perked up to see what she was talking about. "No one's flown one of those in forever."

"No way. This can't be for us. It can't be," Tilly said.

"You mean that heap flies?" Rei asked.

Harrison leaned forward. "It better."

CHAPTER THREE

"Shit. I mean… *shit.* I thought this was maybe some kind of replica or something, you know? The kind of things rich, dumb collectors have restored to its former condition for bragging rights?" Tilly ran her hands over the rough and rusty hull of the helicopter and pulled away when she felt the rust that flaked away on her fingers. "But this really is an absolutely *shitty* aircraft. It's vintage, but not in a good way."

"It has *some* new parts in it. The engine has been updated to current industry standards. The exhaust is brand new. Instruments are up to code and the control kiosks are modern. We've packed it with more modern weapons and sensors. My people tell me it's state-of-the art. Mostly." Harrison pointed out the bits and pieces he was talking about as he walked around the enormous helicopter. "It's fine. It's a perfectly safe vehicle."

"But why?" Tilly asked. "I'm baffled as to why you'd pack all that good shit into this fucking cow's carcass? Why not update an older shuttle model? Maybe something with VTOL?" Technically, a helicopter could take off vertically and land the same, but most craft from the last twenty years used multiple rotors, allowing the aircraft more maneuverability and stability than a double rotor model. Tilly hadn't even seen an old-school helicopter in flight training. The military didn't use them for combat or literally anything else anymore.

"Look, it's what we have. If you can't do it, we'll find someone who can."

Tilly couldn't take her eyes off the old craft, but with a wave of her hand, she said, "Calm down. I said I could fly this, and I can. You updated the twin engines? They look like shiny versions of the old ones. I guess I didn't realize when you asked if I could fly it, you were making a dare of some kind. If I'm not wrong, this is a Sikorsky one forty-eight. *CH-148*, I think they were actually designated. A Cyclone like this was used by the Canadian navy, maybe? The Greeks used a variant of it in the twenty-thirties, I'm pretty sure? What? You couldn't get a hold of a Russian MI twenty-six?" While she'd never seen one up close, she'd studied helicopters in flight school. It was a requirement. Tilly climbed inside and into the cockpit. Harrison was right, the controls were much more familiar to her, more modern, more intuitive than an actual old-school copter would be. There was a co-pilot seat, but it seemed redundant, with most of the same readouts and controls. She adjusted the seat forward and fiddled with it until the back was straight, like she preferred.

"If you're all comfy, maybe we can load up and get ready to lift off. We want to be wheels-up in three hours," Harrison said as he leaned forward from the crew cabin. "I'll be in the copilot seat, so don't mess with the settings there. Okay?" He didn't listen for a response and walked back to the open side door.

At both doors were tripods and slings, where heavy machine guns could be mounted for in-flight use. Further back, she could see a stock of mortar-like rounds she assumed to be for bombing or launching at other craft. Harrison's little talk about finding their scientist and only bringing along a few people 'just in case' began to sound like bullshit to her. He was expecting some kind of trouble, but she didn't know what.

For fun, she leaned over and pulled the copilot seat all the way forward as far as it could go. Harrison would eat his knees when he got in. It was a small thing, but it made her happy.

Tilly felt a little nauseous as she walked around the old bird. It was, as far as she was concerned, a relic. From the outside, it smelled like petrol and rust.

"You're the one who has to fly this ugly thing?" Rei asked. "Good fucking luck." He leaned against the fuselage, half-smiling, almost posing as he put his foot on the outer step and leaned in to look at the cabin.

"Thanks, I sort of thought your company would spring for

something a little more modern... I don't know, *more advanced* than this."

"I heard them talking about logistics for other expeditions, and it sounds like some of the defense stations in China use detectors to follow the signature of modern engines. They aren't calibrated or programmed to follow the trail of shitty combustion engines as easily."

"That doesn't make sense," Tilly said as she stalked around the craft, noting the rust and the mismatched panels, the poor soldering work at the seams.

"The vapors emanating from the helicopter tend to match the chemicals in the clouds throughout China. The factories, the furnaces, all those things spew a mix of crap into the sky. It's an actual benefit of the blanket of pollution." Rei looked in the windows of the craft, but didn't seem to want to climb in. "There's a lot of shit in there. Glad you're not taking too many passengers."

Tilly turned her attention to the area Rei was referring to. "Shit." She found there were newer thirty caliber door guns mounted on each side, each fitted with EMP extensions. In the back was a wide workstation of new computer equipment linked by black cables to lidar and other scanning systems bolted near the doors. "Look at all of this." The new equipment and weapons had to have added a half a ton to the payload, easy.

Nearby, Harrison stared at the clipboard in his hand as he ambled toward the building nearby. Tilly tapped him on the shoulder. "Hey. Hey, Harrison."

"So, can you do it or not? In the interview, you said…"

"I can do it," Tilly said. "I can *definitely* do it."

"Good."

"But I need to know what happens after that."

"I'll brief you in a few moments with everyone else."

"Fine," Tilly said, "but the thing is super weighed down with all those guns and the extra equipment installed in the back. It changes a few things as far as cargo balance and whatnot. What do you think we'll need that stuff for?"

"We told you. The situation in China is more… *fluid* than we like. We need people with experience in combat and…"

"Why?"

"Miss Coleman, there could be any manner of dangers out there," Harrison said. "You know all about them from your time in the country: rebel armies, Chinese nationalists, American profiteers, the Koreans, Japanese treasure hunters, German jack-offs with surplus weapons and an urge to use them. We need people with survival skills and a familiarity with combat, and none of the armies of any of the nations are willing to help us at the moment. We leave in three hours. I'm assuming you're still in."

A deep breath gave Tilly a moment to consider her words. The money would be good, but the thought of the dangers, the vague perils Harrison alluded to, gave her pause. She'd fought various Chinese factions in the war against The Alliance of Asian Free People, and managed to come back in one piece, but she was a part of a real army then, not flying an ancient helicopter into the heart of the country with an unfamiliar crew. "Yes. Of course. I took the job. I said yes, right?" The helicopter sat on a wide-open area of the docks off the sound, situated between rows of orange shipping containers. "Why do we need to take off here? Wouldn't an airport be a little safer?"

Harrison raised his arms in frustration. "You have a lot of questions. Are you planning on doing this throughout the job?"

"I'm flying the helicopter. I need to know if we're going to ram into traffic as soon as we leave the ground, thus killing us all. Are there ships off the coast ready to cause us undue difficulty? I need to know if I'm trying to duck someone's radar to keep from getting arrested. Most of China is touchy about who enters their airspace right now. I need to know if someone might shoot at us for any number of reasons so we all can keep our blood inside our bodies if possible…"

"Okay. Point taken."

"No. Here's the point," Tilly said. "I'm generally a quiet person. I go with the flow and I'm good at following orders, but what I'm bad at is putting people in danger because someone has a secret or two. Tell me what I need to know, and I'll shut up real quick." Her hand shook a little at her side. She'd never dreamed of talking to a superior officer like that, but in the private sector, she might get away with it.

Harrison nodded silently. "Got it." He pointed to a large warehouse behind them. "We're going to meet up there in ten minutes and run through the flight plan with you and the others. I'll elaborate on what you need then. Fair enough?"

Tilly smiled. "Fair enough."

The nearly empty warehouse smelled like motor oil and burnt popcorn. Half the lights were out, except for a long line of them brightly illuminating a table toward the center. It seemed Tilly, Rei and Harrison were the last to arrive, as a handful of others were already gathered in the glow.

"Alright. Let's gather up. Introductions–These men are my team." Harrison pointed to the trio of men on one side of the table-including Rei. He was by far the youngest in the room. The other two men looked like security guards or hired local thugs of some sort. If Tilly had to guess, none of them had seen any military service. "They'll be operating the additional equipment we're using to trace our missing lab. Names are Hyatt, Decatur and Rei. They've worked for us previously and know how to handle themselves. On the other side of the table are our mission specialists, Ned, Saburo and Tilly. The three of them all have experience in China during the war, and Miss Coleman will act as our pilot on the trip." He elaborated no more, not even giving the full names of the others.

"We don't have much time to get all the shit done that needs done," Harrison said. The others settled themselves, looking up at Harrison and the screen he'd set up behind him on one side, and the easel on the other with a map of China. "You're all here for the same reason. We're headed into China to find a mobile research facility that stopped checking in when it should. Its mission was to explore the Huang He, or Yellow River." The screen behind him lit up and displayed a schematic of the lab. "This is WHEEL Sixteen."

The sheer size of the floating laboratory surprised Tilly. The picture she saw at the interview didn't do it justice. It looked like an enormous white and green hockey puck. Supplemental photos showed the prototype floating in what appeared to be the Thames, if she knew her bridges as well as she thought. It dwarfed the sailboats passing in the middle of the river, and it looked as if it might have a problem going under bridges if it wasn't careful.

From the looks of it, the scientists on the expedition had it better than in most four-star hotels. The upper floors had living quarters, a cafeteria, recreation facility, laundry. There was a small theater on the third level, ice machines, drink dispensers, the works. The middle floor contained labs and offices for the doctors, as well as another smaller barracks area for the half dozen security officers accompanying the lab on its journey. The lower level had cages, dozens of them, presumably for the animals they were rescuing.

"They built the WHEELs to help study the environment in several locations around the world. Telford Biotech is proud to be a partner with many other conservation efforts within governments and private sectors." A video flickered to life on the screen showing the Hōfuna corporation's efforts to save various endangered creatures around the world. There was no sound, so Harrison continued. "They built this one to search for animals on the brink of extinction and rescue any viable mating pairs. They are also trained and equipped to take samples, if rescuing the creatures isn't necessarily possible. In light of the recent turbulence throughout the region, the corporation felt it was urgent to send the lab into China to save whatever they could."

Thinking about the schematics, Tilly could only discern a few people responsible for defending the lab. There were no outer guns, missile launchers, lasers, or even so much as pointed sticks.

She apparently wasn't the only one who noticed. Ned spoke up and said, "They went up the Yellow River with only six guards? I mean, this was immediately after the war ended, right? Were they not expecting trouble?"

"Seems like a foregone conclusion at that point," Saburo said. The two smiled and punched fists. Saburo wore a cap with a blue and black camo pattern which the Navy had phased out decades ago. If the woman was formerly in the military, they hadn't issued her that cap.

"I wasn't involved with the prep for his expedition. Whatever their reasoning, they sent what they sent. Our job is to find them, yeah? Here's the breakdown. We're flying into the former Chinese territories to find this conservation team we've lost contact with. We'll fly across the Yellow Sea here." Harrison positioned the easel so the group could see it better, scraping its metal legs across the concrete with a high-pitched screech which made half the people at the table groan. A large map showed the route on a dotted line from their position in Japan, over the sea, and onto the Chinese mainland. "This area is fairly stable and quiet. It's neutral territory, and no one really gives a damn about it right now. The area could heat up in the future, depending on the NATO talks in Paris, but it's good for now."

"When you say it's 'good', do you mean you're not worried about the rebel factions, or the scavengers, or any automated defenses left behind, or do you mean 'good' like everything's been cleared out?" Saburo asked. "I mean, you hired me because I have experience in China, right? There were problems with piracy along the coast way back when I was in-country. I don't guess it got any better."

It took a moment to figure it out, but Tilly spoke up. "That's why we have a helicopter and why we're leaving from a shipping center in the middle of the night. The helicopter fumes give off a heat signature easily mistaken for the normal smog from factories and smokestacks, if I understand right. It should all cover our arrival to anyone who might be watching. Am I right, Mister Harrison?"

With a nod, Harrison said, "Correct. If anyone picks us up, we'll look like the rest of the crap clogging the skies. Doing it at night helps us keep our cover a little better."

Ned caught the importance of Tilly's comments. "So, we don't have permission to enter the Chinese airspace at *any* time, from *any* of the controlling nations, am I right? So, if anything happens along the way, we could be arrested? Or worse?"

"Let's not get dramatic. All of China is pretty much up for grabs, and none of the nations involved would want to see an incident ignite things again. Worst case, you'd be held for a couple of days and released once my company makes a few calls." Harrison shrugged. "Easy. We're just avoiding the usual permissions in order to get to our team faster. Okay?"

With no further dissension, Harrison continued. He pulled another map out and placed it in front of the first. "We'll follow a basic northerly course from there and land here to the south of Zhengzhou. There's an abandoned stadium there some of our contacts have been using as a base of operations. They're allowing us to refuel and rest for the night. They'll share their intel with us about the area and maybe even feed us."

"From there, we move north again to the river. We'll get there around the city of Wenxian, which is where they were last stationed. The last transmission from them reported they were moving upstream to a new position."

"Wenxian? That's not along the river, it's a little way inland," Tilly said. She'd remembered that much from her time in-country, at least.

"It is now." Harrison shrugged as if the discrepancy were no big deal. "The flooding there has been quite extensive."

"And how long ago was this?" Ned asked. "When were they last transmitted?" He'd been silent until then, squinting at the maps and screen.

"A little over two years."

"Why wait so long to go looking?"

Harrison looked annoyed by all the questions. "No idea. I didn't make the call. Not my job. The corporation felt the region was too unstable. They assumed the doctor was busy. They thought he could handle himself in the area. Pick one."

Saburo followed up by asking, "Do we even know if he's been attacked or killed out there? It's pretty rough in some areas."

"I *just* said I don't know what the situation is, didn't I?"

"What's your guess?" Ned asked.

"I don't have a guess. Any scenario is as good as the next."

Tilly sat back and wondered about the whole scenario. Why make it look like a job interview when all they needed was to hire a few street thugs or a group of mercenaries easily found on the streets or on the online dark exchanges? It wasn't illegal or hard to manage in a place like modern-day Japan. There were probably occupied regions in China where it could be done even cheaper. Harrison had gone to the trouble to actually ask standard interview questions and opinions, rather than asking what weapons they were proficient in, or how many confirmed kills they had. Looking back at her meeting about the job, it almost felt like they'd avoided proper questions deliberately. She considered Saburo. Surely a girl like her could handle herself in combat, but she wasn't what Tilly would consider the rough and tumble fighter-type most people looked for when they hired private protection or armed guards. Ned was certainly not the type either: scrawny arms, thin goatee. The kid, Rei? Not hardly a hardened killer. None of them made sense to her.

"And from there, we'll make our way up the river until we find them."

Ned shrugged. "Make our way upriver? I mean, isn't the Sanmenxia Dam about two hundred fifty or three hundred kilometers up the river from there? How the hell could they have made it further than that?"

"I was about to explain." Harrison laid a clear plastic sheet over the river map. "Toward the end of the war, the AFAT rebels began a campaign of bombing and destroying some of the major dams along the Yellow River. These did major damage to the river itself and changed its course. They caused intense flooding and destruction of the communities and businesses along the banks. With little warning, there was substantial loss of life in the towns and settlements in the path of the floods. Wiped away many military bases as well." The map overlay showed a significantly changed river. There were now wide areas where other rivers and lakes joined the Yellow and made what looked like an inland sea in a couple of places.

"Jesus," Ned said. "That gives us hundreds of additional kilometers to search for this hockey puck rather than what might have been a hundred to start with."

"Right, we're hoping to get lucky and find them quickly."

"I'm hoping to find a laundry bag full of weed and a million dollars in cash, but it's not likely," Saburo said.

Harrison glared at her. "It'll take as long as it takes." Saburo nodded back at him aimlessly and he continued. "Any actual questions?"

"Are we expected to engage with any locals on this little trip?" Ned asked.

"Engage?" Harrison looked lost.

"Engage. You know. Shoot? Are we going to be asked to shoot anyone on your little field trip?"

Still taken aback, Harrison said, "Shoot? No. No, we're not *expecting* you to shoot anyone."

"To be clear now, so there's no confusion when our bullocks are flapping in the breeze out there in the middle of nowhere," Ned said. "Are we *allowed* to shoot anyone who gets in our way out there?"

"I don't expect..."

Tilly interrupted to provide some clarity. "Usually in the field, we're told the rules of engagement by our commanding officer, you know? *'Don't shoot anyone'* or *'shoot when fired upon'* maybe *'never fire your weapon for any reason,'* shit of that nature. Dude is asking *now* what those rules are, so he doesn't have to stop and clarify those things if something goes wrong *out there*. Saves time in the middle of a sudden confrontation or conflict of ideologies."

"This isn't the military, okay? You are free to shoot when you feel... I don't know. When you feel threatened."

"You sure?" Ned asked, grinning.

"You're grown adults, yes. That's what I think. Shoot if you feel threatened."

It was a bad idea, and Tilly knew it right away. Of course, it left no room for doubt: *Fire away and ask questions later*. There are a lot of things a person can feel threatened by, she supposed.

"Great. That's settled. Let's run through one more thing." Harrison changed the slide on the screen to bring up a photo of an older man in a lab coat. "This is what Doctor Edward Oscar looks like. In case we somehow find him at a fueling stop or something. It's unlikely, but if there was difficulty with the WHEEL, maybe he left it for some reason." He clicked again to bring up a picture of a tall, overweight man with long hair and the start of a beard. "This is Seely Green, one of the lab assistants." Another change. "Here's Karen Ishe, another lab assistant." He continued through four assistants, two more researchers, the half dozen security, and a guidance crew of four. A total of seventeen living and working inside the massive laboratory.

"You're not just missing a doctor, then." Saburo asked. "It's an entire team. We're talking about the entire team here."

The annoyance in Harrison's voice was unmistakable. "Right. It's his entire group. But the doctor is the most important subject of this search. We want to bring him home more than the others. He's done so much for our corporation and is one of few minds in the world who can do what he does. He knows more about the DNA of various endangered species than every other expert in the world."

"What about the lab itself?" Saburo asked.

"We need files and other information from the lab, and it can all be downloaded onto a drive. We aren't trying to salvage the WHEEL, or bring it home, if that's what you're asking. Anything else? No? Let's get ready to go." He turned and walked away, leaving Rei to collect the laptop and the papers Harrison had left behind.

Tilly approached the young man as he tidied the table. "What's your role in this rescue mission? I doubt you were in the war. Little too young."

"Oh, no. I'm only the errand boy. Drive the truck. Load the crates." He held up some papers from the presentation. "Stack the notes and whatnot."

"Ever seen any combat?"

Rei shrugged. "Outside of video games? I'm a Beta tester for a couple of game companies. Ever play Scatter Sea Wars? I was the first to reach the admiral when that came out."

"So… no?" Tilly asked. "No actual fighting?"

"Nope. Haven't even punched a guy before. But it's cool. You guys are here, right? Should be a simple job for people with your skills." He paused and leaned closer to her. "Unless you want to back out? I mean, we don't have to go. Say *'fuck it'* and we could stay here. You and I could go out drinking tonight. My friends have a band, and we can go back to Nagasaki in the morning to see them play tomorrow night." As he got nearer, she noticed his eyes turn from light green to a shade of reddish violet.

His suggestion flattered Tilly and left her more than a little flustered. It was an offer, a proposition, a date of some sort. She wasn't sure if he was kidding or actually flirting with her. "As much as I would love to blow this off, I'm not sure if it's the best course of action for me here and now. Don't get me wrong..." He was likely ten years younger than she was, probably more, though age didn't really bother her. And if she didn't really need the money, she'd have given it serious thought.

Rei waved his hand at her. His pupils turned black quickly as he turned away. "No. I was kidding. There's no… There's no… I really need to finish cleaning up so I can help with the equipment load-in and get changed." His reddening face made her wonder even more if he was coming on to her. Some papers slipped from the kid's grasp, but he left them and acted as if he didn't notice. He stumbled off toward the lighted hallway. Tilly wondered who was more embarrassed, *her* or him. She took a moment to consider whether she'd misread his signals, but the expensive mood contact lenses in his eyes were hard to dispute. They'd turned traditional colors of amorous, then hurt. She decided she'd tread lightly when Rei was around.

CHAPTER FOUR

"Hello, you old, fat, tin foil bastard," Tilly whispered to the panel in front of her. "Feel like flying today?" The blades began to spin on the helicopter and Tilly studied the various gauges and readouts intently to make sure all systems were working the way they should. She familiarized herself with the location of each of the most important instruments so she could find them easily. As the rotors got up to speed, she felt a wobble that worried her. Despite Harrison's assurances they had fully fitted the aircraft with newer guidance and other systems, she wasn't so sure. The cockpit tactical display, flight management and communications systems seemed to work, which was good news for her and Harrison, as the two nesting themselves in the pilot seats. She scrolled through the info as the tactical workstation gathered it. The interior of the copter smelled like stale beer and petrol from the moment the rotors spun up. Harrison was unfazed and assured her it was normal, and merely a by-product of the air filters and sea air. Tilly was dubious. She took a permanent marker from her flight suit and drew a primitive bird on the console near the door for luck.

"Thinking of leaving soon?" Ned asked from the back. "I think I have to piss." It was enough to elicit a few chuckles from the others over the comm.

"Are we there yet?" Saburo asked. She looked around for some confirmation what she said was also funny and smiled when Ned bumped fists with her.

"Oh, sure. You folks are going to be a fucking barrel of laughs. Here we go." Tilly checked her foot placement on the anti-torque and guided the copter into the air slowly. It was nothing like the modern VTOLs. It felt like a fight from the first moment, like juggling a host of different skills while trying to forget a handful of others. "We are off like a herd of turtles."

The flight computer lit up and displayed a three-dimensional flight map and destination coordinates in a manner she was more familiar with, and she breathed a slight sigh of relief. The rest of Oshima Island became a list of new information, building heights, energy sources, lists of civilian defense gun emplacements, location, and speed of all aircraft for miles. She reminded herself not to get too comfortable with the dearth of knowledge. They were cleared to take on fuel at Jeju International Airport in South Korea, but after that it was only a matter of hours before they fell into The Moat, a zone of electromagnetic interference blanketing a long swath of China, deep into the middle of the country. No intelligence agency could figure out the sources or counter its effect. Aircraft flew without the luxury of satellite guidance or other long-distance communications. Speculation always fell to the Chinese government attempting to confound the original attacks on their country and the ongoing occupation.

In Tilly's experience, the best they could hope for is a line-of-sight radio or radar signals. It was a benefit for any clandestine missions during the war, as no one really saw aerial attacks coming, but it was hell for the pilots who had to fly them. Without the detailed flight information they were used to, they had to rely on their wits, reflexes, the breadcrumbs radar gave them. And a lot of good karma.

The copter settled into a grumpy rhythm and allowed Tilly to guide it where she wanted with minimal frustration. Once they left the last of the Japanese islands behind, they soared over the open water where the Sea of Japan and the East China Sea fed each other. In the back, the passengers had mostly fallen asleep. The only ones among them who appeared awake were Harrison's men, Decatur and Rei. Decatur read a book, or a manual of some sort, as he sat behind a computer array they'd loaded and hooked into the helicopter's system. It appeared Rei was alert, but staring out of one of the side portals at the sea below.

To her relief, Harrison himself was quiet in the seat next to her. She'd feared he'd be nosy about her flight choices, or too specific in how he wanted things done. Worse, she was worried he'd be a talker. She remembered her flight to Japan after her discharge. The woman next to her on the plane would simply not shut up. She told Tilly about her dogs (Schnoodles) and her kids (brats) and droned on about her job with the Kellogg's corporation in which she developed new packaging ideas. In a stroke of luck, Harrison was neither of those people. He asked occasional questions about procedure or what the objects were on the displays, but that was it. In fact, he stared out the front screen for long swaths of time, concentrating only on the skies ahead.

The airport in South Korea was possibly the friendliest she'd flown to. Harrison woke the team up and told them to hit the facilities. A small man with an orange helmet led them across the tarmac and into the building. He pointed out the lavatories to use while their helicopter refueled on the tarmac.

"I would think they'd at least check our papers or our identification before we could go in," Tilly said. "Security is shit here."

"We do a lot of business with them. They know me." Harrison pushed into the men's room before Tilly could even form the word *bullshit*. She knew very well a handshake and a smile never got anyone into a foreign airport in the history of air travel. Certainly not this close to China. She swallowed her comment and walked into the women's restrooms. She took a paper towel, wet it, and ran it over her head. An older woman came out of one stall and stared at Tilly while washing her hands. She smiled and spoke in Korean while shaking her head.

"Sorry, I don't understand."

"She says she thinks it's weird when women shave their head like you." Saburo walked in and stood by the sinks. "She thinks you look weird. Like a peacock or something with your hair."

"That's wonderful. I was hoping to hear what the locals thought of me." She dried her hands with the loud air dryer and smiled widely at the old woman. "Thank you." She bent over and stuck her head under the hot dryer, feeling the droplets of water zip down over her cheeks, chased by the torrent of wind from the rusty metal nozzle.

On the way back to the chopper, Tilly stopped and bought a couple of sodas, a chocolate bar and two bananas for the flight across the Yellow Sea into China. She shoved them into the pockets of her flight suit and headed for the door where they'd entered. The man with the orange helmet who had initially met them out on the tarmac sat on a stool nearby and nodded to her as she approached.

"Ready to start your preflight routine?" The man asked in English.

Tilly nodded. "If I hurry, maybe have time to take a quick nap before we're off and running."

"Good. Good. I have a strong feeling about you," he said. "Much stronger than the others. I'm sure you'll find what you seek." He opened the door for her and motioned her through.

"Thanks." Tilly was already outside and moving toward the Cyclone when the awkwardness of the Korean man's words struck her. Did he mean he liked her better than the rest of the team? It was merely something lost in the man's attempt at English, she was sure. And how much had Harrison shared with him? Why would he know what they were looking for?

Tilly managed a decent thirty-minute nap, awakened by the rest of the group piling in.

"Did you review the coordinates and landmarks I gave you? It sounds like a simple trip, don't you agree, Tina?" Harrison yanked on the harness and snapped himself in.

"Yep, and it's *Tilly*."

Back in the air, the Cyclone bucked and shook as Tilly struggled to keep the stick steady. A light sprinkle spawned a rogue thunderstorm from out of nowhere, defying the forecasts and reducing the already terrible visibility over the Hwang Hai or Yellow Sea. The notorious smog that smothered China like a blanket suddenly cropped up two miles from shore and intensified as the helicopter passed over Hangzhou Bay. It clung to them as they went over land. As they approached the general area of The Moat, she could see Harrison fidgeting with his paper maps and pens, marking routes and circling landmarks, preparing to lose digital online maps and directional assistance. She'd already programmed the route into the computer, and it would still guide them based on their direction and speed. It used a preset list of accurate enough directions, assuming they stayed on course. If they were to deviate, it would be useless.

"We're approaching the Chinese mainland." Harrison peered out his window as he announced it to the rest of the passengers. Tilly guessed he couldn't see anything but water for the moment with the rain all over the windows. "Everyone be on your toes. Communication is about to go down the shitter."

Below them was nothing but sea, and despite her best efforts, Tilly could see nothing but darkness. Not even the moon graced them with a sliver of light.

CHAPTER FIVE

Six Years Earlier

"Look, he's going to get better." Her father's friend and business partner, Hirata Sato, sat across from Tilly at the kitchen counter. He took a sip of his beer straight from the bottle.

"No. It's kind of you to say. I appreciate it. But why would I be here if that was going to happen?" Tilly said. "He will not get better. The doctors have said as much. You know it."

"I think the treatments are draining him, wearing him out. Once he gets used to them, he'll bounce back. He won't be in bed nearly as much. He'll get his lust for life back."

Lust for life. In all the eighteen years she'd lived with her father before she joined the army, she'd never exactly described him as having a lust for life. *A mild interest in breathing* was how she'd describe it if she had to. It was Tilly's turn to take a drink. She'd put hers in a glass out of some attempt at good manners. She finished the glass, leaving only a long line of foam sliding down the side. "Want another?"

"Still working on this one."

She opened another beer and poured it into the glass. "If he gets any better, it won't be enough to get him back to work. Certainly not full time. The doctors said it already. He's the backbone of this little business the two of you put together. Without him…"

"You've been practicing. You're getting good," Hirata said. "You could pick up a little of the slack, couldn't you?"

That was the idea. Tilly had left the Air Corps on a family hardship discharge so she could be with her father after his diagnosis. He'd scoffed at the idea of dying. Everything was a setback to him. Nothing was final, never permanent. When she first arrived in Japan, he looked fine. To her, he looked nothing like the frail and weak old man her military liaison had made him out to be. Her first instinct was she allowed herself to be pushed out of the military for nothing. A poor sentiment, she knew, but flying with the troops was all she knew then.

In the following weeks, she discovered the strange sense of normalcy was an act. Her father slept a lot, ate little, but kept up his stoic facade.

"I…" It was hard to figure out what to tell Hirata. He loved the business as much as her father did. "I'm proud of him for coming all the way to Japan, to Nagasaki. I mean, you both made this happen here." She took a deep breath and then another drink from her glass. "I've loved helping out, but I'm like a robot here. I can do the things you need, but it's a process. They're done by memory, not out of art or craftsmanship. I appreciate you think I'm good at this, but seriously, Hirata, none of my heart is in this." It made her chest tighten to say it. She couldn't imagine saying those words to her father. It was hard enough to say it to the man's best friend.

He was silent for a few moments, but it didn't appear to Tilly he was disappointed, though he'd always been hard to read. "I understand what you are telling me. Craft without heart is missing the most important aspect."

"That sounds vaguely like something from a fortune cookie."

"And *that* sounds vaguely racist."

Tilly stuttered to correct herself. "I didn't…"

"I'm kidding. It sounded a little too… perfect?" He laughed. "Maybe I heard it in a movie or something. Besides, fortune cookies aren't even Japanese. Or Chinese, for that matter. But I get it. If you're not doing what you love, it sucks. How's that?"

"Better."

"Did you know according to legend these kites, these tako, could fight off evil spirits? Tako came here to Japan from China in the Nara period in the seven hundreds and were mostly used in ceremonies and things then."

"Do you think the kites will save my father? Does *he* believe it? He's never explained his sudden interest in them. Maybe that's why." It sounded stupid her father might believe any such thing, that these kites would ward off evil spirits or cancer. He wouldn't allow himself to believe it, not after a lifetime of ignoring the unknown. He'd just as soon believe in the magic of sawing a woman in half or a legit card trick.

"Your father isn't a terribly religious or spiritual man; I think you know. If he is of the belief kites will stave off cancer, he's never conveyed the idea to me." He shook his head. "No, I think your father likes kites. Enjoys making things with his hands. Always a good enough reason, isn't it?"

"Well, he was allergic to church, so I doubt he moved to Japan because he started believing in ghosts and demons." Their neighborhood was primarily Baptist in South Carolina, and their neighbors were church-goers, but Henry Coleman quietly resisted their calls, wishing everyone well on their way to Sunday services, but choosing instead to sit at home and read the paper with his dog on his lap and a coffee on the end table. It didn't bother Tilly in the least. She never felt she was missing out on anything, and she used the extra hours on the weekend to read comics and watch cartoons.

"But do *you* think kites will ward off evil spirits and chase away the cancer?"

Hirada thought about it and smiled. "I don't suppose it would be any stranger than other shit people believe, would it?"

"Are you comparing God or Buddha to a kite?"

The older man laughed and held up his hands. "Did I say that?"

They sat in silence and finished their beers. The house was dark except for the lights of the city bleeding through the curtains as the night dragged on.

Before excusing himself to go home for the night, Hirata pulled on his coat and when they got to the door, he took both of Tilly's hands. "Look, I don't want you to stay if you don't want to. I'll look for an apprentice, or a fast study to take over. There's a trade school not far from here. Maybe a student would be interested in helping. Can you stay on in the meantime?"

"I'm here for my father, no matter how long it takes." She was sure it wasn't exactly what Hirada wanted to hear, but it was all she had at the moment.

When he was gone, Tilly sat on the couch and watched the lights of the air traffic over the harbor. She could tell which models of drones were which from the configuration and shape of their lights. The late-night shuttle crafts carried partiers from one bash to another, and the security forces took the ones that got out of control off to nearby police stations in the sleek white hovering vans with the red and blue lights on the top and bottom.

Next to the couch, her NaNi buzzed. The digital voice squawked at her, "It has been forty-three hours since you last logged practice time. It has been forty-three hours since…" Tilly tapped the 'dismiss' button on the device, and then lowered the volume, hoping the disturbance didn't wake her father. She listened for him but heard only the normal apartment and neighborhood noises.

There was no beer left in the fridge, so Tilly changed into her sweats and brushed her teeth. She quietly cleaned up the bottles and put the glasses in the sink. She headed to the couch to try to sleep, but stopped at the door to her father's room. His reading lamp was still lit on his nightstand, and she had to hold herself back to keep from turning it out. She'd found it sometimes disoriented him in the night if there wasn't a light on, and he preferred it to be the one closest to him.

He grumbled in his sleep, and she stared at him, wondering what annoyed him in his dream.

CHAPTER SIX

"Another seventy-five kilometers, and we'll hit our destination. It's a safe site in open territory. Mostly." Harrison's gaze weighed on Tilly as she guided the craft low over the trees and burned-out buildings. "Look for a half-collapsed football stadium."

She'd lost herself in thought as they traveled. With little to occupy her mind, she thought of her father and his life in Nagasaki. The same memories seemed to rerun in her mind, like they were on a loop, a file on repeat, though some things that sprang to mind seemed random and unimportant. The thoughts were the minutiae of daily life with her father. Medication times, meals, offhand comments.

"Fucking hell," Tilly said as she worked the collective controls and the speed. "How many elderly aircraft did you have to Frankenstein together to get this bird to fly?"

The relic she piloted still handled about as well as she expected: it shook if she pushed it too hard, it pulled to the left, and it rattled in distracting ways. The controls were nowhere near the level she was used to in the craft she'd flown in the war. But she was sure she could handle it, as long as the craft kept itself from flying apart, which was frighteningly out of her control.

"It was modified by our techs and flown for the appropriate test hours to insure the safest craft possible. No one complained about its performance until you happened upon it," Harrison murmured from the seat next to her. "I see no problems."

"One of your men vomited in the aft cargo area ten minutes ago. I'm not sure if you can smell that over the other stenches of this piece of shit."

"What did this shithead eat?" Saburo asked over the headset. "It smells like candy corn and mayonnaise back here."

"Fuck you," Hyatt mumbled across the link.

"Watch your language," Harrison said.

"Yeah. There are ladies present." It was hard to tell if Ned was really trying to defend the honor of the women present, but Tilly found it sort of sweet. Almost as charming as the fact he was strapped into his seat with every buckle and brace he could find. He stopped short of having someone tie him into his chair with rope and zip ties.

The trip felt longer than it really was for Tilly, owing to the lack of electronic help and the smog which never let up. It was dark from the moment they entered what used to be Chinese airspace. She considered moving the copter upward and using the pollution to mask the craft from prying eyes below, but she had no idea what else could hang out there, what else was using it for cover. It was paranoia on her part, but Tilly didn't want to take the chance.

Squelches and muffled voices on the headset suggested someone wanted to talk, and Harrison fiddled with the radio almost immediately. He spoke in nearly perfect Japanese in reply, as he had when talking with the people who had interviewed Tilly about the job. Her own grasp of the language was fair enough to understand Harrison was checking in with the tower in their landing zone and confirming conditions and preparedness for their arrival. He'd run their communications through some of the equipment installed in the back. They still couldn't receive satellite signals, but anything line-of-sight came in with some difficulty.

"They're ready for us," Harrison told Tilly. "Change course and head east at the beacon. Landing site should come into view in about six minutes after that."

"Confirmed. East at the beacon." The idea of an airport ping filled Tilly with warmth. Everything they'd passed over was broken and cracked; destroyed in the war. The only real landmark she'd clocked before that was the campfire where the soldiers took potshots at her. She took a deep breath and flexed her right hand, replacing it with her other hand on the stick. The fight to keep them airborne and on course shook the hell out of her arms and they hurt like a bastard. She shook out her other weary limb. "They tell you how long until the beacon?" She asked.

Harrison grunted and conversed with the ground crew again. Tilly gathered something was wrong. Apparently, they'd missed the beacon. Or it was possible it was no longer there. Either way, it freaked Tilly out.

"Come around and head east now."

Tilly nodded. "Did we miss our waypoint?"

"Do it, now. The sodding signal must be off for some reason."

"Fine, we can work with that," she said. "How far off are we?" *I can work with that. I can work with that.*

"Just..." As Harrison spoke, there was a bright flash on the ground below, followed by the sound of every alarm in the Cyclone blaring at once. Clanging and beeping filled her headphones in an asynchronous mess of noises.

Tilly checked the flight computer, then looked to the right outside of the cockpit. *"Fuuuuuck.* Buckle in and hold on to something. We have a surface-to-air missile locked onto us."

"What?" Harrison shouted through the mic. Tilly could see panic on his face. She ignored him.

A chorus of voices shouted their incredulity at the situation, which didn't help Tilly think any better. "*Shut up.* Our beacon is out because someone knocked it out."

Harrison clicked in beside her and Tilly could clearly hear his own barrage of choice British expletives through her headphones. He cursed the people in the tower, cursed their families, and had some choice words for whoever launched the heat-seeking weapon at them. Whoever fired the missile destroyed the beacon to ambush any aircraft or repair crew dumb enough to come for it, and Tilly's flying hog was the lucky winner.

Tilly jerked the stick to both gain altitude and bring the craft to the left. She hoped the maneuver would force the pursuing missile to correct course and give them slightly more time to get their shit together. "Evasive maneuvers. Harrison, prepare to launch countermeasures."

Harrison did not reply.

"Tell me this thing has some sort of chaff or something to

confuse missiles. I don't care what. *Anything.*" It dawned on Tilly that Harrison sat in the copilot seat, not because he had any sort of flight experience or particular insight into how this mongrel of a craft worked, but because he *wanted to*.

"I don't know…" Harrison held his hands up. Tilly looked over to see red lights reflecting off his face as he scanned the panels, dumbfounded.

"This is your hunk of shit." Tilly jerked the stick and pushed the throttle hard, tossing the craft into a sudden bank again, trying to stay ahead of the missile. "*Find* the controls for it. There has to be something."

Harrison frantically scanned the buttons, switches, gauges, and readouts that made up the panel in front of them.

"Come on."

"I don't…" Harrison stopped. "Suppression? I don't see the word 'countermeasures', but there's a panel for suppression."

The warning klaxon had gone into overdrive, beating a staccato yelp which made Tilly's temple throb in unison with it. "Yes. Activate it. *Now*."

A sudden series of thumps rattled the aft of the copter and, with a little manipulation of the collective, the aircraft pulled up and was climbing almost vertically. The crew in the back shouted and cursed, but it didn't sway Tilly to change her course. She wanted some distance to get away from the possible ensuing explosion.

A pinging sound rang in her ears, getting faster and faster, indicating the missile was in close proximity and inching closer to the ass-end of their copter. Still in a climb, she pushed the craft to go faster. The pinging reached a crescendo and then stopped. Tilly braced herself against the hard walls, hoping to ride out the coming explosion, but after a few seconds, nothing happened. The warnings on their headphones stopped and the blinking lights on the panel no longer danced. Tilly leveled off the craft, took a deep breath and looked at the others.

"Everyone okay? Still got all your toes and eyelashes?" Tilly's head still pounded in time with the now-extinguished alarm.

"What the hell happened?" Harrison asked. He slouched in his seat, clutching his safety harness and visibly shaking.

"No idea," Tilly said. She turned in her seat to look at the main cabin and the startled crew there.

Saburo seemed the least shaken of the group. "Same dude threw up back here again."

"Sorry," Hyatt murmured.

Tilly guided their aircraft back around above where the missile stopped pursuing them. In the jagged terrain below, the fiery glow of their countermeasure flares burned bright on the ground. From the information she could pull from the combat computer, the missiles followed the countermeasures and buried themselves in some building debris. "What the hell?" Harrison shifted in his seat and looked down at the area where their pursuer had disappeared. "Where's the boom? Why isn't there an explosion?"

"I don't know. Maybe it was a dud, something fried when they launched, hard to tell." Faulty weapon or not, Tilly could feel her heart thudding inside her flight suit. With the adrenaline still coursing through her, she rechecked the map and guided the helicopter back toward the area where the missile had first acquired them.

"What are you, crazy?" Harrison shouted. "They could fire again."

"You have deck-mounted thirty caliber machine guns, don't you?" Tilly said into her mic. "Use one."

The men in back slid the side door open and, as the copter circled the area, they spotted the SAM site that launched on them. A half-dozen people ran around it in a frenzy. There was a new missile already loaded, but it hadn't launched, and Tilly got no sign it was trying to lock on to the copter. "We haven't got all day, people. We got places to be."

The roar of the side gun was loud enough to be heard over the din of the helicopter's engine and propellers. Tilly watched as the men on the ground ran for cover, hiding behind debris and the missile launcher itself. The heavy machine gun ripped through the trash on the ground and cut the people there down easily. It was harder to get the ones finding shelter behind the blocky launcher, so

Tilly circled it a little faster, taking the men there by surprise. She watched as Decator killed them with a barrage of gunfire that danced across the ground, into the men. When all the men were dead, the fire continued, with the new target being the launcher. One tire blew out, and the launcher tilted to one side before sparks shot from the control section.

"Enough," Harrison said. "Let's get to our LZ so I can chew someone's ass out for this."

Tilly nodded and pointed them to the east. She wondered how anyone living in the wild, violent world of postwar China would handle threats from a man like Harrison, whose pressed combat gear probably still had the price tags on them.

The faint flashing lights of the football stadium came into view when the helicopter grew closer. Tilly used them on her approach and circled the structure, as instructed by a man on the radio with a heavy British accent. "What are they guiding us with, a flashlight?"

"Could be," Saburo said. The woman was leaning up close behind Tilly's seat and staring out the front window. As the aircraft moved around the structure, she commented on the damage she saw. Fire blackened the stadium in several areas. A gaping hole replaced one section. "This place has seen some things, hasn't it?" The destruction was extensive, carving a 'u' shaped hole in the side which took out all three decks of the stadium there and left only rubble scattered across the ground level. "I guess it makes sense to create a base in something that's already been destroyed. It's a good hiding place."

"Looks like a portion of the western curve is gone. Bombing run?" Ned asked.

"Probably a good guess." Tilly guided the copter around into the center of the field, which was overgrown with weeds and small trees. She was glad the rainstorm had let up, or else the landing might've been even more interesting. "Here we go." Touchdown was graceful, despite the lack of usual airport amenities. As they landed, the helicopter relaxed and rested on the ground. Before Tilly even powered down the rotors, Harrison and his men were out and on the ground, strolling toward an approaching ground crew.

"He's always in a hurry, isn't he?" Ned asked as he took off his headphones and placed them on an overhead hook before exiting the craft.

After everyone else grabbed their gear and left, Tilly stopped pretending to run through her post-flight checklist and placed her clipboard on the copilot's seat. Her hands shook and she could feel a shooting pain in her spine as she let the reality of their recent peril course through her body unchecked. She put both hands on the console in front of her and gripped it, waiting for a wave of nausea to pass. She wouldn't puke, but her whole body would convulse as if she were. It happened with all the close calls she had when she was flying in the war, so it wasn't a new sensation. There was never an occasion she could remember where she'd cried. It wasn't sadness she felt in the proximity to death or even fear; it was anger. She was mad she allowed death to get so close to her and her crew. In the thick of things, her reflexes took care of everything. She guided each craft she'd flown almost magically, commanding them with gentle feather touches and mental instruction. But when the danger was over, she paid for her private wizardry with these agonizing betrayals from her nervous system.

A series of long deep breaths calmed her, and Tilly got out of the chopper and walked around it, doing a visual inspection for damage. It looked like a long, jagged scrape along the door might have been the point of impact with the missile, but the damage was nothing compared to what could have happened. With every step, she took more soothing breaths until she'd circled the craft entirely. After she was sure she was out of sight of everyone, she leaned against the Fat Pig and closed her eyes. She could handle whatever was coming. If the worst that happened was a close call with a dud missile, the mission would be a cakewalk. Easy. She reached in and picked up her clipboard to make a note of the condition before hanging the list back on its hook on the dashboard.

In the dying light of the early evening, Tilly looked up, hoping to see some stars or the blinks of satellites passing overhead, but the smog clouds hadn't relented, even this far inland. She turned her attention to the stadium and the field where she landed. Other than the gaping hole at one end, the rest of the seats and stairs seemed intact, although black from the elements and pollution. In the press boxes at one end, she could see several figures moving in the dim glow of an array of work lights. She guessed those enclosed areas served as their airport tower, as they were the highest point for miles around. She grabbed her things and walked slowly toward a familiar face.

"Tilly? You sure took your time," Rei said. His eyes were blue and white, relaxed, happy. Probably half-drunk already. "Everyone else is in the lounge. Harrison said we could. You should grab a beer and join us?" He had somehow already changed his clothes into a silky red shirt and jeans, in off-duty mode.

In her mind, she was already having that drink, and it felt good. But she knew better. She knew what flying with a hangover felt like. She shook her head. "No thanks. I want to hit the head and then find a place for some rack time. I don't want to feel like crap when I wake up." Flying took more out of her than Tilly was willing to admit sometimes. It was especially bad when she was flying what was basically a combat mission. She was always alert and searching for anything that could present a problem. The focus it required drained her. "Gotta be ready for dust off early tomorrow morning."

Ned and Saburo were not far behind Rei and chimed in on their conversation. "Oh, no worries. Didn't you hear? Harrison says we aren't going tomorrow. Weather is supposed to be a pisser. Rain and storms all day." Ned pointed down the east tunnel. "Beer is this way." He sauntered down the corridor, nearly dancing as he approached a trio of people Tilly didn't recognize. She stared after him, wondering why she would be the last to know the morning flight had been scrubbed. She also considered the abundance of alcohol, which surely waited in the mess hall. There would be food, too. *If she wasn't flying the following day, why not have a drink or two?*

She nodded to the other members of the group and they all walked down the ramp into the dirty concrete tunnels running below the grandstands. The once-gray concrete was blackened with age and mold, possibly scorch marks and bullet holes, though Tilly didn't stop to examine them closely enough to determine their origin. Small vehicles and supplies lined the walls, covered in tarps. Leaky barrels of fuel and oil sat exposed near the kitchen, reeking. The mess hall was a converted concession stand with plastic tables and chairs set up nearby. It was less a dining area and more of a section of tunnel cordoned off by office dividers for walls. Not counting the people she'd arrived with, Tilly figured there were about thirty people eating and drinking when she walked in.

She zeroed in on Harrison, sitting with his detail, eating, and approached him. "Why didn't I get the message we were grounded for tomorrow?" She asked.

Harrison looked up from his rice and what appeared to Tilly to be some sort of blue tofu. "Where have you been? We had a quick huddle and talked about the storm front moving in. We could dust off late tomorrow, if things go our way, but it would leave you flying in the dark."

"We could have discussed the option if you'd waited and consulted me."

His fork clanked on the plastic tray as he dropped it. "Look, we would have consulted you if we'd been able to find you."

"I did an inspection of your helicopter to make sure we hadn't taken damage from small arms fire or something. It took me five minutes."

"Five minutes? We landed nearly two hours ago. Where the hell did you go after your five-minute inspection?" Harrison's companions nodded in agreement and looked up at Tilly. Rei agreed with their assessment.

She stepped back and looked up at the walls, searching for a clock. "I did my checklist and came in." They had to be wrong. There was no way she could have taken so long to inspect the Cyclone.

Harrison's face softened. "Listen, I get it. I know flying in these conditions can be exhausting. Shit, the flying you did had to be a bitch on your body. Get something to eat. Have a drink. You've got all day tomorrow to rest up for the next leg now."

Not wanting to further admit being confused by what had

happened, she downplayed it so as not to concern anyone and possibly get herself grounded. "Where can I bunk?"

Harrison stared at her, trying to read whatever he thought he saw on her face.

Saburo spoke up. "Hey, they already set me up. There's plenty of room. Let me take you." She had shed her blue camo and was wearing black workout shorts and a green tank top with flip-flops. "Grab some chow before it's gone. It's not half bad." She carried two bottles of beer by the necks and used them to motion to the concession stand window where the line had dwindled. "Avoid the chunks of meat and go for the veggies, though. Just a tip." The girl wrinkled her nose and shook her head.

"Thanks, I appreciate it." Tilly filled a bowl with rice, corn, and broccoli, grabbed a hunk of bread, stuck a bottle of water under her arm, and nodded for Saburo to lead on. They walked down the cavernous hall, passing a few stragglers headed in the opposite direction for food. She kept a general count and figured she'd seen about forty people at the base, not including her party. They were disheveled and dirty. There were maybe two banners with the Telford logo on it, maybe a few Telford hats on the crew. She wasn't sure what she expected, but the entire operation at the stadium seemed small, disorganized, and shabby for a company like Telford Biotech.

"You're thinking this place is pretty nasty, right?" Saburo asked.

Tilly was taken slightly aback at the question. "Is it that obvious?"

"Written all over your face. Plus, it was exactly what I was thinking when I walked in. You should've seen the awful bathrooms at the entrance. Ugh."

"Are you intimating there are nice toilets somewhere in the filthy, decaying stadium?"

"God, yes. Stick with me and I'll steer you right." Saburo winked. She took a long drink of her beer as she walked and tossed the empty bottle in a trash receptacle. "The can in our little quarters is much better. And not even mixed. Ladies get their own. It's almost luxurious," she chuckled. "*Almost*. At least they invested in some air fresheners to cover the stench in ours." They walked to a locker room which someone had recently painted white. *All white*—floors, ceiling, walls. It gave the place the air of a hospital or laboratory.

Saburo led the way toward the lockers, shoved off to the side in what might have been a workout room in the old days. As they continued, Tilly realized the rows of metal containers were positioned to form the walls of their luxury accommodations. The smaller woman pointed to one small room created in such a way with a bed and a grey metal chair. "This'll be yours. These rooms are great." Saburo moved to the wall and opened one of the many lockers there. "Plenty of storage. You probably have twenty-thirty lockers for your shit. And the best part about these rooms?" Saburo moved over to the opposite wall. "You can push these lockers a few feet out and your suite is suddenly bigger."

"It's great," Tilly said. "But no doors?" There was a gap between locker sections that served as a doorway, but nothing covered it.

"Eh. Four walls seem to be the best they can do here. They have plenty of these sections of locker, but doors seem to be in short supply."

"And these famous wash facilities?"

"Other way down the hall. Can't miss it. Showers and all. Soap and whatnot, too."

Tilly nodded and looked around her quarters. "I guess I'll get to it." She tossed her pack on the low bed and spooned some food into her mouth.

"Would you like some company while you eat?"

Trying to be delicate, Tilly shook her head. "No. *But thanks*. I think I'm going to eat a little, hit the head and get some sleep."

"Great. Ummm. I forgot. There will be some other ladies coming to their rooms here. And… oh." She pointed at the ceiling. "All the lights on this side are on the same switch. So, they turn everything off at the same time. We'll be stuck with lights in your eyes until like ten from what I hear." Saburo thought a moment before she nodded and moved down the hall. "Okay. I think that's all. *Yeah*. See you in the morning." She disappeared into a gap in the lockers and Tilly heard the springs on the bed creak and strain in the next room.

Tilly opened a locker and set her water bottle on the shelf while she ate more of her corn and rice. She paced the white floor, traveling around the wide-open space, and stared at the sliver of open air where a door should be. True to what Saburo said, a couple of other women walked past, presumably on their way to their own rooms. Both of them took a moment to look in Tilly's direction, nodding and smiling when they saw her.

When she finished, she put the empty bowl and spoon on a locker shelf and closed the door. She tossed her bag on the floor and sat down on the soft bed. She couldn't help but sit facing the hall. Another woman walked by and nodded at her. Tilly took a breath and laid down, facing away from the doorway. She stared at the solid wall of grey lockers instead.

Sleep didn't come immediately. The lights, the passing women, the lavatory sounds contributed to the problem, but she also thought about what happened after they'd landed. She knew she hadn't been out there as long as they said. She walked around the helicopter, stopped, and collected herself on the other side, out of sight. Afterward, she walked in and saw Rei. How did it take hours? She never sat down once she got out. Was it possible she fell asleep standing up as she leaned against their bird?

Another woman passed by Tilly's room, but this one had a man with her, and he lingered a little too long at the gap in the lockers. It spurred Tilly to throw back the blanket and get out of bed. She gripped a row of lockers by the inside shelves and pulled. The metal legs scraped across the concrete floor, wailing and screeching as the whole thing moved. She got a better grasp on the metal doors and pulled some more, increasing the racket of steel screaming across the solid floor. The gap that created her doorway slowly got smaller as the two walls of the room got closer until there was no gap. It wasn't pretty, and the wall wasn't exactly straight anymore, but at least no one could easily walk in on her or stare as they passed.

The problem effectively solved, Tilly got back into her bed and fell asleep.

CHAPTER SEVEN

Six Years Earlier

"I'm good at making the frames. Simple. Easy to do. Why can't I just make frames all day? Hell, I could have so many of these done in one day. My productivity would be through the roof." Tilly sat back in her chair, resigned to the belief her fingers were too fat to paint. Her level of creativity was far below that of the average zoo monkey. Her father and Hirata had temporarily given up asking her to create an original design for a kite and gave her one Hirata had already sketched a pattern on. All she had to do was paint it and outline it.

"You have to walk before you can run," Tilly's dad said.

"Ugh. Haven't heard that old gem of advice in a while. Isn't it the same thing you told me when I was learning to cook spaghetti?"

"Doesn't make it less true, wren."

"You haven't called me wren in years."

"You haven't been around for me to call you that."

"Got me there, pop."

Hirata leaned in and straightened the brush she held in her hand. "You need to be a little firmer when you paint, or else you'll have to go over the same spot again and again. Be confident in your strokes."

"I'm not. I'm not confident in my strokes." It was a painstaking process for Tilly, like learning to march in formation when she knew from day one she'd spend most of her hours in the air, rather than on the ground with the other troops. "You didn't say why I can't just make frames."

"Jesus, girl. You always have to have a shortcut?" Her dad placed his own brush down on the table and stood up slowly. "You can't make frames and only frames because each of these tako is custom, they're one entity. You can't do it piecemeal. You must take the time to see what illustration fits with what frame. What tail completes the spirit of the kite. It isn't a damn assembly line. We aren't making cars here. Robots make cars." He trudged away, turning at the hall that led to the stairs.

"Dad," Tilly said. "You're overreacting here. I've only been trying this for a couple of weeks."

"Your father is frustrated, you both are." Hirata cleaned his own brush and set it aside before returning to the tables where most of the shop's work was done. "And this may surprise you, but having you here isn't necessarily making things better."

"*He* wanted me here. His request dragged me out of the army. If I'm making things worse for him, why did he ask for me?"

Hirata wiped his hands dry and picked up his soda. To Tilly, the man was a stoic teacher, incapable of humor or fault. He was a teacher long before he met Tilly's father, instructing college students on art and design. *Infinitely patient and wise*, was her dad's over-the-top description on the phone before she arrived. It would be impossible to live up to such a thing, but he came close. She saw Hirada through her father's eyes foremost, so to watch this beautiful man slurping soda through a red and white metal straw was incongruous. It was like he used his entire face to suck in the drink. His cheeks imploded, and his brow raised. When he finished, he exaggerated a sigh of refreshment. The entire spectacle nearly made her forget what they were talking about.

"He wants you here, Tilly. I assure you; he wants you here. Now you have arrived, he feels his request was selfish, that he took you away from a life you can't go back to again. I'm sure he believed that once he passed, you could hop on a plane and take your place in the army back. When he sees you struggle, it only reinforces his idea he took something you can't get back."

"He told you this?"

"No."

"So, you sort of telepathically intuited this from him?"

"Maybe."

"You're aware he already thinks you're some sort of magical Japanese sensei guru-type thing, right?"

"Did you know, in the strictest definition of the word, sensei means 'someone born before another?' So, it follows your father is my sensei. He teaches me things, I teach him things. He showed me how to make a complex and delicious rib sauce. I would never have considered it without him."

"His Carolina rib sauce? He stole it from a wing joint in Myrtle Beach, you know? He didn't magically create it. And he tried to teach it to me as well."

"And how did it turn out?"

"Burnt," Tilly laughed. "I burned the ribs, the sauce dried up, and it was really just awful. How did it go for you?"

"Burnt. My sauce stuck to the pan because I didn't pay enough attention to it. Burnt… the first time. But I tried again."

"Is this some sort of analogy for me failing to paint a kite?"

"We're getting to know each other," Hirata said. "We're just getting to enjoy each other's company as we work." After another long slurp of his drink, he picked up a brush and got back to work on his own kite.

"So, I paint the design in full color, and then what?"

"You take the sumi, and you paint black outlines around the design to give it some depth."

"Right. I have my black ink right here." Tilly stirred the dark liquid with her brush, watching the swirls the motion created, and observing the way it clung to the bristles. The container was half full, and she made sure to keep the ink from spilling out onto the floor or her clothes. Some spots looked nearly white when the overhead shop lights hit them perfectly. Tilly made a game out of stirring away any parts that didn't look quite black, but each stroke only created another ridge which caught the glare, turning pale again.

"That's impressive," Hirata said. He was laughing as he stood and came over. "You said you were not an artist. But look at your creation."

She looked up from her ink bowl to find him staring at her kite.

The paper, mere inches away from her, was complete in both the design and outlines. Hirada's dragon face design was fully decked out in oranges, yellows, and reds. It was even expanded on to make the simple dragon face more complex and frightening, almost more realistic, with intricate scales and bloody teeth. Something about the face was now more familiar to her, like she'd seen it before, but it wasn't the sample that hung on the walls all around the shop.

"Where did you get this idea from? The painting technique is not like what I taught your father." Hirata walked around the table, taking in the finished kite from all angles. "I don't know what to say."

Neither did Tilly. She only remembered stirring the darkness in the bowl for what seemed like mere minutes, only to stop when Hirata startled her. She looked down at her hands and found them to be a mess, mostly red and orange from the wrists up to her elbows, with her fingers and palms encrusted with black. She stared at the dark ink as it dripped from her fingertips onto the floor.

"I…"

"Modest. You work a little harder and practice, you'll be flying solo soon enough, little wren." Hirata smiled as he continued to marvel at her work. "Why does he call you wren?"

"We used to see these birds back home in Carolina. They were always active and moving around. I guess I couldn't sit still as a toddler. I think that was where he got it from."

She stared at the kite with no comprehension of how anyone could make something so intricate and beautiful, let alone do it herself. She wiped the black ink on her apron, trying to clean off her fingers and arms.

CHAPTER EIGHT

Come morning, the rain dropped early, waking Tilly from her sleep. She dug a rain poncho from her pack, pushed the lockers slowly apart as quietly as she could, and hit the head. In a few minutes, she was standing at the entrance where she'd arrived the evening before and stared out at the overgrown field and the silhouette of the helicopter in the middle. There was a dark tarp covering it from nose to tail—likely several tarps, considering the size of the Cyclone. She assumed the ground crew did it in anticipation of the coming storm.

Tilly thought of the dream she'd had of her father. It was a pure memory of how things had been, a remembrance of one of their training sessions. Except it had gone off the rails in her dream, everything true until the sudden completion of her painting. She'd never gotten so good, had never experienced that look of wonder and admiration on Hirata's face.

It was still dark and a quick check of her NaNi told her it was a quarter past three. The sun wouldn't rise for over two hours, and then she'd have a whole day to sit and stare at the rain.

"Don't walk around out there, even with your gear," an armed guard approached Tilly from down the hall. "The rain's nasty. Hell, it's what fucked the field up so bad. Even with the bombing this place took, we could still get out for some football once in a while, but once these nasty rains started, the bleachers crumbled and the grass withered. Soon enough, there were divots in the field and our games ended. Hard to run the field with so many holes in it."

"Like acid rain?"

"More or less."

"Is it this bad every time it rains?"

"No. It really depends on the prevailing winds," the guard said.

He pointed over the top of the press boxes. "When it comes in from the east, it brings the smog and debris from some nasty manufacturing plants down the way." As he motioned for Tilly to move back inside, his rain gear crinkled and swished, further breaking the silence of the calm morning.

It immediately occurred to Tilly the rain was why someone had covered the helicopter, why the horrible smelling fuel was in the hall and why the field itself was so barren of equipment.

"Good luck tomorrow. Should be a nice day for flying, if the weather models are to be believed," he said. He waved, swishing louder this time, and continued around the hall. Tilly waved back and thanked him for the thought.

She stood there watching the rain for a few minutes before retreating deeper into the concrete base. They stored all the equipment for the maintenance of the vehicles along the way, intensifying the stench of petrol and oil. Trucks and transports of all kinds lined the corridor–everything from military grade combat machines to patched-together pickup trucks with guns mounted in their beds. The more she thought about it, everything the Hōfuna organization had seemed to be rigged together and barely functioning. It was a wonder they didn't run out of ventilation tape out here in the middle of nowhere. She'd seen it before in active combat zones, supposed it was no different in a post-war zone like the stadium.

When she reached the stairs to the press boxes, she climbed the cold concrete steps and entered the room where the reporters and announcers must have perched to watch the matches once upon a time. There were some nice soft chairs, rummaged from some office somewhere and lined up near the windows looking out onto the field. She followed a light from another room, entering what had to be their communications hub and command center. There were large, older-model computers and monitors set up around the room, with several server towers against the back concrete wall. Two men looked up from their screens and nodded.

"Good morning," Tilly said. She received low, noncommittal grunts in return. Larger computer monitors were bolted to the walls and showed weather and other readings in large green globs. "Looks like we'll get to leave tomorrow?"

From the next room, Harrison entered. "It looks good. We should be able to leave before sunrise so we can stay undetected as long as possible."

"Expecting more missile launchers?"

"No, *that* was a fluke, I think. No reason to believe there will be more. Opened my eyes, though. Not expecting more of the same, but not discounting anything." He smiled almost cheerfully and stood reading his pages.

Tilly didn't find the guess terribly encouraging, but she let it slide. It was too early in the morning to get inside Harrison's brain and unravel his thought process. Though, maybe there wasn't a good time. Maybe the best time to figure him out was before they ventured into a defunct, or possibly active, combat zone.

She stared at the concrete walls blanketed by scraps of paper, pages of notes, and the occasional glossy map with multicolored marks on them. Most seemed to be close-up sections of towns and shorelines. "What's that?" One printout caught her eye—it seemed to be a wider shot than the others, with familiar cities labeled, but features which made little sense nearby. Elevations and distances seemed distorted.

One man looked up. "It is the last good scan of the river we got from about six weeks ago. We did a drone fly-by and contour mapped as much as we could."

"What?" There were definitely many features that matched what she'd studied of the Yellow River, but there were also drastic deviations cutting through the landscape. "But the map you showed us back in Japan was different. This looks *worse* than before? How could it have gotten worse?"

The man nodded affirmatively. "Some pretty serious downpours a few weeks ago upstream have made the flooding more intense in those areas. Maybe it's improved since the scan."

"But there aren't any curves here or here. This part is all wrong." Tilly went along the smooth laminate, pointing out things with her finger. Without satellite guidance, it would be tough to find anything. They could hug the shoreline, but it wouldn't guarantee they'd find the WHEEL. The area they were covering looked more like an inland sea at the moment.

"Many… *Most* of the dams were destroyed in these areas of the Huang He during the war. All the water had to go somewhere. It caused massive flooding, changed the course of the river in some places; it was transformative. Devastating."

"I know *that*. Harrison told us, but I didn't expect the landscape to *keep* changing. If this is from a few weeks back, what does it look like today in these areas?" Staring at the mess of the topography, Tilly tried to imagine how many people had to have lost their lives when any one of the dams suddenly gave way and flooded the communities along the banks. The dams were a vital power source for millions, so much so the military had special details protecting them during the early days of the war. Tilly herself had dropped equipment, weapons, and soldiers at Xiaolangdi Dam. They had anti-aircraft capabilities, anti-tank, and troop suppression ordinance stocked to be ready for whatever came at them. Protecting the dams was a priority, and a vital effort in the war.

"What it looks like today doesn't matter. We're still going to the river and following it until we find WHEEL Sixteen. It changes nothing."

"Sure, it does. With the dams in place, we knew how far your research station could go. It certainly couldn't get past a dam, couldn't climb a canyon, right? Now it could be anywhere along the river. It has no constraints, except wherever the land happens to be." She didn't bother to guess how many hundreds or thousands of miles were possible in the search. "Shit, what if it sunk in this area that looks like a fucking inland sea?" There were many places Tilly could see where an object ten times as large as the WHEEL could hide.

Harrison moved closer to Tilly and pointed out a city along the river. "Look, the lab was assembled at a facility in Puyang with the cooperation of the government before the war. It's a rugged structure and made to withstand all manner of threats. It went through test after test here. I trust the hull's integrity."

"In those tests, did they fire rockets at it and try to sink it with underwater mines?" Tilly asked, genuinely wondering.

Harrison ignored her and the giggles from the men that followed. "Here's the good news: we don't have to search the whole river. We know the bridge at Liuwancun was destroyed and created somewhat of a natural dam, making it impassable to anything as large as the lab. If they continued upriver as planned, they must be somewhere between Huayuancun and Zhengzhou." He marked the points on the map to illustrate their true search area. "It's a pretty small area. A few hundred miles, at best."

"*If* this is still what the area looks like," Tilly said. "And it's not a few hundred miles. Maybe if we flew overland, it would be, but following whatever shape the river is in now? It has to be six, maybe seven hundred miles, minimum. Even if it was a few hundred miles, it's still likely to take a few days, right? Do you have fueling stations and places to rest along the way? Do we have food and other supplies for this long of a search?"

"Look, let me stop you there. I have this planned out. We didn't pick up one day and say *'Let's fly up the sodding Yellow River'* for the bloody fuck of it. Okay? We have spots all along the river to resupply, all well within your fuel requirements. These are stations we have agreements with, and will lend whatever we need. They've got fuel, food, and personnel. It is easily doable."

The differences between the two maps she'd seen within twenty-four hours of one another concerned Tilly. And the lack of a clear way to communicate with these supply depots before they were right up on them did nothing to assuage her fears. She wanted confirmation they were up and ready for a beast like the Cyclone; she wanted confirmation she wouldn't be flying into more corrosive rain, and most of all, she wanted a briefing on any other potential hayseeds with missile launchers. The fewer surprises, the better.

Tilly swallowed all of her questions and comments, all the snide remarks that came to mind. "Great. Well, let me know the status on a morning dust-off as soon as you can."

"Don't worry. This whole affair got off to a shitty start, but it'll be clear sailing in the morning." Harrison pulled a long sheet of paper off the table and folded it expertly down to the size of a pamphlet. "Here. This is a copy of the map on the wall. I've highlighted the route I'd like us to take and marked available friendly landing sites."

"We're loading the same thing into your aircraft's on-board computer, so you don't... you know... have to unfold the map to see where you are." The men in the room laughed. "That would be awkward." It was a good joke to all the men in the room, especially the ones who weren't planning on leaving the shelter of the stadium and getting into a relic in the morning.

"Yeah." She wondered how small she could fold the map and how far it would fit up any of the men's asses. "Sure would."

"Now go, get some sleep. I can't have my pilot drifting off in mid-flight."

Now THAT would be awkward. Tilly left with her map and wound her way through the tunnels. Once she made it back to her rigged-up room, she spread the map out on the floor. The safe landing zones were within safe distances apart, as Harrison said. She found the river was so wide in places from where it had flooded past retaining walls, it appeared more like a series of immense lakes.

"NaNi?" she asked. The familiar vibration massaged her arm, and the bracelet lit up.

"Yes... Tilly? How can I assist you?" The voice was as mechanical and cold as the day they issued her the device.

"NaNi, I need you to scan and store a document."

"Internal memory at... two percent. Would you like to delete some files to free up usable space?"

"Delete some music files."

"Please specify music files or NaNi will delete files randomly."

"Get rid of anything from the twentieth century."

The device was clunkier than a watch, and the band extended further up to the forearm. The bulky part of the face could detach and perform custom functions, most meant for vanity, like hovering to take selfie pictures, but they worked fine for Tilly in combat and other situations. The military had improved the range, making it ideal for surveillance and scanning. However, being so old gave it some limitations, such as a smaller memory and poor voice recognition. Odd glitches bubbled up occasionally, but nothing too serious. It could charge on a combination of kinetic energy and solar power, which wasn't the best combination when flying into the cloud-shrouded Chinese mainland. She only hoped she could find power outlets at their fuel stops along the way.

"Would you like to test your knowledge of the common housefly with a trivia challenge?"

Tilly shook her head. "No."

CHAPTER NINE

There wasn't any damage Tilly could find when she walked around the Cyclone in the morning's dark. She held a pen-sized flashlight to insure there were no new dings or pocks on the hull from the acid rain. She had them drive over a bucket truck so she could get a better view of the rotor for exactly that reason. If those were unbalanced or compromised in some way, the flight would be a short, messy one. Once convinced there was no damage, other than the craft being a piece of shit, she did one last walk and watched them refuel the tubby vehicle.

When Harrison and his men came out, they were all once again wearing matching combat outfits that made them look more like a drone racing pit crew, or a boy band than a search and rescue team. They wore jumpsuits with digital camo patterns wrong for the area they were entering. The zippers were exposed, shining in the bright lights on the field set up for lift off. They carried their packs and black helmets like suitcases, while the combat vets slung the packs across their backs as intended. The only one who seemed to have a lick of sense was Rei, who'd modified his threads a bit; black duct tape covered his shiny zipper and the teeth all the way from top to bottom. The tape also covered his suit at the wrists and the ankles, likely a precaution against anything getting in he didn't want there. He lugged his pack over his shoulders. Less practical was the lightning bolt and the letters TCB emblazoned across his back in glowing green paint. He winked as he walked by, showing the light blue of his contacts. She didn't want to know what mood it indicated.

One man from the control tower walked up to Harrison. "We got a scout report about new incidents of craft in your target area. Would you like to hold up so we can send through a sweep drone?"

"No. We need to get out of here. Maybe we'll get lucky, and those bloody Hags will leave us be," Harrison replied.

Tilly looked back at Harrison briefly. "Hags? What's up? What the hell are hags?"

"Smog Hags," he said. "They're damn pirates who cruise the clouds for cover and then swoop in on unfortunate passers-by. They descend on unsuspecting boats, mostly. Rob them for whatever's useful. Usually kill the crews, too. Fucking nuisance, if you ask me."

They sounded to Tilly like more than a nuisance. Marauders casually dropping from nowhere and kill entire boat crews sounded like more than a petty annoyance.

"But we're in the clear?" Ned asked. He tossed his pack into the copter and joined the group. "They'll leave us alone?"

"I didn't say that."

"How much of a problem are they?" Tilly sighed at yet another hitch in a straightforward job. "Why would this guy warn us if he, or someone else, wasn't concerned?" She sat down in the helicopter and cranked up the main panel. She focused the radar and then pushed it out as far as she could, looking for anything unusual in their course, but nothing came up.

The tower man leaned forward and looked at Tilly and Harrison. "Look, Smog Hags are scavengers and thieves that crawled out of the woodwork after the war ended to capitalize on the sudden lack of military power along the rivers. They stole heavy-lifting drones from some of the abandoned factories and modified them to their own specs. Instead of autonomous robots doing pre-programed tasks, they fixed them to work both manned and unmanned. They use these things to fly their missions and carry off anything they need."

"Sounds like some pretty low-tech shit," Ned said.

"Good word for it. Our spotters prefer to call them 'low-fi,' but same difference. They wouldn't normally be a problem, but they also raided some weapon caches and started tricking out the stripped-down drones with whatever they could get. Some of these low-fis have heavy machine guns on them, some rocket launchers, shit like that, but no guidance systems, no targeting computers.

They're basically flying and shooting with their asses hanging out the window. Any good pilot should be able to out-maneuver them. And your gunners certainly have the advantage as far as firepower."

It didn't sound like a new problem to Tilly, but it seemed like something someone could have apprised her of early on, like at the interview or the briefing. Another combat mission rather than a search and rescue might have made her think twice about going into China again.

"You're not concerned?" Harrison asked.

The tower man waved it off. "Nah, I don't know of any instance of them attacking aircraft. It's usually boats or caravans. You guys are loaded for bear. I'd guess they'd leave you alone."

"Great. We're wasting darkness here. Can we move this fat bastard into the air?" Tilly felt it was best to pull the bandage off quickly and get moving. The more they talked, the more someone was likely to piss her off. "Is everyone ready to rock? Those door guns loaded and armed? Better assign people to them for safety's sake."

"Okay everyone. Let's load up," Harrison said. "Hyatt and Decator, you're on guns. Rei? We're getting close to the river, so start manning those search algorithms. Let's go." He clapped and waved people toward the helicopter like halftime was over and the big game was about to resume. The crew grabbed their gear off the tarmac, tossed it in, and claimed their seats. Hyatt and Decator gingerly locked the opposing guns in place, one port and the other on the starboard side before clipping themselves in overhead and then locking the sliding doors open. Both of them stared like they'd sucked a lemon as they tried to familiarize themselves with the more technical capabilities of the enormous guns.

Tilly did her preflight check until Harrison tried to climb up into the copilot seat. "Nope." She held her hand up to his face and blocked him from moving forward. "After your less-than-stellar performance in our last flight, I think we should consider putting someone with flight experience in the seat."

"Who?"

"Someone. Anyone," Tilly said. She clicked the mic on and

spoke into it. “Anyone else onboard have even a basic amount of piloting experience? Anyone?”

It was quiet as the men in the back shook their heads and looked around.

“I used to fly a tourist shuttle back home in Taiwan,” Saburo said. “You know, one of those things people rent to take them out to sightsee and shit? But it was a tiny thing. Six-passenger, VTOL, lightweight. Tiny.”

“We have a winner. Lady, you’ve got yourself a job. Get your ass up here. Harrison? Maybe you can help your men with the search? Your equipment could probably use another set of eyes?” She was trying to be as delicate as possible while not skipping the point she didn't want the man anywhere near her while she was flying. Harrison looked from one woman to the other and frowned. “Seriously. You can tell me anything you need via the headset. You can even switch to a separate channel if you need to curse me in private.” She tapped her earphones to emphasize the concept. She didn’t want a confrontation with him, but in the safety of what she’d come to call ‘The Fat Pig’, she wasn’t giving him another chance.

Harrison looked at Rei sitting behind the bank of search equipment. He subtly nodded and moved back to the tech section, bumping into Saburo along the way.

Quietly, off-mic, Saburo leaned in and told Tilly she was rusty, and it had been years since she’d done any really flying on her own.

“Perfectly fine. Anything is better than Mister Harrison. He bums me out. Like having your teacher looking over your shoulder all the time.”

“He does seem like a real come-down.”

“Plus, I’m betting you’re a better conversationalist,” Tilly added.

Their headphones hissed, and Harrison’s voice barked from them. “We leaving anytime soon, ladies? I’d like to make it to the river before dark, if you please.”

Saburo and Tilly traded looks and smiled. They talked through the startup process for the elderly conveyance they found themselves in. Within minutes, the craft was airborne and headed toward the river. They flew close to the ground, nap-of-the-earth as much as they could, keeping an eye out for the stray campfire, missile launcher, sniper, or crumbling skyscraper, but it was uneventful as they glided among the trees and fields. No alarms, nothing on the line-of-sight scanners and nothing that concerned Tilly in the least. When she needed a break, her copilot proved quite adept at flying on her own. The two of them held an ongoing discussion of the state of pop music, the decline of films, and the best places to score weed in Tokyo.

"So, should it be this quiet?" Saburo asked during a lull in the conversation.

"What do you mean?"

"There's no chatter or anything. When I flew, I had other aircraft, various towers, and the remnants of ground signals giving me a headache constantly," Saburo said. "Here, it's nothing. It's eerie."

"There's not much out here that still works. Signals can't penetrate the cloud cover, so we get mostly stuff from other craft and towers that can see us. It's like living in the early days of aviation."

Saburo rolled her shoulders and turned her head back and forth to work out the kinks of sitting in one position and staring straight ahead. "Kinda sucks. All this quiet isn't natural."

"True enough."

Soon after, they came upon a large pond near a row of splintered houses. Much of the material from the homes was now floating in the water, likely blown there by the shock of an explosion, or tossed there by a storm. A trail of smoke brought their attention to a small boat half-sunk with its bow on fire near the north shore.

"There's no lake on any of the maps," Harrison said.

"Are we off course?" Saburo asked.

"No, there's just no lake or pond or anything for miles. We'd have to be *way* the fuck off our route. Most likely it was created by flooding at some point," Tilly said.

"Why would the little boat still be on fire, though?" Ned asked. "It couldn't still be on fire from weeks or months ago. It would have burnt out by now, right? Has to be something new. We should see if anyone is in trouble down there."

"Fuck that noise. We have shit to do." Hyatt said.

"Come on, we're here already. Someone might need help." Ned said. "We can circle and see what we see."

"Right. It won't hurt to do a quick check," Harrison said.

As she slowed the craft and began an orbit of the smoky wreckage, a thought occurred to Tilly. "How far to the river?" She had a sudden inkling Ned was right. Partially, at least.

"Uhhh..." Harrison shuffled papers before Saburo chimed in with the answer. "Six or seven minutes, according to the computer."

Tilly yanked them back onto their original course and increased their speed.

"What the hell?" Harrison said. "What are you doing? I said we should bloody check it out."

Operating mostly on a hunch, Tilly pushed The Pig harder. "I heard something. I think it's a trap for anyone that happens on it."

"I didn't hear shit." Ned's voice on the radio was louder now.

A new crackle interrupted the hum of the scanners in the back through Tilly's headset. The sound went from the static that had become the norm since their liftoff to the buzz of something trying to break through. Since the atmosphere, active jamming, and the cloud cover in the area had left their flight path a dead zone for about any noise she would have expected from a normal run; no cross chatter from other aircraft, no ground control, no satellite pings, no nothing. Complete radio silence until this sudden squelch.

It stopped as suddenly as it began, without revealing its source or making any kind of coherent sound. Had she heard it any other time, she would have ignored it completely, but considering the prevailing silence, she was curious. Her last trip to the region hadn't been at all like it. There wasn't as much smog, and the jamming stations were routinely bombed into the ground once they were located. The Yellow River at the time was a hotbed of sound and activity. But here, the slightest static set her on edge.

Tilly ventured a look behind her at Harrison's team, huddled over infra-red scanners, side sonar, and image enhancing stations, and although they all had headphones on, none of them seemed to have picked up the subtle noise. Harrison, himself sat behind them with a tablet connected to it all, so he could see what they saw, hear what they heard, and he hadn't looked up. The gunners were sitting back out of position to shoot anything in a hurry.

"I didn't hear anything," Rei said.

"Let's go back," Ned said. "There could be injured people back there."

Tilly shook her head, though no one but Saburo could see. "Harrison, maybe you filled my head with irrational fears of bandits and rebels, but I think we need to stay on course and keep moving. You're paying me to fly this thing, so let me do it."

He didn't argue, instead he gave her a warning disguised as a compliment. "I'll let you do what you think is right."

"You hired me because I have combat experience, so let me follow my instincts."

Rei's laugh came through the speaker next. "He hired you because no one else wanted the job."

They were silent for a while, and Tilly felt silly for jumping at shadows. What if there was someone who needed help at the lake?

"What was it?" Saburo asked from the copilot seat. "You look concerned."

Saburo had been so quiet and unobtrusive. Unlike Harrison, Tilly had nearly forgotten the poor woman. "No. I don't know. Did you hear anything?"

"Like?"

Tilly shrugged. "I don't know. A different static over the rest of the static?"

"Sorry, no," Saburo said. "I turned the sound down on my headphones. The buzz was giving me a headache, and I could barely think. Why?"

"I thought…" As Tilly spoke, her headphones picked up a loud rumble. "I have a contact. Scratch that…" The sound grew and split into more distinct sources. "... I have multiple contacts."

"What?" Saburo sat up and fiddled with her own headphones. "I only hear some sort of crackling. How do you know…?"

Rei shouted, "I have several signals on the enhanced scanner." They'd fitted the Pig with comprehensive radar tech used to combine multiple returns to form a better 4-D image of approaching craft or land features. "Four targets dropped out of the dense cloud cover. Thin craft, I'm having trouble getting a profile for them," Rei said. "The things must be pretty flat."

"Smog Hags, has to be," Harrison said.

Shit. Tilly thought. *Just great.* She gripped the stick tighter and guided the copter down and slowed their speed. She wasn't sure how badly she needed the job now that she was getting chased by Hags and shot at by missile installations.

"If these are Smog Hags, we need those door guns hot and ready," Tilly said. "And make sure the rest of you are strapped in. This could get crazy interesting very quickly."

An alarm went off throughout the control panel and it took a moment to find its source on the cobbled-together panel before she could turn it off. "One of them launched something at us." She scrolled through the information the defensive threw up onto the screen as fast as she could. "Some kind of guided mini-missile. Hold on, we need to drop away from it quickly." Tilly shoved the stick forward, sending them into a steeper dive. A chorus of curse words inundated her over the headphones, suggesting the crew hadn't buckled in as she'd instructed them to.

"Level it off, and we'll try to scramble it," Decator shouted. Tilly listened and ended their dive toward the river. She had to trust they knew what they were doing and had come prepared for such an eventuality, even though nothing in their experience so far bore that out.

As the warning lights and buzzers went crazy in celebration of the danger ahead, Decator let loose with his gun. Instead of the usual whine of a heavy machine gun, his weapon hissed and shook the entire craft as it released several rings of light which Tilly could see on the relic's rear flight camera. The pursuing small objects exploded in clouds of metal and fire immediately upon contact with the orange glares.

"I had the stadium crew service those EMPs on the door guns

while we were stuck there." Harrison sounded proud of himself. "They work as advertised. I'd say."

Before Tilly could warn him not to get too excited about the minor victory, Saburo shouted as the port windscreen next to her shattered in a series of pinprick bullet holes.

On the radar, Tilly could see two Hags hanging a couple dozen feet behind and below the copter. The other two were moving in from above, which meant none were in range of the craft's door guns. "Hold the fuck on to something, everyone," Tilly said.

She went into an automatic mode in her head, reacting and acting in equal measure, staying out of the Low-fis' sights, but giving the men on her bird the best possible angle of attack to fight back. Quickly, a thump somewhere off their tail indicated one of the Smog Hags caught a bullet and burst into flames. She watched it go down quickly and vanish into the trees off the shore.

"Nice shooting," she said. "Three more."

Climbing in the air away from the marauding pursuers, the helicopter rumbled in protest of some of Tilly's more acrobatic intentions. She reminded herself she was basically flying a bulldozer instead of the sports cars she was used to. The Cyclone was built for search and rescue initially and modified for combat transportation later. No one anticipated stunts and rolls, or acrobatics.

"Come on Tilly, we need to get out of their crosshairs," Harrison shouted. "Move this thing."

"This thing doesn't move so well," Tilly replied in a calm voice. "It's several tons heavier than those lifters the hags are using." In time to prove her point, one of the remaining Low-fis caught up with them and raced past the front of the copter like they were standing still. It was close enough Tilly could see the skull painted on the pilot's helmet and could almost read the serial numbers on the gun the Low-fi's pilot pointed at the copter. She followed it, rather than turning away, hoping it would give the gunners a better shot at the attacking craft, or a longer period to shoot. One of the guns behind her rumbled with the effort, but the craft continued uninjured.

Over in the co-pilot's seat, Saburo looked only slightly less uncomfortable than Harrison had. At the very least, she had the presence of mind to look at the combat computer rather than the weather information.

In the time it took The Pig to pursue the first craft, the other Low-fis lined up behind it and open up with their ragged weaponry. Tilly knew the enemy had gained the advantage as soon as she heard the telltale thuds of heavy arms fire punching the outer hull of the Pig and the new warning buzzers telling her something important took a hit. The shouts of terror from Hyatt were a big clue too, as he was standing in an open doorway on the side which got strafed.

"Jesus and Mary, can't you do anything about this, Tilly?" Decator grunted into the mic for all to hear.

"I'm doing everything I can. Suggestions would be welcome." She dropped their altitude again until they were nearly skimming the surface of the river. The Low-fis followed, undeterred, and began firing anew. She heard the familiar zip of an EMP pulse from one of the copter's guns, but it had no effect. Their pursuers were too fast and too maneuverable to get caught by it.

A new alarm sounded, and Saburo shouted. "Missile. A new missile warning, and it looks like it was fired really close."

Tilly nearly froze. There were too many things going on and not enough brainpower to deal with all of them. Too many variables in the sky. Too many attackers, too many weapons, too many choices regarding how to deal with them. And she was far too unfamiliar with the Cyclone to push it to any limits or coax any tricks out of it. Still, she tried. She got the helicopter to climb and head for the direction of the forest, doing her best to get them away from the water. It might make for a better landing, but if what she was told about the Smog Hags was right, the Low-fis would likely strafe and kill any survivors spotted in the water.

Explosions burst around the copter, rocking it. She could smell what was most definitely some sort of electrical fire as smoke drifted into the cockpit. They skimmed right above the tree line, with Tilly fighting with the controls the whole way. More explosions shook the copter as the Low-fis strafed the starboard side with more rocket-propelled grenades.

Hyatt shrieked in pain across the comms immediately after the last burst.

"Shit," Harrison shouted.

"Oh, my God. He's gone," Saburo said. "The gun placement snapped, and Hyatt's gone. He fell out of the helicopter with it. He's gone."

Tilly wanted to turn and look. It seemed like she needed to confirm the man was dead, but she had more pressing matters in keeping the bird in the air, so the others didn't suffer the same fate as Hyatt. She scanned for a clearing or any other suitable spot to put the aircraft down and found a wide area near a thin stream that ran into the Yellow River. It was their best, possibly only, choice with everything going on.

Behind her, Harrison and his men were shouting and carrying on about Hyatt, so Tilly unplugged her headphones so she could concentrate. As she did so, she saw Saburo yell at her as well, but she couldn't hear the woman over the clunk and hiss of the helicopter dying around them. The tail rotor caught a tree and sent them spinning as she tried to correct. The whole thing twisted like its namesake, faster in circles as they careened toward the clearing she'd spotted. It was hard to tell if the thuds behind her came from equipment shifting, bodies tumbling or more explosives homing in on the craft. She didn't have the time to turn and clarify which it was, nor did she really want to know. There wasn't much more that could be fucked up on their transport, and her only mission as they spun toward the earth was survival.

At the last second, something set the bird tilting sideways, whether it was a tree, a bomb, a rock, whatever, it didn't matter; they hit the ground and slid across the shore into the stream, where it came to rest half-submerged and smoking. Sparks flew all around her as she tore the headset off and unbuckled her harness.

She grabbed Saburo and helped her out of her safety restraints. "Are you okay? Shit, you're bleeding. Your forehead, it's bleeding." Her hand went quickly to the other woman's head. "Come on, let's get you out of here. Let's get everyone out of here before something happens."

"*Something happens?*" Saburo asked. "What do you call this?"

She swung her free arm around at the damaged craft and the fire and smoke. "There's another *something* that could happen?"

As they pulled along through the chaos of the crash, they splashed into the water that seeped in and collected in the cabin from the stream. There were fewer voices in the mess than she expected, and she hoped it didn't mean there were fewer survivors as well.

"Hello? Anybody?" Saburo shouted.

"Hello?" Tilly splashed ahead, still trying to support Saburo while shoving the debris of Harrison's tracking equipment out of the way. She looked up at the side door, which was now more of a skylight, looming above their heads. Through it, she saw the outlines of two Low-fis zipping over them.

"Fuck," Ned shouted. "*Fuuuuck.*" In the rear of the craft, he stood slowly up, unsteady on his feet. He hobbled over to the two women and helped support Saburo.

"Help me up," Tilly said. There weren't many exits from the huge craft, and she took it upon herself to find one everyone could use. After the cockpit filled with acrid smoke, she decided it wouldn't be viable for an exit. The only way out seemed to be through one of the doors. She stood on an ammunition crate and reached up for the open air. Saburo and Ned gave her a boost so she could reach one of the fixed seats. From there, she strained to pull herself up to the gun emplacement to escape the craft.

"Fuck that, we're never going to get all these people up there and out," Decator yelled up to her. He charged into the clouded cockpit and vanished from Tilly's sight. She could still hear him though, as he coughed and wheezed through the smoke, and soon she could hear him pounding on the front windows until one shattered.

Overhead, she heard the Low-fis returning, their whining, sputtering engines cutting through the mayhem unfolding inside the helicopter. Tilly stared at them and thought about the weight of the pistol at her side. She could easily pull it, but didn't have the power to bring even one drone down.

"Tilly! Help me set up this rifle," Saburo shouted. "Hurry."

It took a few seconds for the two women to piece together a long rifle with a huge scope. Tilly hadn't seen one like it since the war, carried by a sniper on one of her troop drops.

Cradling the weapon, Saburo squinted into the sight. She took a second to check the rifle, then steadied it on the metal wheel housing of the Pig, scanning for the Smog Hags as they approached. Tilly lay flat next to the woman, watching the craft skim in from the east, barely above the treetops. Tilly stared, breathing lightly so as not to disturb Saburo's own breathing. Her eye rested near the scope, sighting the vehicles in as they came. It didn't seem to Tilly the Hags were interested in any sort of evasive maneuvers. They likely assumed everyone was dead. She heard Rei shouting from his hiding place, trying to convince her to get to cover. She pushed his voice aside, focusing her concentration on the danger at hand.

"Two near the tree line, yeah?" Saburo asked.

"Agreed. Ten o'clock." Tilly watched the way the drones rode the wind, the way they fought gravity. They were like hummingbirds in the way they flitted and corrected on the wind. The one she'd seen up close appeared welded together from several crafts: the roll bar probably came from a truck or a dune buggy of some sort, the frame was a cargo drone, the weapons from ground troops or trucks, and most of the flight controls worked similar to a fighter of some sort. She filled some blanks in from what she could see as the Low-fis approached.

The buzz of the craft grew unbearable and Tilly braced for their attack. The long rifle jerked slightly next to her head, roaring some fiery obscenity at the Hags. Tilly looked over the trees to see the first shot didn't seem to hit. Saburo followed up with two more shots in rapid succession. The first of them shattered the Smog Hag's cockpit. The second appeared to impact the pilot's helmet. While it didn't kill the pilot, it made them react poorly, juking right to avoid more gunfire, and moving directly into the path of the other Low-fi, which hadn't registered the threat and wasn't trying to evade. They collided at high speed. The second craft sheared off the first's aft rotor and sent them both spinning into the trees to the north.

Tilly scanned the forest, waiting to see if more Smog Hags appeared by air or on the ground, but nothing came. After minutes of holding still, she looked at Saburo, who hadn't moved. "You okay?" Tilly stood, scanning the forest again.

"Any more?"

The air was devoid of the drones' buzzing rumble, though the coughing and sputtering of the dying Pig made it hard to be sure. "I think you handled it."

"We better move then." Saburo was already breaking the gun down, carefully sliding pieces into her backpack's housing.

A small plume of grey smoke rose from the area where the hags went down. Tilly took a deep breath and thought about the people onboard, thought about the lives they'd just ended. Was it worth the one person from Harrison's team who died? The gun in her holster felt heavier than before.

"Let's go," Saburo said. She was on the ground already, and the rescue mission crew were already nearing the foliage for cover. Tilly found her footing to jump back into the copter to get her own gear but stopped as she saw Saburo was still waiting nearby. The former co-pilot held up Tilly's pack, carrying twice the gear as everyone else. Tilly waved and slid down the hull to the ground.

"Thanks," Tilly said as she joined Saburo. "I appreciate it."

"I didn't know if it was going to go up in smoke in there or not."

"Are you okay? That's the question. It looks like your head stopped bleeding."

Saburo nodded. "A little banged up, but I'm good. I don't even feel the cut on my head. You?"

"I'm fine." It wasn't until that moment Tilly could feel an ache in her shoulder. She had no idea when she might have injured it in all the chaos, and she didn't dwell on it. She hoped it worked itself out quickly and didn't hamper whatever she needed to do next.

"Let's catch up. I'd hate to get lost out here."

Tilly grabbed Saburo's elbow. "Did you see who got out? Did everyone else make it? I know about Hyatt, but…"

"I think so; I mean, it was a mess in there, but I think so."

Ahead of them, the group was moving without them, and Tilly assumed it was at Ned's behest. As the only soldier in that group, he likely would have suggested the crew get off their butts and move on before more of the Smog Hags showed up and tried to finish the group off. The likelihood of them coming was high. They'd probably want a little revenge, sure, but they'd also want to scavenge whatever they could off the Cyclone, too. If any of the guns or equipment was still useful, it would help to create better Low-fis somewhere down the line. Whatever the motives, Tilly didn't want to be anywhere nearby when they showed up.

"Hey, why don't you move on ahead and catch the group?" Tilly said.

"You're limping. Why don't I cover the rear and you go ahead?"

"I'm fine." Tilly wanted the girl, as well-intentioned as she was, to get away. She felt all the emotions from the crash catching up to her and didn't want to have to share them, didn't want anyone putting their arm around her and telling her it would be okay, and the crash wasn't her fault. "Seriously, we can switch off in a couple of hours. You should go ahead," Tilly said. "Honest. I'll be fine." With a nod, Saburo patted Tilly's arm and increased her pace to reach the group as it disappeared into some trees.

Once the girl had vanished into the woods, Tilly turned and looked at the broken, smoking helicopter. She'd forgotten how much she loved the feel of flying and, as much as she hated the Fat Pig that was the Cyclone, she could feel herself shaking as she thought about the loss of it. While she stared at the crushed carcass of the copter, she could see the shape of it transform in the smoke, flames and water. It broke down as supports gave way, gear melted. It looked like something completely different from the Pig, but she couldn't decide what it was. The shattered front windows and the twisted metal of the cockpit looked like an enormous mouth, and the smoke streaming out appeared to be from a mythical monster preparing to breathe fire. It no longer resembled a bird; it looked more like the tattoo covering her arm from shoulder to wrist—a fire-breathing dragon. She watched it burn and thought about all the other things it looked like as it died a slow, crumbling death.

CHAPTER TEN

Six Years Earlier

"You did all this while I was gone, pop?"

Tilly picked up a rod and looked at it. It seemed like the most primitive thing she'd ever seen. She struggled to remember the last time she held something that wasn't made of metal or plastic. In her time in China, she'd seen her fair share of trees and shrubs, twigs, and grass, but there'd never been a need to bring them inside and make something. It was counterintuitive. Part of their job, their duties as soldiers, was to keep their living space clean, free of dirt, dust and things like… sticks. But here in her father's apartment were piles of sticks or dowels or frames or whatever they called the pieces from day to day. There were scraps of papers, bits of cloth, glue droplets, and a million other things a vacuum wouldn't pick up. It was maddening for someone conditioned to keep her personal space tidy.

"What in the world possessed you to move from the States to this place and take up this particular profession?"

"I saw a documentary on the art of Japanese kite making. They interviewed this man, and he talked about how making kites transformed him, made him a different person. It was this Zen thing for him."

"Zen thing? Dad, you've never used the word Zen in your life." Tilly carefully dropped a dozen or more scraps into the trash and wiped her hands.

Her father laughed. "Yeah, well. I'm still not entirely sure what it means, really." He took a deep breath, paused, and then took another. Tilly noticed he'd been breathing heavier and deeper in the last couple of days. His nurse said he went through spells like that, and they seemed to get more frequent.

"In this show, this documentary, they talked about how Japanese kite making was barely a thing anymore. Nobody was learning to build kites the old way anymore. Too much manufacturing and robots. Who has time to make a kite? Who cares how it's made? Robots, apparently. Robots and machines make the kites now."

"And that sounded perfect for you?"

"Yeah, why not?"

"A fifty-seven-year-old office manager from Chicago? You crunched numbers and yelled at people for a living, right?"

"Yeah."

It was like twenty questions, trying to get him to explain his thinking on why he made an enormous life change, relocated, and tried to resurrect a dying art. He made it sound like no big deal.

Tilly kept pulling at the threads he gave her. "So? You came here based on a show you watched? That's it?"

"Look, when I was a little shit, your grandfather and I, well, the whole family... There was your grandfather, grandmother, your uncle Leon, aunt Silvie, my cousins Mack, Teresa, Evan…" He paused, stuck in a memory. "There were others. Anyway, it was a bunch of us. And we'd rent this house in South Carolina, with a beautiful view of the beach and the ocean. Amazing. But your grandfather and I would fly kites on the beach all day. Well, most days. We knew nothing about *making* kites. We always bought these cheap plastic things from the store and flew them while the rest of the family was swimming and fishing." Her father pointed to the stick in her hand. "Plastic rods, plastic facing, cheap synthetic line. We didn't care."

"Grandpa Nick? He didn't seem like the kite flying type."

"Is there a kite-flying type? Doesn't everyone like flying a kite?"

"No, pop. They do not. There are most assuredly people who are not kite people," Tilly said. "I hope you aren't in charge of advertising for your kite company. Because 'Doesn't everyone like flying a kite?' is a terrible ad slogan."

He nodded and took a deep breath. "I suppose so, but we keep busy, you know?"

"You and Grandpa Nick spent all day with kites? Did you wear shorts there? I don't remember you ever wearing shorts. *That* seems unnatural. At least for you."

"I was a kid, and we were at the beach. Of course, I wore shorts."

Tilly laughed. "I can't picture it."

It was a few moments before her father said anything more. "I'm tired. I'm ready to go to bed."

"You're in bed."

"I'm ready to *sleep* now, smartass. I need my lights off and the music on."

Tilly gathered the scraps off her father's bed and then walked around the room, shutting off lights. "Okay. I understand."

"Not that light."

"What?" Tilly was all the way across the room.

"Leave *that* light on. I like it." He motioned to the lamp she'd just turned off.

"Why?"

He shrugged. "I like it on. Can you leave it on? What's the big deal? Maybe I want to go jogging later, *Jesus*, girl."

She laughed, enjoying how he could turn from happy to cranky to sarcastic on a dime. "Okay." Tilly clicked the light back on. "You know, all these things can be automated. Computerized. They can go off and on automatically." She turned on the radio and tuned it to the jazz station. "Your music, too."

Her father grunted and turned on his side.

"I can help with it," Tilly said. "I set it up for myself in my room, back in the military for my barracks."

Her father didn't reply.

"Okay then. I guess I'll see you in the morning." Tilly walked to the living room and sat on the couch where the glare of the street's nighttime lights flashed on, covering the entire area. She considered drinking a beer before she went to bed, but the buzz of her NaNi distracted her.

"*It has been fourteen hours since you last logged practice time. Should we practice now?*" The female voice asked.

"Sure." Tilly picked up the kite making kit her father had given her to learn with and set aside the bamboo, the thin strands of string, and all the other parts except the patterns, paper, and ink. She was to trace the pattern and learn the general shape of the kite, the way the faces and figures were created on the surface, the way they fit in the frames. She'd practiced the framing, working with the bamboo, but she was clumsy with it. She liked the art portion. The painting, the drawing was fun, although she despised tracing the patterns. It was better to create her own characters and patterns.

She smoothed out the paper and focused on it. If she stared at it, maybe she could imagine what belonged there: a dragon, a face, a dark cloud. Sometimes when she stared at the perfectly blank pages, she imagined what it would be like if she dumped a can of ink on it. She wondered if the slowly spreading ink would form a figure, eyes, nose, mouth with jagged fangs.

Most likely, her father would yell at her for wasting supplies and precious time.

CHAPTER ELEVEN

The trudge through the fields was tiring and nerve-wracking. The forest ended and their only path forward was through a series of flooded fields that likely were originally for planting rice or wheat, maybe tea leaves. The water reached their waists, but the upraised paths weaving a crisscross checkerboard pattern through the farms were impossible to see until they'd already tripped over them. The entire team was soaked within minutes, not only from falling at the paths, but from slipping in the mud all along the way.

"I can barely lift my feet. I think there's three inches of muck stuck to my bloody boots," Ned said.

"At least." Saburo, being much shorter than the lanky Brit, was having a tougher time. For her, the water was nearly up to her chest, and she had to hold her rifle high over her head as she struggled on.

Tilly stayed far in the back. Since the crash, she'd gotten nothing but dirty looks from Harrison and his men. Not one of them came back to check on her or fill her in on the plan of where they were going or what they would do now they were earthbound. No one was thrilled with her to be sure. That attitude is to be expected when you plow an aircraft into the trees of a foreign country. Forget she kept them all alive in that disaster, forget she'd kept them from being shredded by machine gun fire, and incinerated by missiles.

She stopped walking as the thought hit her: she hadn't kept them all safe. She knew when they were flying that Hyatt was thrown clear of the helicopter after being hit by the Low-fis. In the heat of the battle, she'd compartmentalized that information so she could focus on keeping them in the air. In the crash's chaos, she shoved it down to keep herself and everyone else alive again. And in the march to flee from danger, she'd forgotten about it to keep herself alive. Standing ass-deep in muddy water was not the time she wanted to unpack the memory, but it was too late to stop it. She pictured Hyatt flying out of the damaged doorway and off into the air and the ground below. Her body wouldn't let her escape the man's face or the terror he must have felt. She could have helped him if she was a better pilot, if she'd reacted faster to the attack, or if she'd forced Harrison to wait at the soccer stadium for more intelligence on the Smog Hags. She found a raised path and knelt there, without climbing up to stand out of the water, and stared at the mud all around her. She wondered what the hell had brought her to that point, wondered why she didn't stay in Nagasaki and take a real civilian job. Why she couldn't work a little harder at her father's business. Any of those things. If she'd done any of those things, she wouldn't have been with the group. Maybe he wouldn't have died.

Or maybe they *all* would have.

Off in the distance, Harrison pointed the group toward the nearest tree line, likely hoping to get some higher ground. It would make the trek less miserable, besides giving them cover from anything that may come their way. Tilly slogged through the water to catch up. She knew full well if they were still in the war, he would be the last person she'd follow. Despite her disdain for his instincts, this idea worked out, allowing the group to walk on a relatively flat surface in only a few inches of water. They only needed to dodge some tree branches and wide leaves.

It was colder once Tilly was out of the water. There was only a slight breeze, but the wet clothing felt like an icy burden. She wiped her smooth head dry as she could and pulled on her cover. The others were likely colder with wet hair beneath their hoods. She'd love to tell everyone she'd shaved her head long ago with situations like this in mind, but if she was being honest, she'd done it because it looked cool and was easy to take care of. It was also the reason she had the ink done on her arm. The rest of her unit got a small dragon wrapped in a sword on their left shoulders - their unit's insignia - and Tilly did the same, but she also got a full sleeve done on the opposite arm. The bright red and orange dragon started at her shoulder, wrapped around her arm, and ended with its mouth opening wide at her wrist. No one could deny she looked intimidating when she showed it.

As she cursed the flooded fields to herself, she heard a rustle in the trees on her right. The first time she noticed, she assumed it was the damn wind that had dogged them throughout the hike, and she ignored it. The second time however, the noise took on the rhythm of someone walking on dried leaves, one crunch after another. Ahead of her, the rest of the group had moved out of view, which made Tilly wonder if the sound in the trees could be one of her companions.

"Hello?" She stopped moving, so she didn't confuse her own footfalls with someone else's. "Saburo? Is that you?" The steps stopped, but there was no response. She took this as a good thing. She wasn't imagining the sound. "I can hear you, you know. You're crunching up a storm over there."

The line of trees was thick enough Tilly could barely distinguish one from another. The darkness in the trees descended with the afternoon clouds that thickened the smog. She wondered if the acid rain they'd been warned about at the stadium extended so far into China that it might come down on them if the weather turned.

The sound of rustling and dry leaves returned, rhythmic as before. She brought her rifle level and swept the woods. The weapon shook a little in her hands and she fought to steady it. "I'm not going to play this game. Come on out or I'll fucking come in after you." It felt stupid right away. What if no one was there? Was she cursing at a swinging branch? Tilly's finger tightened on the rifle's trigger. "Come out." The lack of response sent her forward, making good on her threat.

Fine.

She stepped carefully over the tall grass obscuring the area, minding the roots and the branches jutting from the dirt. Ahead, she saw movement, not a limb, not a phantom of her imagination, but the form of something moving close to the ground. Her guess, it was an animal. The wide-open fields, trees, and lack of humans would be conducive to wildlife. If she was still guessing about it, the thing approaching could easily be a sun bear, big cat, or a pangolin. It approached slowly, and Tilly stood still with her weapon ready. She was ready to relax when the form suddenly stood up and moved to a tree like it might climb it.

Tilly wondered if the creature had stood before it got to the tree, or if it had climbed up to a semi-standing stance using the tree. If it was a bear, it would make sense to stand on its own, but any other creature wouldn't look quite so large. She slowly reached over and activated the light on her NaNi, increasing the brightness, hoping to get a glimpse of the thing. Even at full power, the beam wasn't strong enough to cut through the distance.

"You wanna smoke?"

Tilly swung the rifle toward the voice and stopped short of pointing it in Saburo's face. The light from her device washed out the young woman's face.

The woman raised her hands to shield her eyes and backed off. "It's me, it's me. Wow, you *do* need to toke up a little. What the hell? You seem pretty fucking tense."

Tilly lowered her gun and looked back to the tree where she'd seen the form. Whatever it was had melted away. "Sorry. I saw something in the woods. Guess my imagination got the best of me. I was fixing to catch up when you startled me."

The click and sudden glow of a lighter let Tilly know Saburo had already moved on from the incident. The girl puffed out smoke and handed a joint over to Tilly with a smile.

"I volunteered to backtrack and locate your ass. Harrison was super broken up about you falling behind." She made a jerking-off motion with one hand and took the joint back with the other. "Mind clicking that off?" She pointed to Tilly's flashlight. "It's cool, though. Is it part of your little phone thing?"

Embarrassed to have the light still on and potentially attracting the attention of anyone or anything in the area, Tilly shut it off. "Yeah, sorry. It's an old one, and pretty beat up. I'm sure you have a newer one." She took the cigarette back and took another hit. She knew it was a bad idea standing around in a field smoking, knew she'd be impaired as they moved on, but she needed to calm down. The creature she'd seen in the woods was a figment of her imagination, nerves surfacing after the crash. If she didn't have a way to settle herself, she'd be jumping at shadows for the rest of the march.

"I don't have one of those things. Never been able to afford one, really."

Tilly was surprised. Back in the U.S., they handed them out like candy. "Didn't you get a basic model in the army? Our unit did, and I even managed some software upgrades necessary for my unit's job functions."

"We were deployed when the quartermaster sent those around. When we got back, they were mysteriously out of stock and back-ordered." Saburo shook her head. "And our quartermaster's kids were mysteriously going to a better college."

"Wow. Jackass move."

Saburo shrugged. "Eh. After that, I never felt the need for one."

"Not missing much, to be honest. Especially out here. Phone, mapping, and all the other features are blocked by the smog."

"You still have music and maps you downloaded before you left. Pretty awesome."

"Well, I ditched most of the music, but yeah. I guess." Tilly thought about remained on her NaNi—not much. Pictures, the latest Yellow River maps she got at the stadium, calendars, and a few videos she saved of kite-making lessons. Nothing that would do them much good in their current situation.

It was clear by the way she suddenly changed the subject that Saburo had something on her mind. She casually asked, "So what do you think the story is with the Brit and his mannequins? Are they for real here, or are they going to get us all ganked?"

A quick glimpse of Hyatt standing at the door of the helicopter flitted into Tilly's mind before she pushed it out. "Your guess is as good as mine. He does seem to be trying to get us all killed, though, bless his heart."

"Right? His men aren't soldiers, so why bring them, you know?"

"I think he wants to surround himself with his own people. Makes him feel safe. Since they work for him and the company, I suppose he thinks they're more loyal or they'll *have* to listen to him," Tilly said. She wondered if they were there because Harrison knew something he wasn't saying.

They walked together, in no hurry to catch up, until their cigarette was nearly gone. "You saw something in the woods, huh? Animal, vegetable, or mineral?"

"No idea. Probably some animal. Gone now, I guess. We need to watch out, make sure nothing and no one is dogging us."

"One person with their nose up our ass is no problem, but many more, and I'm not sure we can engage with a positive outcome." Saburo inhaled deeply and wheezed as she let it go. She flicked their roach into the water nearby. The ember hissed as it disappeared.

They both laughed.

"Engage with a positive outcome? That's one I haven't heard for a while. Takes me back to the first time I was in this country. I don't know what the hell to expect this time around."

In mere minutes, the pair caught up with the rest of the group, who had all stopped to rest and wait for them. Harrison and his men gathered in a semi-circle, hunched over a paper map with a small flashlight. Rei hung behind the others, disinterested and sleepy looking. Tilly noticed his eyes had gone black again, the contacts suggesting he was tense. His black Hōfuna cap was turned around backward, and his rifle hung loosely around his neck. It looked like he was snacking on a beef stick or something, rather than paying attention. Ned stood a few clicks up the path by himself, looking back and forth with his rifle cradled in his arms.

"Well, look who finally made it," Harrison said. "Next time we'll keep going and you're on your own."

Tilly could see he was angry at her, but probably too exhausted to give her the malice he'd intended. Was he angry they didn't have the helicopter, or because Hyatt was dead?

"Yeah. You looked absolutely heartbroken about me," Tilly said. "If you think you'll make it out here longer without me, you're welcome to light out on your own."

The two men seated beside Harrison had trouble folding the map back down into its original compact size. Tilly smiled when she realized they'd been looking at a common auto club-style road map of China. It showed highways, cities, parks and interchanges, all useless information in their current situation. Worst of all, there was no way something like that could show the current state of the Yellow River or the damage it would have done to the surrounding area.

"I'm not sure if you're aware of the situation, but *you* are one of my hired gun monkeys, so maybe show a little more respect and a little less mouth," Harrison said. "And now that our helicopter is gone, you're no more special than the next person only here for money."

"Hey," Ned interrupted. "It looks like there's some sort of rise a couple of clicks ahead. Could be a road that passed through these fields. Maybe it leads to a town somewhere where we can find transportation."

"You really think it will go somewhere?" Saburo asked.

"Has to go *somewhere*, right?" Ned replied.

"Huh. Makes sense, I would imagine." Saburo tightened the straps on her pack and checked her rifle. "I'll take point, if no one minds." She bounded off up the tree line without waiting for anyone's response, rifle at the ready.

"She's not too bright, is she?" Harrison asked when she was out of sight. "Anyone with half a brain wouldn't go off like that alone." Decator chuckled at the observation.

Ned stepped closer to the group. "Did you say the same thing about me when I took point and went off alone?" He gave the men a hard stare.

"Look," Decator was still smiling as he held up his hands. "Just joking around. I mean, the girl probably weighs ten stone soaking wet with her equipment on, and she barely comes up to my belly button. She's a joke."

"Why the fuck did your man Harrison hire her, then?" Ned shoved Decator, nearly knocking him to the ground. "And I'll tell you something. I'd follow her or Tilly long before I would follow any of you strapping lads into a fight."

When Harrison put his hand on his pistol, Tilly dissuaded him of the notion. She raised her rifle and nudged it into his side. "Let's not be stupid. Man's only stating his opinion, not threatening anyone."

"He shoved *my* man."

"Then they probably should settle it themselves, yeah?"

Rei paid attention when the weapons came out, though he made no play for his own. His eyes turned red, and he looked to Tilly for some indication of how to handle the situation. If the minor argument got out of hand, how far would they have to go to put it down? If it were to go beyond shouting and shoving, Tilly had her money on the combat vets.

The clack of a pistol being cocked startled Tilly, despite the already tense situation. She raised her rifle and scanned around to see who pulled the gun and whose side they were on. It confused her to see she was the only one with a weapon at the ready until she heard a voice behind them.

"None of you lot move," a man said. "You there, drop your gun."

CHAPTER TWELVE

Tilly slowly did as told and turned to see her group surrounded by at least a dozen soldiers emerging from the nearby weeds on both sides. Dark paint camouflaged their faces, and they wore a mishmash of various types of military fatigues.

"Who in name of fuck are you?" The man's voice was relatively quiet, and Tilly wondered if he was worried about attracting some sort of unwanted attention.

"We're with the Hōfuna group. We're looking for a missing scientific vessel that got lost somewhere on the river," Harrison said as he stepped forward.

"Was that your helicopter that went down? We were on our way to check it out."

"Yes," Harrison said. "We were trying to find some sort of shelter in case the Hags came back to finish the job."

"Hōfuna?" the leader asked. "You were supposed to land at our camp and refuel a couple of hours ago."

Relief flooded Harrison's face. "You're with the United Nations group? Thank God. I was afraid we'd be lost out here for days. Can you get us back to your camp?"

"Sure."

Tilly asked, "Is your camp any safer than legging it through the brush? No offense."

"None taken. It's safe. I'm major Collins, with the U.N." The leader lowered his weapon and signaled his people to do the same. Both groups relaxed. "The Smog Hags generally leave us alone. We have plenty of defenses and a good number of troops. Also, it seems like they know exactly where the territory boundary is and they're reluctant to pass over it. Probably afraid to incur the wrath of the United Nations' mighty security forces. Start an international incident if they did."

"Good," Harrison said.

The atmosphere tensed again when a woman's voice shouted, "Everything good over there?" It was Saburo.

"What are you talking about?" Harrison seemed annoyed again, and it took Tilly back to the fight brewing before Collins and his troops came in.

"Who?" Collins asked.

A red, laser-generated targeting dot appeared on Collins' chest. When the man realized what was happening, he reached for his sidearm. Tilly put her hand on his.

"It's okay, Saburo. We're all good here. You can come back. These soldiers are going to escort us to their camp. We're good. Don't shoot."

It took a moment, but the red light went out. After a few beats, Saburo came trudging through the brush, rifle still at the ready. "You okay here?" She asked again, eyes scanning the soldiers she didn't know.

"Yes." Tilly smiled and patted Saburo's arm. "Nice job covering us. Good to know someone had our backs out here." She looked at Harrison and lingered, trying to stare daggers into the man. She heard Ned giggle at the insult. It was at that moment she knew for sure which companions she could count on in the group and which were along to protect Harrison's interests. She was still up in the air about Rei. He was on the opposite team, but he seemed to have some sense about him.

Collins looked around the group. "Are we all here then, or are there more surprises in the bushes?"

The ensuing march took them back through the flooded fields, though it seemed Collins and his men knew paths that kept them only ankle deep in the water, rather than waist level. It was getting on in the afternoon and already getting dark. No one used lights, though. They walked close to the tall green weeds protruding from the water in the area. The foliage gave them some cover from anyone following them, and the sweet, sugary smell gave their nostrils a reprieve from the stagnant stench of the decaying grass of the previous fields and stagnant mud. It also covered the way Tilly's clothes reeked of pot smoke.

Darkness fell during the hour it took to get to the camp. They walked in from the east up a steep muddy path until they came to the first part of their encampment. Here, stacked in rows of three, were enormous concrete pipes. Tilly guessed they had to be around eight feet tall at the mouth and maybe twenty or twenty-five feet long. Cloth or a blanket fixed to it concealed the opening of each pipe. As they approached, people stuck their heads out from behind the coverings. The pipes stacked in the second and third rows had rough ladders leading up to them.

"What's this?" Ned asked.

Collins sighed. "This was supposed to be new living quarters for our soldiers and their families, but every time we tried to build, something came along and fucked it up royally. The pipes were supposed to be for the new sewer system, but now they're the closest thing these people have to luxury apartments. Some of those fit two homes. Block off the middle and you've got a two-family walkup on the third floor."

"What keeps stopping you?" Saburo asked. "I thought it was U.N. territory and no one would attack it."

"No, the Smog Hags won't attack. They only want to survive. All the other factions would love to take this area if they had a shot. Mostly the Chinese and the rebels, I suppose. They'd love to claim this if they could get away with it. That's why there's so many people here. They all came to avoid the attacks on their own encampments. But the Hags? They don't want trouble with us."

The village comprised rows and rows of the pipes and other dwellings made from what must have been the supplies to build proper houses. Fencing, two by fours, and the occasional doors were all representative of do-it-yourself housing units. Kids' toys littered the ground in many areas, fires raged in old oil drums. It was like many settlements Tilly had encountered during aid missions in her early years flying for the military.

They passed through the village and followed a muddy stone trail up to a camp with more conventional buildings. They looked a little different from the dwellings Tilly had stayed in during her training. There were a couple of corrugated buildings that likely served as barracks, and several other wooden structures. One of them had a big red cross on the outside, and the other looked more like a long mess hall. In the distance were two more sewer pipes standing on end next to each other, reaching some twenty feet into the air.

"This is our home, sweet home. You got your infirmary, your command center, chow hall. You can't see them from here, but we have latrines further back, so they don't contaminate our water up here," Collins said. "I'd imagine you want to get out of those wet clothes and have a nice meal. We can loan you all some clothes, and I'll have someone show you where you can change and hang up your stuff."

"Thanks," Harrison said.

"While you're doing that, I'll get a cook to get some dinner cracking for you," Collins said. He grabbed a nearby soldier and pulled her close. "This is private Nancy. Nancy, show our visitors to the shed so they can change." Nancy nodded and pulled the group along with a wave.

"We'll get you changed in the storage shed, and then I'll see if we can set up some sleeping bags while you eat, good?"

"Sounds great." Ned followed Nancy a little closer than the others as they walked toward the far corrugated building. "I'm most certainly tired and hungry, so I guess that covers it."

"Don't trip over yourself," Saburo said with a disapproving sneer.

"Nancy? Is that your last name? Or is it your first? Can I call you Nancy?"

"We just got here, dude." Tilly shook her head, assuming Ned was trying to make a friend for the night.

Nancy let them change into some ill-fitting clothing, then led them back to the mess hall to eat with Collins and a few others under his command. It was simple, much like at the soccer stadium. There was rice, some sort of juice, fresh water, plenty of greens, and even some piss-poor Japanese beer. The group ate whatever was placed in front of them, wave after wave, without question.

"You've no helicopter, and I assume no backup airship. And I'm guessing you haven't found whatever it is you're here for." Collins sat down with a mug of some neon orange drink. "So, what do you do now, son? What's your plan?"

Everyone looked to Harrison for his plan on how to move forward. Tilly was as eager to hear his intent as anyone else. If he'd said a word about it to anyone, it would have been when they were huddled with their auto club map out in the field before Tilly and Saburo caught up with them. If anything had been ironed out, they hadn't shared it with her.

"We barely hit the river when the Smog Hags attacked us and hadn't really begun our mission. When the Cyclone put us down, we were at square one." He drank in a dark cup of coffee and thought for a second. "I don't know what the hell to do, honestly. I guess we'll leg it up the river from here to continue the mission."

"Really?" Saburo asked with a full mouth. "You don't want to turn around? We have no idea where to find this hockey puck of yours."

Private Nancy cleared her throat, sitting at a table away from the rest. "You want to continue up the river?"

Harrison and his group turned to Nancy. "Yes, we'd like to. I mean, we don't have too many options. That's one of them."

She nodded. "I mean, if Major Collins could see his way clear to let a few of us go for a bit, I think I could help you out."

"No." Collins sounded startled by something.

"No?" Nancy asked. "What else are we doing around here? Least we can do is help."

"We already helped," Collins said.

"What's going on?" Harrison asked.

"Come with me," Nancy said.

"*Nancy,*" Collins growled.

"Just a little show and tell, sir." The group pushed away from the table and followed the private out of the mess hall and up another trail until the sound of the river got more intense. There, right on the water, an overgrown path led to another building they'd not seen before.

Nancy yanked on the rusted door until it creaked open, and she ushered everyone inside. They stood in the enormous corrugated building and stared at three rusting boats bobbing in the filthy water. Tilly had the same feeling in her stomach as when she first saw the copter that got them there. These were elderly vehicles whose usefulness had long passed. The three might not have been quite as old as the copter, but they were close, maybe Vietnam era, or Korean war. The three of them were likely called fast attack boats at one time, though their speed was probably relative at this point. The largest could hold a good dozen people, but the other two were made for what Tilly guessed was a three-person crew. A heavy gunner for the principal weapon at the fore of the boat, another soldier for the lighter guns, and a pilot.

"They run?" Harrison asked.

"Do they even float?" Saburo asked.

Private Nancy puffed up her chest in a show of mock indignation. "Do they run? Do they float? I am hurt. This *wounds* me. I offer you a thing you require, and you question my veracity? Fucking wounded, I am."

"Well?" Harrison said. "You have to admit, they look a bit run down."

Nancy hopped from the dock onto the deck of the larger boat and held her arms out. "Look at it. I can have a man with a hose here to spritz this place down in minutes. A little elbow grease, some wire brushes, and they'll be sea-worthy. Extremely sea-worthy. These are the best boats you'll find anywhere on the river."

"I literally haven't seen another boat on the river," Harrison said. "Not a one."

"Then you will *rule* the waters." Nancy's smile widened at the declaration.

"Jesus, Nancy." Collins shook his head. "I don't think these things are a good idea. I mean, shit, they haven't been out in a couple of years."

Tilly stood behind the others and scanned the boats herself. She was quickly becoming a believer in turning back. Her whole reason for being there was to fly a helicopter which no longer functioned. She knew how to handle a gun, and was good at being a soldier, but it wasn't why she had signed up. If these boats could function, then best they head back downriver with them, pilot to a city on the map that still actually existed and run back to Japan before something worse happened to them.

"Course, you could always swim upriver. How is your dog paddle?"

"Let's take the boats and head home. This whole thing is a wash," Tilly said.

Puffed up by the sudden acquisition of potential transport, Harrison sounded more confident. "You know, we've already talked about this. If you want to go home, you can, but you'll do it on your own. I think we can still get to the WHEEL and finish this job. We are going to find this WHEEL." Harrison stared at the gun placements. "Any of those work?" he asked Nancy.

"A few of them. Not all. You can always use the gunwales to steady the soldiers' personal weapons."

"We don't need all these. We certainly don't have the crew to man all three properly," Harrison said.

"I can help with that. If you sweet-talk the major here, we can provide the crew, and all you'll need to do is look for your lost whatever. We can return the boats when you're done. No problem. No problem *at all*." Nancy seemed far too interested in making this deal for Tilly's liking. If the crew was going to rob Harrison's search team, they were going to be sadly let down when they saw how little the group was carrying. And it made no sense why they would go through the ploy of allowing them to use the boats. They could easily have killed the team at any point after their crash landing, if that was their intent.

"I don't know…" Collins said.

There was hope in Nancy's eyes. "If we go, we can find supplies, fruit, things we need. Maybe trade with the Scottish post up the river a bit." She smiled at the major and nodded fervently.

"How can I say no to such an offer? Have some volunteers tidy these things, and we'll salvage what we can from the storehouse,"

Collins said. "And Nancy? I'd like a word back at the camp. Immediately."

Harrison glared at Tilly as he passed her. "If you still plan on coming with us, I suggest you lend a hand with the repairs, kiddo."

Standing nearby, Saburo said, "Hell, we'll all pitch in. Look, the faster we find this station and the doctor, the faster we can go home."

Ned laughed at the comment. "Home? Shit, *this* is home now. Home is where most of your underwear is. And right now, that's here."

"Oh, and all this time I was imagining you didn't wear underwear, Ned." Saburo rolled her eyes and walked on.

Tilly took a moment to stare at the dark river beyond the building and the dangers that awaited there. The Hags were still somewhere in the area, there were rogue teams with missile launchers and God knows what else, fanatics out to kill anyone in their territory, and now they were preparing to continue in boats smelling like latrines. But if she quit now, odds were good she wouldn't get paid. And that lessened the chances of going home to the Carolina beaches. With a sigh, she grabbed a wrench based solely on the hope of Saburo's words. *The faster they did the job, the sooner they could get home.* Wherever that was for her now.

CHAPTER THIRTEEN

After some preliminary work, they walked back up the rocky path to the ratty little camp where the soldiers lived, some small distance from the main living area of the civilians. They, too, lived in poorly built shacks and huts, with the center of their camp made from two enormous pieces of concrete sewer pipe. Unlike the villagers, though, these weren't laid on their side for people to live inside. Their openings were pointing toward the heavens. They each had to be a minimum of thirty feet tall with a ten-foot diameter.

"Come." Nancy motioned for the group to follow as he led them around to the far side, where they found two crudely chiseled openings, one in each pipe. The closest had two soldiers casually guarding it on the inside. Beyond them, every available space on the wall had racks drilled into it. All held some sort of weapon, explosive, or piece of military equipment. On the floor, crates were labeled with black markings indicating they contained an odd assortment of goods: MREs, kitchen supplies, lanterns, cassette tapes, and yarn were ones that caught Tilly's eye. Above them, an enormous blue tarp stretched tightly over the top.

"This one is our equipment storage and armory. Anything we find out in the world that could be of some use to our efforts ends up here for safekeeping. We have guards on station all day and night." She nodded to the filthy camo-clad soldiers above them and continued to the next pipe, which had a series of mismatched tarps attached to the top of the pipe, forming a funnel which emptied into a trough at the bottom. "This thing is our crude attempt to reclaim rainwater for cleaning and bathing. The refugee camp uses purified river water for everything."

"You don't have the acid rain problem here?" Harrison asked.

"No. It usually dissipates by the time it gets to us."

"Usually?" Ned asked. "How do you know if it's safe to drink or not?"

"If the water is hissing, or if the barrel seems to be melting, don't drink it." She pointed to a ladder on the outer wall of the water pipe, then pointed up to a narrow ledge around the outside. "We station a man up there at night to keep watch. There's a little perch inside he can use to sit on, so things aren't quite so precarious."

Harrison tried to be polite, but the speed with which his words emerged suggested he wasn't listening terribly closely. "Thank you for the tour and the offer to help with the transportation. We'd like to leave as soon as we can. Would it be possible to get underway at first light?"

Nancy looked at one of the men following the group—they'd accumulated a bigger following than Tilly realized—and the man shook his head. "No. It'll take a bit longer. Maybe two days. Depends on how the repairs go, I suppose."

Tilly's heart sank. More time out in the Chinese wilderness was not good news. "What's going to take so long?" she asked. "I mean, you said the boats work, right? Then what do you need two days for?"

Harrison shot her a look and held up a hand to her. "I'm in charge here, Tammy."

"Tilly. My name is Tilly."

He turned his back to her and addressed Nancy. "We can wait that long. *If we must*. But anything you can do to speed this up would be greatly appreciated."

Nancy smiled and opened her arms wide. "Of course, of course. There's no need to worry. We'll get you there safe and sound. We're all friends here." She patted Tilly on the shoulder. "Good friends."

The others were silent until Ned spoke. "What in fuck's name are we supposed to do for forty-eight hours in your lovely facilities?"

The red-haired woman leaned even closer to Tilly. "We… *have alcohol*." She laughed close enough Tilly could smell the stench of her breath, a mixture of fish, cigarette smoke, and cabbage that somehow smelled worse than the boats.

And that was it. They were given floor space in the storage building with clean sleeping bags. As everyone jockeyed for the best area for their rack, Tilly gazed at the beautiful trees and foliage lurking outside the ugly, muddy circle of the base. It was a tangle of greens and yellows, browns, and reds.

"What exactly are these people?" Saburo strode up, eating her rice as she walked. "Are these soldiers all with the United Nations?"

"I've noticed a few Americans. Nancy seems to be Spanish. Hang on." Tilly tapped her NaNi and asked it to display the map they'd scanned. She zeroed in on their current position. "Well, according to this map, we're in neutral territory awarded to the United Nations. So… there's that."

"I haven't seen a U.N. flag since we arrived," Saburo said.

It was a problem Tilly faced even when she was a part of the fighting force during the war. A lot of the things that happened only occurred on paper. No one really policed them or bothered to confirm they were running as they should. Even during the war, when satellite and wireless communications were working at their peak, when a simple call or scan would prove the existence of an anomalous force or rogue battle was happening, it rarely happened, and the reason was simple: chaos.

There was so much going on in China, no single government or combination of them could keep track of it all. When a splinter faction of the Chinese military joins up with like-minded Russian and Japanese groups, it wasn't a piddly few hundred or even a thousand rebels to deal with; it was an army in the millions which squeezed old-school China in a way it had never felt before. It would have made sense for everyone else to stay out of it, and let the country destroy itself, which is something the United States had never managed in its long rivalry with them. But the world saw it as an opportunity to weaken China, under the guise of helping them. And once the conflict was in hand, they all had their piece of the continent pie to 'protect.'

After the war, the original Chinese landmass stood at about forty-five percent of its starting area. Over half got chopped up and divided among the interested parties. And from there, no one really monitored each other. They couldn't, with the smog interfering with the satellites and communication.

"Look, this is weird, but..." Tilly wondered if her observation was all that strange.

"What?" Saburo asked.

"Have you seen a single Chinese person since we landed? I mean, how many billion Chinese people are there in China?"

The question seemed to take Saburo by surprise. "*What?*" She laughed. "Well... I mean, I'm sure the Smog Hags were Chinese, right?"

"I suppose, but we never saw their faces. I mean, not right up and personal. There weren't any at the stadium that I remember. I haven't seen any here at the encampment yet."

Saburo pointed in the general direction they'd walked through when they first arrived. "There's an entire camp full of refugees over there. They have to be up to their asses in Chinese people, ya know? It's late, but we can check out their village in the morning if it sets your mind at ease."

"I'd like that. I'm not worried, I guess. Just puzzled." When Tilly had been in the country with her unit during the war, they had Chinese advisors, used combat troops from various factions and assisted in the airlift of citizens from combat ops, it was their country and it made sense they could barely move without stepping on one.

But here, she'd seen so many other nationalities, including representation from every other Asian country. She was American, Saburo was probably Filipino, Ned seemed to be a white mutt, Harrison and his two men were British, and Rei was likely Japanese. Were there any Chinese soldiers or pilots when they stopped to fuel up on the way to the mainland? She didn't think about it at the time, but the man in the yellow hardhat at the airport had to be South Korean. It was an enigma she hoped could be answered at the refugee camp in the morning. Were the people of China all wise enough to move further inland in anticipation or fear of more flooding? Or did something else draw them in another direction?

The evening descended into a more chill affair than Tilly

expected. The soldiers built up a crazy high bonfire in the center of their ramshackle headquarters and pulled up chairs and stumps and anything else they could find to sit on. Tilly sat down on a dirty blanket, drank a strong German lager, and stared at the flames. All the while, Nancy and the other U.N. soldiers did their best to amuse their visitors with strange war stories, some grisly enough to make Harrison and his men visibly uncomfortable.

One stubby blonde-haired woman with a German accent laughed a little too hard at the stories and blurted out, "Oh, and the cat parade. That was good fun."

"Elina, enough," Collins said.

"What's she talking about?" Ned asked. "Cats?"

"No, no. She's drunk. She's talking crazy. One of our patrols caught a woman going through our trash, and they scared her off, that's all. It's a stupid lie which rolls on and gets bigger."

"Where does the cat part come in? How do you get from a woman in the trash to cat people?" Harrison asked. He was apparently intrigued, and leaned closer to Collins to understand his words better.

"There are many Chinese legends about shapeshifters, and through nothing but sheer boredom, someone repeated one," Collins said. "That's it. Small, superstitious minds. They caught a woman and called her a shapeshifter. That is all, that's it."

"I saw it, and so did Shulcoff. Others too," a man shouted from the other side of the fire.

"Bullshit." Ned smiled and shook his head.

"No, the woman had the face of a cat and could leap like a goddamn panther." The other man sounded clear-headed, unlike the woman who brought the subject up. "It was no ordinary woman."

The first soldier spoke again, spilling her beer as she motioned with her arms. "What about the Scots? Huh? They say they've seen cat people and more strange things. The last time we traded with them, they talked about winged monsters and tiger women. What about that?"

"They're assholes. They were fucking with you. It's a sodding sport for them. The Scots barely tolerate us, and only then because we have things they want for trade. Enough of this. I'm not drunk enough to have a serious conversation about your ridiculous creatures stalking the woods," Collins said. "I'm going to drink more, but I still won't want to hear your crap."

The woman mumbled something in German and turned her back on him, staring directly at Tilly. Her eyes were vacant, likely from drinking, but Tilly read something else there, fear maybe. Confusion? It wasn't easy to tell, not considering the things she said, and the effort Del put into discrediting her.

More alcohol passed around the fire led to less talk. People left the circle, off to bed, guard duty, patrol, the latrines. Some came back, some didn't, but no one asked why. Tilly sat between Ned and Saburo, and they remained as far from Harrison and his men as they could, feeling somewhat like they were at an office Christmas party with their boss. They weren't sure exactly how far they could go in enjoying themselves.

"Hey," a nearby shout cut through the calm of the evening. The guard stationed at the top of the pipe pointed toward the woods. "Another scavenger in our trash."

Collins looked at his people and rolled his eyes. "Jesus God, what's so great about our garbage? Someone chase the fucker off." His words sent a trio of woozy soldiers running toward the armory and then off toward the dump with rifles. Thinking of the German woman's alleged encounter with a strange beast, Tilly stood and chased after them, curious more than anything.

"Where are you going?" Ned asked, startled into motion from his own binge. "What are we doing?"

Tilly ran as best she could in the muddy clearing of the compound and followed out into the brush outside the perimeter. The forest got thicker the further they ran into it. Nearly tripping over several stumps as she first came in, Tilly realized the militia had likely cut the trees down to better see any coming attacks. The scavenger they were chasing had closed the distance to the woods in no time flat, leaping from stump to stump until they were well within the thick trees and full foliage.

"Slow down, Tilly," Saburo shouted. "Don't get too far ahead."

It was then she realized she'd left without grabbing a weapon of any sort; no gun, no knife, nothing. If she was running into a fight, she'd be defenseless on her own. Despite the fear of an ambush, she continued on. She did her best to follow in the same area the intruder had stepped, hoping it would help avoid any booby-traps hidden along the forest floor.

After less than a minute, she knew she'd lost the mysterious figure. And she also realized she'd lost the drunken soldiers almost as soon as they entered the wooded area. Tilly slid to a stop and took a minute to listen for any sign of life. The only thing she could hear was the tromping of her fellow crew behind her. They came up behind her and stopped a few feet back.

"What did you do, lose them?" Ned asked.

"You alright?" Saburo asked.

Tilly quickly caught her breath and pointed around the area. "I saw them until right about here. Fucking fast little mother, I can tell you for sure."

"Screw it. Probably some war orphan digging through the trash for food," Ned said. He was panting from the short run, harder than he should have been. "Probably hundreds of them, thousands all over the country. Not like they took anything but trash. Fuck it. We aren't getting paid to guard these people's shit." Ned glanced around and walked back toward the camp.

"What do you think?" Saburo stepped up next to Tilly. "Any reason we should care about this person rummaging through the trash?"

"Probably not." Something nagged at Tilly, like maybe this wasn't just some urchin looking for scraps. They were small enough to be a child, but they moved like a streak of light, like nothing she'd seen before. There was certainly no way she was going to catch up with someone like that.

"I think I'm on edge from being back in this country, you know? I thought I'd be fine, but everything seems different, yeah?" Saburo said. "It's like a different place, I guess. The first time I was with the army, you know? It was all official and whatnot. Now, it's just us. Should we care about this?"

It was something that hadn't occurred to Tilly. In many respects, they were the law wherever they went. Who knew what the law was from territory to territory here? Did anyone enforce anything? Various countries may have claimed territories in the remnants of China, but none of those nations had the people to fill out and occupy the land as the citizens of China itself had. So now there were wide-open swaths of uninhabited land throughout the territories where, Tilly supposed, a person could do most anything they wanted.

"We don't have to worry about anything being official or right or wrong. We only have to do our job here and get home," Tilly said. "And the job description didn't include running down trash thieves." She took a last look and patted Saburo on the shoulder. "Come on, I'm exhausted, and my brain doesn't have the bandwidth for this shit right now. I'm ready for bed." She was aware of how much the booze had affected her in her pursuit and figured she was right in stopping where she had. Any further into the forest and she might have gotten herself lost.

They walked back toward the stench of the bonfire still smoldering at camp. Tilly wondered what type of wood or underbrush they'd cut to make the fire stink like it did. It certainly made it easier to find their way back. *Just follow the reeking smell of decay.*

As they got to the cut back area of trees, the bonfire bathed the camp in its orange and yellow glow, causing shadows to dance across the ground. Before they could move another step, Tilly noticed something near one of the buildings. She silently held out her arm to stop Saburo. At first, she thought it was a trick of shadows, but as they watched, it moved out of line with the fire. A dark figure gliding close to the wall.

"Did the idiot come back already?" Saburo asked.

"Looks like. Wait here. I'll go around and see if I can scare them your way." Tilly crouched and made her way as quietly as she could among the trees, hoping the crackling of the fire and conversations of those surrounding it would be enough to cover any noise she made. When she found cover and peered out to assess the situation, the person was gone. No one stood along the wall, nor had the person dropped to the ground to hide.

From behind her, a low voice mumbled something in Chinese. Whoever said it was well-concealed in the forest.

"Who is it?"

"English." The voice almost sang the word.

"Yes, English."

"I eat their food. They get angry."

"Saburo?" Tilly called.

"They set traps. I break their traps and they get more angry."

Tilly rose from her hiding place. "Who are you?" It certainly wasn't Saburo's voice, and she doubted the woman could have made it over from her position so quickly without being heard. It was definitely a female voice, but garbled, and not necessarily due to a language barrier. It was something else. It seemed the speaker had a lisp, or a swollen tongue—some physicality that impaired her speech.

"I have been watching you and your friends. You are going up the river, correct? You should not."

"Why?"

"Things happen there. Not good things. Ancient things."

Tilly considered it for a few moments. "Like what?" She squinted into the darkness, seeing the dark form moving backward as she did.

There was a crush of branches and sudden shouts before she could get an answer. "I have her," Saburo shouted.

Tilly turned in the commotion's direction, homing in on the noise. "Be careful," she shouted. "Stop. Stop it."

At first, Tilly thought the dim light of the distant campfire was playing tricks on her as Saburo held the woman's head up. Her face was thick and sleek, almost coming to a point at her nose. A light layer of short, white and orange hair, or maybe it was actually fur, covered her skin. She couldn't tell in the light. The woman's large black eyes stared back defiantly. It appeared much like the woman at the campfire described: a woman who looked like a cat.

"What the hell?" Saburo said.

"Who are you?" Tilly asked. She'd never seen anything like the creature outside of a movie. It swatted at Saburo with thick, wide hands and clawed fingers. When she opened her mouth, her teeth were pointed and sharp.

"*What* are you?" Saburo tightened her hold on the woman to get her to answer.

"I am Mingmei," the woman said. "I am why you don't go further up the river." The words came muffled and strained, like she was having trouble getting them out of her tooth-crowded mouth. "Look well on me."

Their scuffle brought people running toward them, zeroing in on the noise. Tilly could see them through the trees, lights bobbing through the branches. She could make out five of them, at least, and knew they didn't have much more time alone with the creature, the person, calling herself Mingmei.

"What's up the river?" she asked Mingmei.

As those from camp drew closer, Mingmei's face turned more fearful. "Let me free, they will kill me. Kill me like the others."

"What's up the river that could do something like this to you?" Tilly felt a pain in her forehead as she thought about the thing before her. She half-remembered the thing in the trees as they'd hiked through the fields. As it struggled with Saburo, Tilly could see more of the tiger-woman's body. Though she covered most of her upper body with a tattered brown shirt, the fur still showed through on her neck and lower arms, her hands, and wrists. Her legs were thick and muscular and fur-wrapped as well.

"You will not find your doctor, only *Kalidas*. And death."

"*What happened to you*?" Tilly asked again, but those from camp had caught up with them. The area was bathed in the white light of their flashlights, and the air filled with their shouts and heavy breathing. They got close enough that she could smell their unwashed clothes and foul breath wafting over her shoulder.

Collins ran up to the group as Mingmei stopped struggling. "Jesus. It's another one. These things get bolder the more they come around." The deep voice of the camp leader sounded disappointed more than anything.

"This is the person you saw before?" Saburo asked.

"One of them."

"There's more?"

"Plenty. All the time. Probably the fifth one we've caught this week, Nancy?"

"Sixth," Nancy said. She sounded sure of her count and as unimpressed as Collins.

"Yeah, six is right, I guess," Collins said. "Kill it and toss it into the woods with the others. Maybe they'll get the hint."

The men raised their guns and pointed them at Mingmei and Saburo. "Get out of the way and let it go. Don't worry, it won't escape." Saburo's eyes went wide in fear she'd get caught in the shooting.

"Whoa." Tilly put herself between the men and the creature. "Wait a minute. This is a living, thinking creature. You can't just shoot it. It… *she's* intelligent. She has a name. What the fuck is wrong with you?"

"My dog back home has a name and knows how to bring me my shoes, doesn't mean it's a person or nothing," Collins said. "Now move."

"What's happening?" Harrison and his men came running up to the back of the crowd.

"The fairy tales they were telling around the campfire weren't fairy tales," Tilly said. "The tiger lady is real."

"Let me go." Mingmei's voice was high and angry.

Harrison and his man stopped to gaze at the thing, stunned. Rather than stand next to them and gawk, Rei passed them and came to Tilly's side, looking at her and Mingmei.

"The thing is real?" Harrison asked. "It's real? He really did it?"

More men and women had gathered around, mumbling, and pushing each other for a look at the furry orange and black woman. Some wandered away quickly, but others lingered with vacant stares, in awe of the thing squirming in Saburo's grip.

"Why did you lie?" Tilly asked Collins. "Why try to keep this a secret?"

Before Collins could offer a reason, Saburo yelped in surprise and pain. Her hands instinctively shot to her face where the woman had clawed her. The creature that called herself Mingmei bounded off into the woods before anyone realized what was going on. In the commotion, soldiers began firing wildly into the trees. Tilly fell to the ground, dragging Saburo and Rei down with her. Soldiers immediately began pouring over them, running into the darkness to catch the woman.

It would have been fine with Tilly to rest on the grass and leaves to contemplate what she'd seen. She had no urge to get up and give chase to the men or the entity they pursued. Her body likely wouldn't have allowed her to stand up anyway, such was the state of her muscles and mind. As the adrenaline of the chase and the shock of the unknown wore off, she found it hard to focus on things around her, harder still to push her way up to a sitting position. She could still feel; she knew Saburo's leg pressed against her, so she hadn't left. Rei held her forearm in a tight grip, and she could hear Harrison's voice fading in and out like he was pacing in another room, but little else.

"The fuck is going on?" she asked no one in particular. "I feel like I've been drugged or something. I can't see. I just..." She fought it, but darkness crept not only into her vision, but her mind until it all went blank.

CHAPTER FOURTEEN

Six Years Earlier

"Come on, Hirata. Whatever possessed you to go into business with my father? I mean, an office manager from Chicago? When did you even have time to teach him Japanese?" Tilly laughed. "He isn't the quickest learner."

Hirata seemed unamused. "Is that what you think of your father? That he was an office manager? He was the manager of international sales for his company. He already spoke our language fluently, along with several others. He taught *me* some Spanish."

There was never a time when Tilly had heard her father speak anything but English, and he'd never mentioned knowing more. She'd joined the military straight out of high school and mainly communicated with him via phone calls and emails, video chats, and text. It left little opportunity for him to show off his language skills, but it surprised her he didn't at least talk about it.

"He said when your mother passed and you left home, he felt pretty alone. Taking classes let him meet people and learn things to feel useful to his company. To anyone, I suppose."

"But kite-making? Come on. This bird-legged old white guy from America comes over to Japan to save the art of traditional Japanese kite making?"

"You do not know your father so well. When he came to me with his idea, yes, I thought he was a crazy person. But he showed more dedication and love for this art than any of my countrymen. He was eager to learn and took direction well. You must admire that, coming from the military? The discipline he showed was truly touching."

In the bedroom, her father's light steps made the floorboards creak. He shuffled out in his ratty bathrobe and grunted a hello to

Tilly and Hirata. "I'm hungry."

"Good to see you too, pop," Tilly said. "There's pudding in the fridge. Your favorite, butterscotch."

"I don't want any damn pudding. And *fuck* butterscotch."

Hirata laughed. "Henry, you get damn cranky when you wake up, you know? You should take it easy today, you're always a little sick the day after a treatment."

"Do I?" Henry grumbled. "I hadn't noticed."

"Dad."

"It's okay. I'm used to it." Hirata stood and grabbed his umbrella. "I was on my way out. I'll see you in the shop tomorrow, Tilly?"

She nodded and opened the door for him.

"Yeah. She'll be there, right under our feet." Henry rolled his eyes.

"See you later, Mister Sato." Tilly closed the door and walked to the kitchen sink to work on the afternoon dishes.

"Dad, seriously. What the hell? Why were you an ass to him?" Soap bubbles already covered Tilly's hands. She wiped them on the dish towel and tossed it on the counter. "Maybe we need to consider going home. You aren't making any friends here, that's for sure. Maybe go back home to South Carolina. You still have some friends there. You have family - your cousin Martin, Aunt Lisa, right?"

"Marty's a damn dog's ass, and Lisa hasn't spoken to me since your mom left. I'd sooner pound my dick flat with a wooden mallet." He was nearly asleep, drained from the day's treatment. "Look. You don't have to be here. Hirata can help me. He said he would."

"No offense, but Mister Sato isn't much more spritely than you are."

"He's fine. *Shit.* He's healthy as a horse, with all the stuff he eats and drinks. Raw vegetable juice and seaweed. Ever eat that kale stuff? Ugh. Nasty."

"Dad," Tilly said. "I'll stay. I'm fine with staying, but it's confusing here. I don't know my way around. I don't know where the hospitals are, the treatment facilities. I can't help if I don't know my way around, you know? You would be more comfortable back home."

"Aww. That's not home anymore. Hasn't been," her dad said. He coughed and his voice became somewhat clearer. "Hell, what do you need to know about this place? I'll point to the grocery for you, and all the medical bullshit is written down. It's easy."

"This place is tiny." She could barely muster up the strength to keep talking and her own arguments sounded weak in her head, and worse, out loud. The apartment she shared with her dad was small, but no worse than the barracks in the military, or a sleeping bag in a tent. The couch was plenty big enough for her, and the master bedroom was perfect for her dad and all the medical equipment and monitors he needed. The kitchen was fine for them-small but easy to clean. It had a stove, a sink, and a microwave, all the necessities. The front window let in good light and gave them a view of both the ocean and the constant construction on the docks. It wasn't spacious by any means, but it was enough.

Her real problem was she was bored.

The army was structured, busy, and fulfilling. No downtime, not a moment to wonder what to do next. If she had time to think about what needed to be done, she would work on her shuttle or whatever craft she was flying at the time. Software could be updated, or at worst, she could clean it inside and out.

But now, every morning, she cleared her sheets off the couch, put her pillow away, vacuumed the floor, and squared away her night clothes. After fifteen minutes of calisthenics, she did the breakfast dishes, showered, and dressed for the day. She kept her clothes and other belongings in her long green duffle and, despite her father offering her a chest to keep her things in, she refused to unpack it. After finishing her morning routine, she sat down on the couch until time to go to work. With her work ethic, and all her free time, it seems it would be easy to find time to practice building kites. But she couldn't bring herself to enjoy the process. It was tedious and delicate. The papers easily tore. The frames were flimsy.

"Little wren, if you want to go home, *go*. If you want to join the army again, *go join*. I don't want to be what makes you miserable."

There was no way she'd ever get back into the army. She knew that. “Dad, you will not make me miserable. I love you. I’ll be here, but I want you to be taken care of properly.” The idea of being stuck with her father wouldn’t make her miserable, but she knew, even then, it wouldn’t make her happy.

“Still hungry.”

“Pudding?”

“Do we have the chocolate fudge in the little cups I like?”

Tilly nodded and moved to the fridge. “Sure.” She held up a cup and waved it at him. “Last one.”

“Fine.”

Tilly gripped the cup and pulled at the flimsy plastic lid. When it wouldn’t give, she switched hands and pulled again. It was tough, but she heard it crackle a little as it gave. When the top came free, she lost her grip, and the contents of the cup spilled out over her hand. Some of the black pudding dripped over her fingers and onto the floor, dropping in long tentacles of black splatter on the linoleum. It went on longer than she expected, spilling much more than she thought the container held. The drips dangled from her hand like tendrils reaching for the floor.

CHAPTER FIFTEEN

Tilly woke with a start, sure she would find herself lying in a pile of strange animal and human bodies, thrown there by the militia. Instead, she was in the sleeping bag loaned to her by the group, alone in the metal hut. She felt like she'd been swimming in a hot spring all night. When she ran her hands through her hair, it was wet, nearly dripping. She used her t-shirt to wipe the sweat from her brow and sat up. The light outside, such as it was, streamed through slotted blinds over the windows.

"NaNi?"

"*Yes?*"

"What time is it?"

"*Local time is... eleven hundred hours and seventeen minutes.*" The device on her arm said. "*Would you like to know what time the sun will set tonight*?"

"No."

"*There are several types of edible insects native to this geographic location. Would you like a full list*?"

"No."

"*Your body temperature is elevated by one point one degree and has been for the last several hours. Should I make an appointment with your physician*?"

"No."

"*Would you like me to scan my files for things that could cause elevated temperatures in humans?*"

"No." Tilly said. She rubbed her eyes and forced herself up. She had a nasty headache, but otherwise felt fine.

"*Shall I take a blood sample for analysis*?"

"What? No. No. Don't do that." NaNi had never asked that question before, and Tilly was unaware of whether the little device on her arm could actually perform the action. "Let's stop with your questions and diagnosis, please. You can go back to standby mode." The device vibrated once on her wrist and went still.

Seeing she was alone, Tilly quickly changed into dry clothes and laced up her boots before stepping out into the compound. She turned toward the latrines. The men and women there were as active and nonchalant as when Harrison's group arrived. Nothing seemed urgent, and no one gave her a second glance until Saburo and Ned intercepted her.

"Holy hell," Saburo said. A bright smile suddenly lit her face. "We wondered whether you were going to wake up soon. How are you?"

"I'm good, I guess. A little temperature, and I'm thirsty. Otherwise, good."

"You fell over and went to sleep right there in the woods," Ned said. "And you weren't the only one. Like, two or three others fainted dead away. I don't know if they woke up yet or not. Harrison figured something about you fainting or passing out from the shock of seeing the cat lady and whatnot. I don't know what he was talking about. I helped carry you back."

"Thanks for helping, Ned. Speaking of… cat ladies. What happened after I blacked out? Did they catch her? Or…"

"Got away. No one could find her. They looked for hours," Saburo said as she leaned in close. "And today, it's like nothing happened. No one has said a word."

Ned nodded. "Like the most natural thing in the world. Like it's a common fucking thing."

"What about Harrison? Before I blacked out, I heard him say, 'He did it' or something to that effect. Did he elaborate on it?"

"I didn't hear him," Saburo said. Ned shrugged. "Anyway, he vanished into his tent right after the encounter."

Tilly thought about it and pointed to the bathrooms. "I really need to hit the head. Give me a minute and we'll figure things out." She ducked into what amounted to a poorly built outhouse made for three people with zero privacy from anyone else that might have to go. It was rank, and she stepped mindfully around the stains and puddles dotting the wooden floor.

"Hey, if you're feeling up for it, we can go check out the refugee camp and see what we can find there. I know you were interested in seeing who lives there and stuff," Saburo said.

Though her companion was still outside, Tilly could hear her clear as day through the thin walls. "Sure."

"You missed breakfast. Some sort of fish stew and biscuits," Ned said. "You're probably better off. It looked and smelled like vomit with fish in it."

"That was fish?" Saburo asked. "*No*."

As Tilly left the facilities, she washed her hands with a hose hanging on the wall. "Sorry I couldn't be there for that, but I'm sure there will be other opportunities to feel gross on this trip."

"I did snag a pear for you." The trio walked toward the refugee camps and Ned passed the fruit over to Tilly. "They seemed like the least threatening food on the table."

She nodded thanks and immediately shoved the pear into her mouth. Though thrilled to miss the stew they'd described, she was hungry. The juice spilled out over her lips and chin the instant her teeth bit into it. More spilled down her shirt. She wasn't sure if it was the night's strange encounter that had thrown her senses into chaos, or the natural properties of the fruit, but Tilly was positive it was the best thing she'd ever tasted. Not just the best pear, or the best fruit, but the best food she'd had the pleasure of consuming in her lifetime. She laughed as she tried to keep more of the liquid from pouring out.

"Wow," she said. "That's delicious."

"I guess so," Saburo said. "How many have you had now?"

Tilly swallowed the remaining pear meat in her mouth. "What do you mean? I've only taken a few bites."

"I gave you three of them," Ned said. "You must have been hungry."

"What?" she stopped and looked around. They were already in the refugee village, surrounded by log huts and the sewer pipe sections they'd seen on the way in. Behind them, the military barracks were nearly a mile back.

"I don't understand." She looked in her palm to find two pear stems neatly twisted together in a braid, and another pear half- eaten. "I was only eating the first one."

A group of children ran past, bumping into Ned. The kids laughed and kept going, dragging a broken box kite behind them. None of them appeared to be more than six or seven years old, though it was hard to judge with each one caked in dark mud. Even with the layers of filth, Tilly could tell they were mostly white kids, with a few black, but none were obviously Asian.

She continued to glance around, disturbed by the missing time. Was she so hungry she'd eaten three pears and not realized it? Had she blacked out like the night before, but kept walking? Saburo and Ned were looking at her, so she played it off and laughed about being so hungry.

On the top row of concrete pipes, a dark-skinned woman sat dangling one leg over the side. She stared back at Tilly, looking her up and down with a critical eye. The woman wore a simple blue sundress with a wide black belt. Her hair spilled out from under a baseball cap pulled down over her forehead.

Tilly waved and shouted, "How's it with you, miss?"

"I don't know how far you want to go into the camp, but I don't see a single Chinese person anywhere," Ned said. "From the sounds of it, they're Brits, mostly. Maybe a few Aussies. I think there was a Somali family back a bit."

Still fixed on the woman who hadn't responded, Tilly said, "Yeah. I can take your word for it." She glanced around in the camp, but didn't see anyone remotely Asian, let alone Chinese.

"So, what does it mean?" Ned shrugged. "I'm fuzzy on what this proves."

The woman on the ledge got up and disappeared into her concrete tube, pulling a red curtain across the opening as she did. "I'm not sure, honestly," Tilly said. "I guess I expected to find actual Chinese people in China."

CHAPTER SIXTEEN

The next morning, everyone awoke to the loud thumping of boat engines turning over in the building where they'd first seen them. Word spread the boats were ready to go. The crew was loading up ammunition, food, and other supplies into each of the three craft. Outside their storehouse lodgings, mumbling soldiers were calling Nancy the captain of the expedition.

Despite the urge to stay up all night for a chance to see the tiger woman, Mingmei, Tilly had fallen asleep. She'd eaten a bowl of some sort of rice stew, which thankfully hadn't contained fish and hadn't looked like vomit. And while the others returned to their nightly inferno and flowing alcohol, she had snuck off and zipped herself into her sleeping bag.

Harrison's group struck camp and packed their gear in the morning. Each member of the team, Harrison included, moved at half pace, weighed down by a couple nights straight of heavy drinking, smoking, and lack of rest. It was the first time in years Tilly felt like the sensible one of a group she was part of. She took no joy in it, however. It forced her to take up some slack in loading her group's gear, waiting for the hungover and the ill to get their shit done in slow motion. Harrison himself moved particularly slow. He supervised the loading for most of the project, then instead of studying maps and charts, he stared off up the river. She thought about how to approach him, how to ask about what he'd said, and when to do it.

Seeing one last metal ammunition case sitting on the dock next to a box with 'batteries' written on the side, Tilly picked up both and shouted to Nancy, "Where do you want these?"

"Main hold." Nancy pointed to the stairs that led below deck. "*Please.*" She sounded as poorly rested as the others, but was still functioning, reviewing papers and fiddling in the larger boat's wheelhouse, familiarizing herself with the controls as she played with the steering wheel absently. The boat had "*The Myrtle" painted* in black across the bow in block letters.

Descending into the boat's dark storage area, it surprised Tilly how large it was. It was larger than it should have been. There were side compartments with materials that seemed newer than the rest of the vessel, markings and bolts that looked like they'd been used in the last few years, rather than decades ago. She figured they'd used it for smuggling at some point. It certainly wasn't unheard of in the military during the conflict. Tilly had been called on to chase down more than one boat and several transports flying illegal goods from one side to another.

She ducked as she moved toward the bow, and eventually stopped where she found herself somewhere below the wheelhouse and forward gun placement. She set the box near other supplies and slid the case next to a couple of stacks of ammunition.

As she turned to go, Tilly noticed a gap in the boxes. While the other supplies seemed neatly stacked and squared away, the containers around the gap appeared jarred and haphazard. She assumed there was some mechanism below the bow turret that could be accessed there, and they had left a path in case emergency repairs were needed quickly.

She sat listening to the men and women walking around on the deck above, thinking about the journey ahead and the path thus far. It was no different from a wartime mission, only with better pay and less support. She was concerned about the number of unknowns they were headed into. She considered turning around and heading back downriver to be the sensible choice. But if they rallied against Harrison, they would face consequences down the line. He seemed to have contacts all the way up the river, so maybe his network extended down the Huang He as well.

A box shifted nearby. It fell off its stack and clattered to the metal deck. Tilly turned, startled. There was a sudden hiss of surprise, and she considered whether she'd made the sound herself. A scraping sound from behind the boxes suggested someone else was in the hold with her.

"Hello?" She was prepared to let it all go, blame it on the boat scraping against something on the riverbed-a stick, a rock. "Is someone there?"

Another scrape on the metal hull, like nails on a chalkboard.

"NaNi? Light, please? One quarter illumination." Her device vibrated twice, and a dim light brightened the area centered on her wrist. The boxes and tight passage were slightly less daunting with the soft glow, and Tilly moved until she came to a gap between the supplies and the hold's front wall. The gap was maybe three feet wide, and as she moved to explore it, she found herself face to face with the cat creature she'd seen the night prior. Her heart thudded, her pulse quickened.

"Look. I'm going to come in, okay?" Tilly discretely patted her side to confirm her sidearm was there. She unsnapped the holster, just in case, and squeezed into the gap. She wanted to believe Mingmei was a friend, an ally of some sort, but after the cat creature took a swipe at Saburo, she couldn't take a chance. "I'm coming in. I'm not going to hurt you. And I don't want to fight." More scratching and shuffling met her words, the sounds louder than before.

Rather than attack with the element of surprise, the thing shrank back into a corner. It curled defensively in the darkness. "Get away," Mingmei hissed as she retreated. "Stay back."

It took a moment for Tilly to gather her wits about her. She stared at Mingmei, her feline face barely lit and looking more animal than human in the dark hold. "It's okay. It's okay. I'm not going to hurt you." She took a deep breath and lowered her voice, wondering if she could hurt the creature or if that was a pipe dream. If the quick glimpses of the cat woman's arms and legs were any indication, Tilly would be in for a real fight. "What are you doing down here? There are men on the boat who would want to kill you. It's not safe down here."

"I heard you talk. You and the others. You want to find the doctor."

"Yes, we do."

"I say this is a bad thing. The doctor is not a friend to anyone. He is a monster." Her speech sounded forced. She slipped into a low growl.

"A monster? What do you mean? Where did you see him?" The men up on deck talked louder. She heard Harrison call her name. "They might come down here looking for me. You need to leave before we get underway."

"*You have to stop this.* The doctor has awakened something he does not understand. *Go home.*"

The siren sounded on the attack boat. The engines sputtered.

"Stay hidden, okay?" Tilly said. "Stay down here, and we'll figure out what to do with you. I have to go or they'll come looking and discover you." She crawled away, careful to move the boxes behind her to cover the gap, and climbed into the empty part of the hold. She brushed herself off and thought about the woman hidden in the hold. Could she, should she, keep it a secret? What the hell was it, exactly?

"Hey, there you are," Saburo said. "Didn't you hear us? We've been looking for you."

Her mind still churning over the tiger-woman, Tilly said, "Yeah, I spilled a bunch of stuff out of one of the boxes, and I've been cleaning it up. Sorry." She climbed onto the deck and waved a sheepish hand to everyone nearby. "Sorry. I feel pretty stupid now." As she scanned the bleary-eyed crew, she realized none of them cared much.

They shoved off, and the boats were underway, the two smaller craft flanking *The Myrtle.* They moved up the river at a slow, steady pace. *The Myrtle* was very much like the Cyclone they flew in on. It was loud, smoky, and made frightening noises as it clawed their way along. The attack boats at their sides were antiques as well. They glided across the water easily, though, silently, except for the trio manning each one. They seemed to have the time of their lives. They swerved the boats from side to side, creating wakes that slapped the shores and each other's craft. Occasionally, they swooped closer to shore to check something out, but it never amounted to more than garbage.

"If your men think they've spotted our WHEEL, you can tell them to stop. The thing is massive and quite hard to miss," Harrison told Nancy. "It wouldn't be hidden by some bushes."

"They have orders to keep an eye out for anything they can salvage," she said. "Anything to fetch us a penny or two on the market. You never know, the Scots might need some shit from the bushes and trade with us."

"Whatever. I want to get where I'm going."

Nancy took out a pipe and stuffed it with tobacco. "Only a few days ago, you were going nowhere. And now you're in a hurry." She lit the pipe and leaned back in her chair, obviously enjoying herself. "Shit. I say you need to enjoy the ride and shut the fuck up."

It was a personal joy to hear someone tell Harrison off. Tilly wanted to do it herself, but held her tongue because she had no other way home. "No one seems phased by these cat people," Tilly said. "I have to say, it's a shock for us. Shock for me, at least. How long have these things been around here?"

"They've been raiding our trash and stealing our things for short of a year, I suppose. Believe me, we were shocked. We were shocked plenty. Had a few people go mad, if you follow me. It was harder for some to grasp than others."

"But now?"

"Now we don't give two shits. I know it's weird for you. But we just got used to them. They're no big deal." A plume of blue smoke drifted from Nancy's pipe as she chewed it absently in her mouth.

"No big deal? When you first encountered them, did you not think the rest of the world might want to know about them? Couldn't you have sent word to someone about what's going on here?"

"We did," Nancy said. "We sent out several messengers in boats over the course of a few months. Some of our lads even put together their own version of a Low-fi and sent them off to get the word out, but we never heard from any of them again. We figured we were stuck with them."

"All right, let's go." Harrison all but shoved Tilly away from Nancy. "I need to talk with the captain and work out our search patterns. Give us a few minutes here."

For a moment, Tilly considered shoving the man back. Maybe even punch him in the face to express her anger, but she didn't have the energy to let Harrison get to her. The thing that kept her from telling him to fuck off was the same thing that dissuaded her from knocking him on his ass. Starting a fight in a boat, chugging down the Yellow River, held no appeal to her at the moment. Though she knew that sentiment could change at any time. Instead, she carefully made her way to the aft of the boat.

Leaning against the rail, Saburo cleaned off her boots with a twig and tossed the mud overboard. Tilly sat down next to her and watched the trees and bushes on the shoreline pass by.

"You're an *American*?" Saburo asked. "I thought I heard you say something about being an American."

"Yeah. South Carolina. You?"

"Philippines. An area you probably never heard of called Barceloneta on San Miguel Bay," Saburo said.

"No, I have never heard of San Miguel Bay. Where is it?"

"It's on the eastern side. Hard to explain."

"Hold on." Tilly raised her wrist. "NaNi? Display a map of the Philippines."

"Displaying… *the Philippines*," NaNi said. Immediately, the small device projected a map of the country into the air above it.

This got Saburo's attention. "I didn't know those things could do that." She moved closer and pointed to a bay midway down the coast. "This is it. Right here. This is San Miguel Bay."

"NaNi? Can you enlarge the area of San Miguel Bay?"

The map zoomed into the area Saburo indicated. "Right over here, around the curve, is where I grew up." She smiled as she stared at the tiny dots which showed her town.

"We could probably zero in on your home if you wanted," Tilly said. Her friend was looking far away, smiling at the projected map.

"No. This is good."

"Hey, why don't you keep the NaNi for a while? You can look stuff up, check out maps, whatever I have stored." Tilly detached the face from the wide band around her wrist and held it out to Saburo.

The other woman shook her head. "Oh, no. I'd lose it or something. I can't."

"You won't lose it. Look." Tilly set the face on the deck next to Saburo, then pressed her finger to her wristband. Both watched as the mini turbines jutted out and the face became airborne. "The army liked this model because it could act as a recon drone. Not a great range, but it was good for an aerial view of a combat zone. Plus, if you lose it…" She moved her finger over to the next function and the small, detached piece returned to its place on the wrist unit and locked in.

"*Reattached,*" NaNi said. "*Would you like me to define 'separation anxiety?'*"

"No thank you, NaNi." Tilly held her arm out toward her companion.

Saburo was dumbstruck. "I've never seen one of these before. At least not one that could do that."

"Seriously. Check it out." Tilly handed the face unit back to Saburo. "Give it back when you're done."

"Thank you." Saburo snuggled herself into a cozy spot with her pack as a pillow and experimented with the device.

"*Would you like to know the current air temperature?*" NaNi asked.

With a giggle, Saburo replied with an emphatic affirmative.

If she believed in such things, Tilly would say the pair was a match made in heaven. She turned to watch the shoreline drift by. The river was wide enough in the area that one of the smaller attack boats briefly vanished from sight as it explored the far shore. Harrison watched them through a pair of old-school binoculars he discovered in the wheelhouse. He sighed in relief as the boat came back into formation.

There were occasional breaks in the trees that let faint light through to the water. Tilly marveled at how anything made it through the grey clouds of filth that drifted across the skies. Like her companions, she scanned the shores for signs of anything out of place or even vaguely menacing. It was tough to make that kind of call. Trash covered nearly every inch of the banks; metal, plastic, and other materials washed up from the flooding-so much the crew only pointed out the really strange things. They saw rusted industrial fridges, tractor tires, keyboards, microwaves, cubicle parts, and so many window frames and doors it was impossible to mention them all. Torn remnants of what they assumed was a circus tent with tattered red and yellow stripes flapped in the breeze. Grass and weeds grew up through the junk, limited only by the amount of sunlight that gave them life.

A dreadful feeling rose from the pit of Tilly's stomach. She was out of her element without the helicopter. Boats weren't her thing and never had been. Anyone could carry the rifle she cradled in her arm and do a better job. But if Harrison said there was no safe way home until they reached the station, then she had no choice.

"Mister Harrison," Decator shouted from the back of the boat. "Sir?"

Harrison moved away from the captain to track down the man at the back of the boat.

Tilly took the opportunity to move up and talk to Nancy. "You've never been much further than this? What do you think is out here?" She watched as the captain scrolled through the data on the vessel's computer.

"I don't know what's out here. No one I know does. Can't even hazard a fucking guess," Nancy said. "Beyond the Scot's camp is a black hole on our maps as far as what we might encounter. That's what scares me."

"Why would they need a research station out here?"

The captain shrugged, then quickly flinched from the controls.

"What's wrong?" Tilly grabbed her arm to check for an injury on the woman, wondering if she'd cut herself on something.

The captain pulled her arm away and gripped the wheel with both hands again. "Did you see that?" Tilly shook her head no, unclear what she meant.

"The shadow?" Nancy clarified. "Something cast a shadow across the bow."

Having seen nothing, Tilly left the wheelhouse to explore the front of the ship. She climbed the trio of stairs, sidestepped ropes and boxes of equipment until she stepped out onto the bow. Faint bits of light were breaking through the clouds. Maybe they were strong enough to cast shadows, but nothing was there. Enormous ferns spread out along the shore, reaching their branches over the river. She shrugged and looked back at Nancy. "Nothing but trees. What did you see?"

The captain shouted, "It wasn't a tree, damn it! Something moved out there and cast an enormous shadow on the deck."

Tilly scanned again. From the junk on the shore to the sky above, she found nothing out of the ordinary. The captain was making her nervous, jumping at things that weren't there. Instead of returning to the wheelhouse, Tilly moved to the back of the ship to see why Harrison had been called away. Climbing through the narrow area on the starboard side, she could make out both of their escort boats, moving along fine.

Seeing Tilly out on the deck, the gunner on the starboard boat waved and shouted with a smile. He wore his black cap backward. With his clean-shaven face, he looked to be about fifteen years old. She gave him a cursory grin back and waved. The kid laughed and slapped the side of the attack boat before shouting down to someone below. The craft veered back and forth before revving the motor and darting toward Tilly's boat.

The young man stood in his gunner's seat as music suddenly blared from his craft. His smile widened.

For a moment, she wondered who the idiots were Harrison had entrusted their lives with. She lost the thought when a huge, black shape land on the front of the attack boat. The weight of the object drove the bow deep into the water. The young gunner fell forward, slamming his head against the inside of the gun turret. After the motor revved, it lifted slightly above the waterline before the whole back end slapped back down into the dark water. The boat crew's shouting spread to the other craft.

When the spray of water dissipated, Tilly's focus turned to what had hit the bow of the escort craft. It appeared as if a huge, black mass-maybe a tree trunk that fell from the forest, or a rock that rolled down a hill—had careened onto the unlucky boat. But once she got a clear look at it, the conjecture went out the window — the enormous mass was moving.

Shiny black wings unfurled, revealing a large fur-covered creature. It stood some eight feet tall or more, the body of which seemed familiar. "Is that a fucking bear? With wings?" Tilly asked. "Holy shit." Other crew members echoed her words.

The crew of *The Myrtle* stood transfixed, taking in the sight. Tilly felt sick to her stomach and confused in the same way she'd felt when she first saw Mingmei in the forest. Her thoughts stuck together as if coated in maple syrup. On the boat's deck was a creature she'd never seen, never dreamed of. If Mingmei was a shock, this creature was a full-on lightning bolt; a thousand times more insane than a tiny cat person. This was a bear with enormous wings on the bow of one of their boats.

Rei stumbled to the deck near Tilly and lay flat. "I'm going to hang down here. Want to join me?"

"I don't…" She couldn't get her eyes to focus on anything, let alone Rei. Glimpses of the world around her came and went, but the thing on the other boat refused to come into focus until Saburo bumped into her. The woman's shoulder connected squarely with Tilly's ribs, sending a shot of pain through her chest.

Saburo charged toward the forward thirty-caliber machine gun, shoving two men out of her way. Once there, she pulled back the handle. She pointed the barrel at the great blur on the other boat and fired, filling the air with smoke and sound. The gun shook and rattled as it fired. Shells fell to the deck.

The pain of the blow to her torso cleared Tilly's head, and she peered over the rail at the creature on the other craft. A large black and white bear with wings. The wings looked stretched and leathery, like those of a bat. Each one reached eight to ten feet long when the creature completely extended them. It walked on its hind legs like a human, with no inclination of dropping onto all fours.

The gunner in the other boat righted himself so that his butt sat flat on the seat. There was no way he could move the twin guns to shoot his attacker; it was so close, nearly straddling the barrels. This also put it too close for Saburo to fire out of fear of hitting the soldier, forcing her to fire around the creature when she could.

The fact didn't stop others from taking careless potshots from *The Myrtle* and the gunner's craft. The crack of small arms fire echoed across the water and against the trees lining the river. Their efforts didn't draw the thing's attention or break its concentration. It grabbed a soldier in one enormous arm, yanked him free of his seat, and in two quick steps, it was airborne with the hapless man. The beast seemed unfazed by the extra weight. It rocketed toward the clouds with two sweeps of the giant wings.

The gunfire stopped. Everyone followed the shape skyward with the writhing and shrieking gunner. That's when they all noticed more of the dark shapes descending on the boat formation. Tilly counted fifteen before she gave up.

The captain came out from the wheelhouse and shouted, "Fire now, or they'll carry us all off!" She raised a rifle and drew a bead on the closest flying bear. When she pulled the trigger, the clatter made those nearest her cringe in surprise.

She couldn't hear them, but she saw others on the boats follow Nancy's lead. Again, the crew raised their weapons and fired. A woman on the other boat jumped into the now-vacant seat of the twin guns and brought them around to bark fire and smoke at the dark, descending monsters. The other escort boat's guns came to life as well, creating a wall of sound so thick, Tilly thought she'd gone deaf. The pounding of the guns and maneuvering boat motors blocked out any opportunity to hear anything else.

Gun raised, Tilly inhaled deeply, getting the same feeling she got from the tiger-woman in the hold. She felt like these bear things were intelligent and sentient. Her trigger finger was in place, but she couldn't bring herself to pull it.

"Tilly," Rei shouted. The kid stood next to Tilly, but his voice was nearly lost in the din. "Are you okay? Can you fight?"

She shook her head and shouted back, "I can't! Look at them, they're like Mingmei. There's more than just a beast there."

"They're killing our team. Whatever they are, we're going to die here if you don't help us."

It was true, whether or not Tilly liked it. Whatever was going on, the creatures didn't want to talk like Mingmei. These things were content to kill anything moving on the boats. She saw a beast grab a soldier on the other fast attack boat and tear the man with wide, flat claws before lifting off and soaring away with him.

Reluctantly, Tilly raised her rifle, found a target, and followed it across the gray sky. Leading the flying creature slightly with her field of fire, she took a deep breath and did her best not to look at its face. It was impossible. The creature turned and appeared to assess where it wanted to go next. It dipped, only to change course directly. She kept the gun trained on it, following it as it dodged and swooped in a death dive. It sped up as it fell toward her, wings tucked back, barely working to guide the bear like a fat, furry missile plummeting toward Tilly. Less than fifty feet away, the bear popped its wings out to slow itself. It reached out its paws to grab her. Tilly could see long yellowing claws poised to shred and dig into her body as she dropped to the deck for cover.

She felt a sudden rush of air from the creature's massive wings as it flew over. The thing screeched as a nearby gun clacked bullet after bullet, followed by a splash. Tilly stood, leaned forward, and looked over the side where the bear was howling and thrashing in the river. Its injured wing floated uselessly behind it, while the other flapped and swept, determined to get airborne. Its cries turned pitiful as the bear struggled to stay afloat. There was genuine fear in its eyes as it sank down into the water.

A cry of help snapped Tilly back to the surrounding battle. Several of the bears had landed on the opposite side of The Myrtle and the crew were being overrun. Saburo ran for the machine gun mounted on the side nearest her, but stopped short as one of the flying beasts landed face first on the deck in front of her. The body fell with a crunch of bone and metal. Saburo waited a moment, then went for the gun again. She grabbed the stock and brought it around to cover the boat's starboard side.

Tilly focused on three winged bears walking unsteadily on their hind legs, slashing at the crew of the last attack boat. Their combined weight made the slim attack boat dip dangerously low to the waterline. They rocked the craft every time they moved. Only two of the six-member crew still stood, trying to fend off the attackers. The woman who'd taken over the twin guns at the fore now stood and swung a fire axe at her opponent. A male soldier in the back fired his sidearm at the closest of two beasts.

A few feet behind her on the deck, Rei stood and opened up on the second bear in the back, raking it with machine gun fire. The startled creature raised a wing to shield itself from the attack, shifting its balance. It changed the boat's weight distribution. The craft lurched to the starboard and capsized, throwing creatures and soldiers alike into the river's dark water. Tilly lost sight of the humans, but the bear creatures were clearly visible, flailing in the water. She supposed that, normally, bears could swim or tread water. But here, the creatures were hampered by their enormous wings, dragged down by their weight, and stymied by their unwieldiness.

When the soldiers surfaced near her boat, Saburo threw them both life preservers and prepared to pull them both in. Behind her, Ned took up a grenade launcher and fired it indiscriminately at the beasts in the air. His efforts paid off in loud thumps and bursts of light near his targets. The creatures howled and cried as they fell from the sky and splashed into the water below. Reloading, Ned fired at them as they treaded water, causing fountains of water to fill the air.

With the two survivors now aboard *The Myrtle*, Tilly moved to help the other escort craft. Her efforts were unnecessary; the last three winged black bears swooped low over the water before retreating toward the clouds with surprising speed.

A few feet from Tilly, Harrison stood with a nine-millimeter pistol in hand and sweat on his brow. He appeared to be tallying the cost of the encounter. One escort boat capsized and sank. The other escort showed long claw marks and bullet holes across the hull. The damage to *The Myrtle* was not nearly as bad. Harrison and his crew were accounted for. Captain Nancy was still at the wheel. One gunner was dead and two were missing. Two soldiers from the escort boats were dead, and one was missing. The total didn't count the three carried off by the creatures.

Harrison's eyes narrowed at the report. "Alright. Let's get

ourselves cleaned up and moving as soon as possible." He was calm, robotic in his manner.

The crew, some bleeding, some soaked from the river, grumbled.

"Get moving? What the great fucking hell were those things?" Decator asked. "What the fucking hell?" It was the first time anyone had heard such an outburst against Harrison from the man. The rest of the survivors echoed his words, most scanning the skies as they waited for answers. "We just lost a third of our people, at least."

Harrison raised his hands for calm as he tried to reassure the crew. "I have no idea what they are," he said. "I've never seen anything like them. If I had known things like those existed on the river, I would have made sure we were prepared for them."

"Prepared for them?" said a U.N. soldier sitting on the deck. He leaned against the hull in what seemed like an effort to hide himself from an impending attack. "If I would have known about them, I would have stayed the hell home. I thought we were here to pick up some fucking scientist for you and take him home."

"You knew there would be risks," Harrison said. "You lot from the camp knew about these creatures. This is still considered an active combat zone, and I told everyone that when I hired them. Don't act like this was going to be a stroll down Main Street."

The soldier stood cautiously and looked around. "Fucking little trash-stealing cat people are one thing but fuck flying bear bats. We were along to scavenge supplies. *Shit.*" He sunk back into his space, hidden from whatever he thought was coming. "I'll fight a man with my own two hands, but *shit.*"

The men's murmuring died down.

"We need to turn the fuck around." Ned crouched low in the boat. He put his gun down. "This isn't right. I can't do this."

"How far is the Scot's camp?" Harrison asked.

"What?" Nancy said.

"How much further upriver is the camp the fucking Scots run?" He was shaking, but his voice was a steady monotone.

"Another hour or so. It's not far," Nancy said. "But we…"

Harrison interrupted with, "Then let's go. We can make it before darkness sets in. Surely, they can help us and shelter us."

"What if those things come back?" Ned asked. "Those giant fucking things falling from the sky to eat us? What if they come back?" Saburo sat down beside the man and comforted him.

"Then we'll be ready." Harrison gave Nancy a harsh glance, then sat down with his arms folded. "Just keep looking up."

CHAPTER SEVENTEEN

The soldiers on board were less lackadaisical as the two remaining boats continued upriver. They also lacked enthusiasm for their general duties. They were too occupied watching the skies for additional surprises that might fall on them. Harrison and the captain allowed a pair of the U.N. crew to hide below deck in the small quarters. The pair were in more shock than the others, unable to talk, in fact. They jumped at the slightest sound, twitching at the possibility of the return of the winged bear-things. They refused to drink water and wouldn't accept food, so their friends got them settled below at the mouth of the cargo hold, wrapped in blankets. Tilly watched them set up, hoping Mingmei could keep quiet.

Once they were underway and had a few minutes under their belts, the tense silence broke when Tilly inched closer to Harrison. "You really have no idea what to make of those things?" she asked. "None?"

The company man smoked idly as he stared out at the water and trees covering the shore. "You think you deserve some other answer than the others? Are you special in some way? No. I don't know what to make of those things." He aimed his monotone answer at the shore.

"You said the guy we're here to scoop up is a scientist. A conservationist, I think you said? Right?"

"And you think he stapled some wings on a grizzly bear and made it fly? Don't be stupid," Harrison said.

The venom with which the man called her stupid made Tilly's attitude change quickly. "I didn't say that. You need to look around and see what's happening here. We lost a helicopter to rebels, and then a boat and some soldiers to huge flying beasts. We haven't been out here but a few days, and your resources are dwindling almost as low as the morale. You really should be a little more aware of your need for friends right now."

Tilly walked away, shoving past the few men in her way. She settled into a nest of ropes and equipment at the boat's aft and pulled her hat over her eyes. Even if she would not be able to sleep, Tilly had no intention of getting into a deep conversation with anyone. She was unconcerned with pissing off her employer anymore. She patted the pistol still strapped at her side, the clasp still secure.

Nothing was worth the hassle or money. Not getting back to America, not paying off debts, and certainly not the thrill of flying again. She'd done her best to keep her father's business afloat, but the constant barrage of things that came at her was more than she could handle. She tried to learn the language, figure out bookkeeping, marketing and more, but it all crumbled with her feeble attempts to care for her ailing father. Suppliers were unreliable, inventory dwindled, customers came and went. In the end, if they hadn't closed up shop when they did, it would have driven her mad. The Air Corps didn't teach her much in the way of advertising or publicity. Harata wasn't business-oriented, either, though he seemed able to carry the place on his own. Nothing was worth the hassle, certainly not a kite store.

A new murmur on the escort boat got Tilly's attention. Soon, *The Myrtle* was bustling with activity. The crew shouted about flashes of light breaking above the trees. The soldiers got themselves worked up and began gathering, loading, and readying their weapons. Tilly wasn't sure she could handle another emergency, another battle, or another spectacle. She wanted to crawl into the hold and talk to Mingmei, ask her what more she knew about the situation and what awaited them upriver. But there wasn't a simple way to do it without attracting the attention of everyone around her. And no matter their mental states, the men in the hold's mouth would prove a problem if she pressed past them.

Harrison leaned against the wheelhouse, staring at colors that were barely visible. Tilly remained aft, both watching the activity and staring at the shell-shocked soldiers at the bottom of the steps. She heard thuds and crackles, and when the smell of smoke wafted their way, she was sure it wasn't a combat zone or firefight they were headed into. The colors of the bursts were wrong, too colorful, too festive to be a fight between opposing forces. The smell of smoke wasn't quite the same as that in a combat zone. It was sweeter.

"That's about where our next stop is, right?" Harrison shouted to the captain.

"You're right. Run by the European bunch," Nancy said. "Last time we made this stop, it was run by this daft Scot. And by the looks of things, he's likely still 'round."

"Daft? How?"

The captain laughed. "I'd hate to spoil it for you. He's a good chap, I think. A little unorthodox. We're almost there."

As *The Myrtle* rounded the bend in the river, a large encampment presented itself on the boat's starboard side. It was a dingy wooden grouping of buildings with a trio of piers that jutted into the river. On shore, men and women walked between the buildings with no urgency, confirming Tilly's theory about the explosions not being combat-related. The soldiers on the boat relaxed somewhat, but didn't remove their hands from the triggers of their weapons. On the middle dock, a man in a bright red shirt waved his arms and pointed to a slip at his feet. The captain guided *The Myrtle* with effortless grace into the area. "This is Clive. Clive is their quartermaster, harbormaster, Jack-of-all-trades. Careful. He'll charm ya, bargain with ya, swindle ya. Always open for a swap for something he wants or needs. Not too shy to steal something if you don't want to part with it politely."

Such a thing was evident in the way the man smiled. It was a warm smile, an inviting one, and yet there was something behind it that was immediately unsavory to Tilly. His bright eyes seemed to scan the people on the boat, calculating something. Maybe it was easy to say once she'd been warned, but she made a note to be on guard around him. There were similar hustlers in the old unit during the war, but rarely bothered their own people. Their creed was "don't shit where you eat." Bilking the people you lived with day-in and day-out was a recipe for hard feelings, broken bones, and revenge. Instead, they aimed for the transients, the visitors they would never see again, and therefore couldn't be held accountable to. Less probability of things coming back on them.

"Hey," Clive shouted. "Hey, hey." He tossed a mooring line to the soldier at the fore of the ship and, together with the captain, maneuvered the craft up to the dock. "Looks like, what? Looks like some Americans? That right? Americans?" He scanned us as we moved to the ladder to disembark. "I see a lovely Korean or two, yeah? Philippine? The big guy must be a Brit. Has to be. They're the only ones that wear their gear all crazy like yours." He pointed to Harrison and his two men. "Am I right, mate?"

"We're only here to get some fuel and a place for the night," Harrison said. "We were told the commanding officer here could accommodate us."

"I'm not trying to be cheeky or anything. No offense to you. We got plenty of Brits here. I'm only seeing if my guessing skills are still sharp, you know?" His eyes darted from person to person as he spoke. He never actually looked at Harrison, rather at the ones burdened with overly heavy packs and cases. "How about it?"

"Yes, I'm from the United Kingdom. Good guess. Now, about your commanding officer?"

Clive nodded and seemed prepared to answer the question when his eyes widened. He stepped backward, slipping on the dock, and nearly fell into the river. He landed on his butt inches from the edge and reached for his sidearm. Tilly followed his line of sight and it made sense to her immediately. Mingmei had moved from her hiding place and was following the last two crewmen to the ladder to disembark.

"No," Tilly said. "Whoa. Whoa. Whoa." She pulled her own weapon and trained it on Clive. Soon the others had unslung their guns. The crumbling wooden dock was suddenly a crowded chaos of soldiers and mercenaries swinging guns around. Captain Nancy, Saburo, and Harrison all pointed their weapons at Clive. The others were less sure. Tilly noted they appeared less inclined to kill other men than they were to kill the strange animal-thing. The sudden shift to impending violence brought a trio of armed soldiers running from the boathouse.

"Let's calm down, please," Nancy said. "There is no need for this. We're all friends here."

"Except that thing." Clive pointed to where Mingmei had been. In the scuffle, she'd disappeared, likely to her place in the cargo hold.

"That *thing* is with us," Tilly said.

"Yeah? You're its guardian angel, then?" His eyes narrowed.

"Whatever."

Harrison and the rest of the crew appeared dumbstruck that the cat creature had been in their presence and they hadn't known it. "Maybe we need to talk," Harrison said to Tilly.

Clive put his gun away and stood. "Brilliant. Well, I'm fine with you keeping a pet on board your vessel, but I doubt it'll go over a treat with Morrow." He waved the approaching men off. "It's fine. Fine." He drew closer to Harrison and Tilly and lowered his voice. "You do what you want, I don't give a good goddamn. But you may want to keep your mouth screwed tight about her, yeah?"

Harrison clapped Nancy hard on the back. "It's okay people. Let's ease up on the guns, what say? This is all a misunderstanding." The group was slow to react. "Come on. All of you get ashore and get to it. We need to refuel and get the fuck out of here come morning." As they drifted off, Harrison grabbed Tilly's arm and dragged her close to the wheelhouse. "What the fuck?"

"She snuck onboard when we were loading the boats. I figured she could help us."

"The fucking tiger-lady just snuck onto the boat? That's something you should have mentioned before we left," Harrison said. "As it is, I agree with you about her usefulness, but it would've been nice not to find out this way. You saw how the last camp treated them. What if this place is as bad?"

"Not sure it can be."

As the two relaxed, everyone followed Clive toward the camp. Tilly asked Harrison, "What about Mingmei? Think we need to worry?"

"Talk to her," he said. "It might be wise to keep her hidden as much as possible. Can you manage?"

Tilly climbed back down the ladder and entered the small compartment, then crawled into the open equipment hold. Tilly was surprised Harrison had been so calm. He was unpredictable at any rate, and she decided to keep an eye on him and his newfound amicability. She squeezed into the darkness, pushing past the weapons crates and everything else the captain kept hidden in the space below *The Myrtle*. Saburo still had her NaNi face, so she had to make do with the small flashlight clipped to her vest's shoulder. The narrow beam helped her navigate to where she'd seen Mingmei the last time.

"They want to kill me." Mingmei's voice came from the darkness.

"They don't want to kill you. You surprised them, that's all."

Silence returned.

"Can you help me here? I can't find you." The darkness was thicker the further Tilly ventured into the hold.

"I saw the look in that man's eyes. He wants to kill me. I saw it. This body, this face. I'm hideous. I am a monster he wants to see destroyed."

Tilly gave up trying to navigate the dark and put her forehead down on the cold metal of the hold. "Look. He suggested you stay on the boat. I'd say you're perfectly safe down here. Even I can't find you easily," she said. "Not the ideal situation, but I think it's for the best. We'll be leaving at first light." Tilly waited a moment and decided it was best not to pursue the conversation. Mingmei understood, she was sure. "We'll make sure one of our people is guarding the boat at all times, okay? You'll be safe if you stay hidden. Got it?" Tilly maneuvered herself around and crawled back the way she came.

"Your dreams are wrong, aren't they?"

Tilly stopped. "What?"

A low growl came from the darkness. "He remakes your memories and steals your time."

"This Kalidas?"

"Yes. He wants your mind as clean as possible for when he saves you." Mingmei whispered the words, barely audible in the cargo hold.

"Tilly, let's go." On the dock, Harrison waited. Tilly nodded. "She'll stay where she is."

"I'll see to it," Nancy said. Tilly wasn't aware the captain was still there, or how much she knew.

Tilly and Harrison caught up with Clive and the others at the camp.

"The rest of your crew can explore our outpost at their leisure. Maybe find the mess hall, have some chow. They're welcome here, yeah?" Clive clapped his hands together and put on a bright smile that matched his bright red shirt. "But… I'm afraid your weapons have to stay here. We have a lovely locker for them at the gate, but we don't allow visitors to tote their weapons around our compound."

"What? I'll do no such thing," Ned said.

"Right," Saburo added. "What are all the explosions going on over there? How do you expect we protect ourselves?"

"Those little pops and crackles are nothing. It's a celebration. We're celebrating. Nothing but fireworks. The compound is perfectly safe." As if to illustrate his point, bright yellow pops of sparkling light suddenly blasted the sky, crackling through the air.

"You want to keep your gun, stay here." Harrison's decree to the troops didn't make anyone happy. His style of leadership was uneven and spotty, giving in when he should dig in, folding his arms when he should concede. Most of the crew reluctantly handed over their sidearms and rifles, but defiantly kept their combat knives. The more adamant among them headed back toward the boat.

"Alrighty then," Clive said. "Let's go see the big man." He pointed up the trail which led straight up the middle of the wooden huts, canvas tents, and corrugated metal buildings comprising the bulk of the outpost. As the group walked, the encampment soldiers stopped what they were doing to watch them pass. Most only took a moment to acknowledge unfamiliar faces among them, others lingered long enough to make Tilly uncomfortable.

"What is your mission here?" Harrison asked.

"Mission?"

"Your purpose? Surely, you're here for a reason?"

The man took a deep breath. "Well, I suppose there was a reason at some point. We're supposed to occupy this space in the name of the European Union, I guess."

"And how many men do you have here to 'occupy this space' for the E-U?"

It was here the smell of smoke hit Tilly. It stung her nostrils-not quite the same way the discharge of a gun or cannon did, but it was still familiar. The popping and thudding sounds they'd heard on the way in began again, as did a chorus of whoops and shouts from men somewhere far ahead.

"Awww. It's a mess to count troops. Squads come; squads go. I think we officially have two platoons, which should come out to around sixty bodies. But come chow time, it's a damn sight more, I'll tell ya." Clive laughed. "Either that, or our sixty bastards eat more than their fair share."

Clive led the group out of the camp. The mud trail led up a steep incline for a quarter mile before leveling out. Smoke was thick here, but Tilly could still make out the shapes and shadows of laughing and yelling people ahead. "Mind the bottles," Clive said, gesturing toward the sudden appearance of whole and shattered alcohol bottles coating the ground. The path remained fairly clear, but the glass crunched beneath her boots.

"A few of the boys may be a bit steam boated. They're having a wee celebration."

"Steam boated?" Tilly asked.

"Bladdered. Wrecked." Clive laughed.

"Drunk," Harrison said.

She'd gotten the gist, but thanked the man anyway. "What are we celebrating?"

Another solid thud exploded nearby. Tilly moved her hand to her holster out of caution, then remembered she'd handed her gun to someone at the door. Another half mile ahead, a bright burst of blue light startled her, followed by a second crackle of silver that ended with a hiss.

"Are those fireworks?"

"Aye."

"What are we celebrating?" she asked again.

Clive shrugged and pushed a man aside who was blocking the path. "One side, Stewart." Ahead was the platform where the fireworks were being staged. Two men loaded mortars while the third watched and drank. "There he is. Right there." Clive pointed to the man with the controller. "That's the major there." Obscured by the bright lights fading down toward the trees, the man was hard to see. He was shirtless and sweaty, thin in the shadows.

Once the next setup was ready, the major lifted a control box and fired off the explosives. They twisted in the air, leaving glowing yellow fire behind them. Rather than climb skyward, the fireball raced some thirty feet above the ground and burst short of the forest. The explosion brought a shriek of animal terror in the distance, followed by cheers and laughter from the men surrounding Tilly.

Through the thick haze, three figures were visible far down range. This was mostly because of their sheer size and the fact two of them were flying barely above the ground, dipping and weaving. The third figure flapped massive wings, blowing smoke around in whirls and twisters.

"Those are the bear creatures that attacked our boat," Tilly said.

Their guide looked impressed. "You fought these howlin' things in the wild and lived to tell the tale? No small feat. I'd tip my hat if I had one."

"Not all of us lived to tell."

They stopped ten feet from the trio of men firing off the light show and waited until the next round of explosives screamed through the air. At the other end, they exploded mere feet away from the monsters trying to avoid them. She couldn't tell for sure from so far away, but the bears appeared to be chained to the ground. Otherwise, they'd fly off or attack the spectators. A bright blue burst landed between two of them and began spinning in circles, hissing and throwing off smoke. The bears tried to run in opposite directions, but stopped abruptly twenty feet from the commotion.

The two men ran up to the platform and began reloading the mortars and launchers. Clive took the opportunity to dart up to the major and lean close. The other man nodded and glanced at Tilly and the others. Clive waved them on and took the launcher from the major. Harrison and his men led the way, and Tilly followed at a slight distance. The smoke was thicker here at the launch point, the air much heavier.

When they drew close enough, Tilly found her assessment of the major correct. He was skinny to the point he looked ill. His ribs showed through his sweaty, pale torso, and his trousers hung loosely about his waist as if he'd recently lost a considerable amount of weight. He glistened with a coating of perspiration covering his bare trunk. A cigarette hung from his lips, and he looked at them with his head cocked to an angle.

"Were we expecting you?"

"Excuse me?" Harrison extended his hand.

"Do you have some sort of appointment with us? Are you supposed to be here?" The major's cigarette danced on his lip as he talked.

"Uh, no. We're just…"

"Who the fuck are ya, then?"

Clive held his hand up. "I think he wants to know why you've stopped here. What's your business, you know? We don't get much unexpected, uh, company in this place what ain't tryna kill us. Usually soldiers and the like, passing through."

The major removed the cigarette and took a long drink of his beer bottle, staring at Harrison as he did.

"We're looking for a missing researcher. He's been out here with his team for a good long time, and we believe he came this way."

Thick smoke from the major's cigarette billowed into the fog of the pyrotechnics. After he finished his drink, he stared at the group with a look of immediate casual disinterest. "Like, a doctor?" the major asked. "A scientist or something? Unless they can bandage up a cut or sew an ear back on, ain't no "researchers" around here."

"Look, his name is…"

Bored with the way the men were communicating, Tilly pushed Harrison aside and stepped closer to major Morrow. "They would have been floating down the river in a giant-ass lab that looks like a yo-yo on its side. Been a few years now, I'd wager."

The major smiled widely and pointed at Tilly with the hand that held the cigarette. White ash spilled through the air. "Now, lassie. Now you got my interest. We saw the thing, sure. And it landed right here, didn't it?"

Clive laughed in agreement. "Hard to miss it. Big and shiny and green."

"Sure, and I remember the little twat that waddled out of the doors, too. Spectacles and grey hair, the whole scholar look. Important. *Wordy*. Right dull, he was. Steps out of his spaceship and says he's looking for turtles and bugs, yeah?"

Pushing his way back in front of Tilly, Harrison said, "Right. That's him. I'd wager he didn't say he was looking for turtles and bugs, but trying to save endangered species."

"Yeah, he was a right twat, no matter what he was looking for. Pushed his way in here, demanding shelter and food. Wanted me to spare some men to protect them whilst they traipsed into the forests looking for whales and dodos." He took the control box back from Clive and stared off toward the winged bears, who had calmed during the lull. They appeared to be digging at the ground where their chains were embedded in the ground. "Said he was almost there."

"We told 'em to fuck off," Clive said.

"That we did, Clive. That we did." Morrow stuck the slight butt of his cigarette back in his mouth and used both hands to press buttons on the box. The nearby mortars thumped and smoked as they launched more fireworks downrange. The animal-things squealed in terror as their area exploded with sizzling light. As the explosions died down again, Morrow looked at Harrison with a slightly pained expression. He nodded to Tilly. "You wearing some kind of flight suit? It shows insignia from the Army Air Corps. You actually with them, or did you buy a ratty jumpsuit from a thrift store somewheres?"

"It's real," Tilly said. "Only I'm not with them anymore. Mister Harrison hired me to fly them out here to find their lost researchers."

The major sent his bottle sailing into the field, where it shattered with a clatter. "Clive told me you came in by boat. Where's your airship? Whatcha got, one of those spiffy new gunships from the Toledo Corporation? Maybe a high-priced Madison Puma shuttle?"

Embarrassed to speak with someone who seemed to actually know their stuff, Tilly lowered her head. "We were flying a pre-war Cyclone."

"What? A helicopter?" Morrow looked skeptical.

Tilly nodded.

"A Goddamn helicopter? What, with propellers and everything? Shit," Major Morrow said. "Hope they're paying you well." He took one last drag at the cigarette and tossed it to the side. "And what happened to it? Clive says you came in on two equally pathetic patrol boats."

"Shot down," Tilly said. "Smog Hags, from what we could tell."

When Morrow walked past the group, Tilly was immediately taken aback by his body odor. It was hard to tell if the man had taken a shower since his arrival in China from the scent. She did her best to keep a blank face and not react to it.

"I'll let ye stay here if you'd like. For the night anyway." Morrow held up his hands, waving them. "But only because you have a real military person among ya, and I need to keep good relations with the U-S of fucking A. Otherwise, I'd send you out on your ass like your little twat friend."

The winged beast in the middle flopped around, trying to fly on what looked to be one good wing. The other bloodied and crooked wing dragged along behind the bear-thing as it crawled back toward the spike that kept it chained to the ground. It moaned a broken whimper with each movement; the sound rising as it drew within a couple arm lengths of the spike.

"Come morning, you're gone," Major Morrow said. "Understand? Your doctor man went further up river. Never heard from him again."

Saburo drew closer. "What the hell are you doing with those things?" She asked, indicating the tormented bears.

The major walked away without answering her, addressing the

creatures themselves instead. "Where ya goin', beastie?" he shouted. "I still need you to do something for me. Can ya howl? Give us a good, loud growl. You can do it."

The creature continued pulling itself along, ignoring the man.

Morrow rolled his eyes. "Aww. You can do it." He charged out onto the field until he came to a post that seemed to limit how far the beast could reach while tethered to the stake. The ground showed a curved line of disturbed earth, but the creature strained itself to go further. Morrow fell on all fours in front of it and looked it in the eyes. "You feel like calling out to your friends, don't ya? Come on. Call them."

"Morrow," Tilly called. "What the hell are you doing? Let the things go. It's no threat to you now. They can barely walk, let alone fly." She couldn't look at the battered and bleeding creatures. She instead focused on Morrow.

"Missy, don't shout at me. It's my goddamn camp and I'll do what I please," Morrow said. "And for your information, I look at these damn things every damn day. You think they're friendly or something? These troops that wander through our camp? Lots of them ripped to hell by beasts like these, so don't cry for them. They're big boys and girls. Now, if you'd like some advice, I'd suggest you hoof it back to the camp before the celebration really gets underway."

"What are you talking about?"

Morrow waved to Clive. "Take these people back to the camp and get them somewhere safe."

Clive nodded.

"You all can come with me. I'll see your set up with a place to sleep and eat," he said. "Come now, not much time."

"It's early," Saburo said. "We don't *need* to sleep or eat just yet."

"You'll see. Get set up and you'll be right as rain," Clive said. A half dozen dirty, shirtless men pushed in behind the group. "Come on. We're all friends here. Let's keep it that way. What say?"

"It's for your own safety," Morrow said. "Give us a minute and all will be well with the world. Official business and all."

Clive leaned close to the group. "Honest, this will go a long way to making friends with Morrow. If you don't, he might not be inclined to help you out in your hour of need. What say?"

Harrison's brow creased in concentration. It was obvious he not only had no poker face, but was also a terrible judge of character. He finally said, "Only if it helps us keep the relations on an even keel with him." He turned to the rest of his group. "Let's go, everyone. We can eat and set up our kits. Settle in before we speak with them about the next leg of our little expedition." He smiled, but it was weak. It looked like a smile Tilly had seen a dozen times in combat from a new lieutenant or captain walking into a shitshow they weren't qualified to deal with.

CHAPTER EIGHTEEN

They were corralled into an ill-used building with rusted cots and an exposed latrine. There were several narrow windows on either side with dusty, smudged glass and cobwebs in the corners.

"If ya need anything, let us know," Clive said. "But we'll be a bit busy for a spell. I'll have the cook start something extra for you. Something good." When he stepped out, a click followed the slam of the door.

Saburo stepped over and tried the door handle. "It's locked. He locked us in."

Decator pounded on the wall and stepped up to a window to look out. "Hey, what gives? Why are you locking us up?"

"Only for a bit," Clive shouted. "Get comfortable. I'll be back after the party."

Tilly and her companions watched Clive vanish into the crowd that now gathered closer to the camp. Some men climbed up into nearby watch towers, others into trenches lining the sides of the open field.

"What the hell?" Ned said. "Let's fucking bust out of this thing." He kicked the front door with enough force to shake the entire wall, but the door didn't move.

"He's right," Decator said. "First, we have to leave the weapons behind, and now we're locked up? Come on, we can all rush the door and bust it right off."

Uncharacteristically silent, Harrison stood alone by the old bed frames and looked out a window. Tilly approached him as Decator and Ned lined themselves up to charge the door. "Do you see that?" Harrison said. "They're coming."

"What are you talking about?"

"I closed my eyes for a moment," he said, "and felt like I was dreaming. There was darkness. These things were coming closer and closer."

"What things?" Saburo asked. "What kind of things?"

Harrison slowly shook his head. "It was like dozens of hands reaching out for me. But it was comforting. It was warm."

The group exchanged uncomfortable looks. Tilly knew what happened to squads that lost their leaders, no matter how inept that leader was. They lost faith in their mission. They tore themselves apart if someone didn't fill the vacuum quickly.

"What are you talking about?" Tilly asked. "You had a dream or something. We're all tired from the attack, and this entire trip is fucking with our minds." A rumbling in the depths of her mind reminded her of the bears and the cat woman. She also thought about her recent memories and dreams that had taken a turn into strangeness.

"These things…" Harrison began, before being interrupted by a cracking sound from the nearby forest. Everyone turned to the windows to see what the sound was. While Harrison had been speaking, the crowd outside had gone eerily silent. From the window, the group watched a huge tree fall onto the field. More toppled in the forest itself.

From the gap created by the felled tree, a half a dozen creatures emerged. They ran flat out, heads down. From her vantage point, Tilly could see they weren't flying like the bear-bats, or moving gracefully as Mingmei had. These were large, broad monsters with horns on their heads pouring onto the field, all walking on two legs. A dozen followed the initial six and then double that at least. And double again. They created a dark brown stream of angry things flowing toward the chained creatures on the pitch.

"What the fuck are those things?" Ned asked. "Deer people?"

"I don't know," Rei said. "Could be."

From the opposite wall, Harrison said, "Ox. They're ox creatures."

"How the hell can you tell that from way over here?" Ned asked. "I can barely see them."

Harrison sat on the floor and shook his head.

Curious, Tilly walked over to him. "Was this in your dream, or whatever it was? Why do you sound so sure?"

"I thought it was bullshit."

"What was bullshit? What did you think was bullshit?"

"Uhhh… Tilly? You should see this," Saburo said. "Something is happening." She pointed out the window to the field.

Tilly reluctantly moved from Harrison and joined Saburo at the window. On the field and in the towers, men were setting up heavy machine guns and other, larger arms. "They lured the things here with the bear-bats' cries."

When the ox men were within reach of the winged beasts, the soldiers began firing. The clatter of dozens of different firearms shattered the silence of a few minutes ago. On the other side, the beasts twitched and fell from the impact of so much concentrated firepower. The soldiers managed to keep a nearly straight line where they stopped the things. A small stack of bodies showed the limit of the ox men's progress. Smoke from all the shooting quickly wafted over to the small shack with Tilly and her companions. It seeped in through the cracks and irritated their eyes.

A sudden cry from Harrison altered the group's focus. Ned stood next to the man and kicked him in his side a second time. "What the fuck have you gotten us into?" Ned shouted. "What did you think was bullshit?"

Rei grabbed Ned and pulled him away, preventing more violence. "Tell them," Rei said.

"Tell us what?" Tilly asked.

"A messenger made it back from the region," Ned said. "They had some kind of report about what was going on in the area before he hired you all. You're not the first group to come looking out here." He looked poised to attack Harrison again at any moment.

Harrison buried his face in an ill-used cot and sobbed.

"How many have come before us?" Ned shouted.

Through his pathetic cries, Harrison said, "Four. There were four teams before us. None of the others made it this far."

"What happened to them?" Decator picked his boss up off the

cot and slammed him against the wall. "Where are they?"

"I don't know," Harrison whimpered. "We only got scraps of communications sent by drones. They sent mundane reports until they started talking about beasts attacking them. Weird shit. Things that shouldn't exist. They never came back."

Anger rose inside Tilly. The whole thing had been too good to be true, but she'd ignored it. The perfect job for her, right when she'd begun scraping money together for a flight back to America, and as the debt for the store had reared its head again.

She looked at Rei and asked, "You knew about this?"

"I wasn't supposed to know. I overheard bits and pieces."

"You could have warned us."

"I tried." Rei's eye color wavered from black to a jaundiced yellow. Tilly took this to mean he was as confused and angry as the rest of the crew.

Tilly thought about his coy invitation to skip the job and go see a band in the city. "It wasn't good enough, was it?"

"I say we fucking slit their throats and watch them die," Ned said. If the vein throbbing in his head was any indication, it looked like he meant it.

"No. We still need to get out of here, and they have connections we might need." Decator sounded tired as he spoke. He searched everyone's faces, his own eyes wide with fear.

"Fuck this," Tilly said. "Let's get the door open and get out of here while we can." Ned, Rei, and Decator lined up at the entrance. The three of them slammed into it, shaking the entire structure again. "We could probably bust these windows if we had to."

"No, I heard something crack in the frame last time," Ned said. "Let's give it another shot." He and his companions backed up for another run.

"Jesus, it's not stopping." Saburo remained at the window, watching the carnage unfold. "There's got to be hundreds of them running out of the woods and into the field of fire. They're piling up out there like firewood. Why would they do that?"

"Let's go," Tilly said, lining up with the three men. As they rushed the door once more, she kicked the wall next to the doorframe, hoping to loosen the structure even more. The combination worked, and the group managed to splinter the portal.

"Holy shit," Saburo shouted. "Those bear creatures are dropping from above now."

Tilly stepped out of the makeshift prison. A few of the creatures circled above the camp. They dove and grabbed men and women indiscriminately, then dropped some from thirty or forty feet in the air. They slammed others into buildings at full speed. A glance to the battlefield showed the EU soldiers losing ground and the ox beasts advancing.

"I don't think they counted on both groups showing up at once," Tilly said. "Those things dropping in from the sky have turned the tide."

"What do we do?" Rei asked.

Tilly realized the group was looking to her. Harrison was still balled up on the floor. "Well, we make a run for the boats," she said. "If we get there, we might be able to make for the river and convince these things we're not worth chasing. We watch each other's backs. Call out any creatures that get too close and grab whatever weapons you can find along the way. Okay?" The nods told her everyone was onboard. "Can someone help Harrison along? We can't leave him. He might be useful with his connections along the river, and I think he has more to tell us."

"He'll slow us down," Ned said.

"If it gets dangerous, drop him." Tilly evaluated the camp and a way through. It wouldn't be a far run, but there were bear-bats dropping everywhere.

"Affirmative." Ned and Rei grabbed Harrison and got him standing.

They ran, keeping themselves close to the buildings, making it tougher for anything to drop in without warning. Being near the structures also allowed them to notice things they might have missed along the way; they grabbed a shovel, a hatchet, and several short pieces of rebar. Tilly had hoped to find guns, but they didn't have time to search each building. She settled for a thick metal bar and pressed on.

They made it through the compound unfettered. The gunfire from the field had become more sporadic, and the screams and shouts faded as they got further from it. They gathered themselves when they reached the edge of the camp, assessing the open area that lay between them and the docks.

"What do we do?" Saburo asked.

It was an enormous gap with no cover and no way around it. The only solution was to be as quiet as possible so as not to attract attention. It wasn't the best plan, but it was the best Tilly could do. "Okay. Decator and Rei, you help Harrison to the boat. Saburo and Ned, you guard them. Whack the fuck out of anything that comes at you. I'll watch our rear."

Seconds after they broke cover, a bear-bat dropped next to them with a thud. Its black wings kicked up dust. It was the first close look she'd had at one of things, but Tilly couldn't dwell on it. She dodged the thing's attack with its sharp claws and long arms. It wasn't a bear standing on its hind legs, rather it had more of a human stance and physiology.

She swung the thick rebar at it, but fell short as she tried to avoid the massive wings. The creature was slow to react, but its body presented so many potential dangers, it perplexed Tilly as to how to attack. She had to mind the claws and thick arms, avoid the jaws and sharp teeth, and keep an eye out for the sweeping wings. She couldn't help but think a gun would work fine if someone had one.

"Run! I can hold this thing off," she shouted. "Get Nancy and the others to start the boats and help us out."

"Tilly," Saburo shouted. "Take this." She threw the long-handled shovel over and ran after the others. It clattered to the ground a few feet behind Tilly.

The beast lunged then, growling and gnashing its teeth. It used its broad, leathery wings to blow Tilly off balance. It reached for her as she stumbled and fell to the ground. She threw the bar as hard as she could at its head and scored a hit. It thudded against the monster's temple. While the hit only slowed it for a moment, it was all Tilly needed to reach for the shovel and bring it around in front of her. She swung at the charging bear-bat's chest with the metal point and made contact. It drew a line of blood and stopped the thing's charge.

From the docks, a sudden burst of gunfire erupted. The U.N. soldiers that had stayed behind broke from their hiding places to cover Harrison and the others. They immediately killed an approaching bear-bat, sending it spinning into the river. The boat engines clattered to life. The mounted guns turned toward the beastly attackers.

Tilly jabbed at her foe again. She knew the shooters on the dock couldn't help her without risking shooting her as well. The bear-bat swung on her, trying to rid her of the shovel. She reacted by swinging at an exposed wing. She cut a small tear in the membrane. The thing roared in agony and struck her to the ground with a thick, furry forearm.

Her temple immediately ached from the blow. From her vantage point on the ground, Tilly's situation was getting worse. Behind the creature, a group of ox-men were charging through the camp in her direction.

Without a strategy, she stood and ran toward the boats with the bear-bat in close pursuit. Luckily, she was faster and created some distance between them. It roared in anger and leapt into the air. Before it could catch air and pull itself upward, two particularly aggressive ox-men ran it to the ground. They knocked it to the dirt, trampling it before the thing even knew what was happening.

At the dock, the roar of boat motors. *The Myrtle* and its companion were pulling away already. Harrison came to life, shouting and shoving Nancy while watching the action on shore. There was no way Tilly could make the jump onto the deck, so she dove headfirst into the water. She swam underwater as hard as she could, getting a few yards away before the ox-men began jumping off the dock as well. Splashing and grunting soon surrounded her as her new opponents swung and clawed at her while trying to keep themselves afloat. Tilly had the advantage of being lighter and faster. It allowed her to pull away and catch up with the boat. Saburo and Ned helped her aboard, hauling her soaked body onto the deck. She lay gasping on her back.

“Are you alright?” Saburo asked.

Once she caught her breath and had her wits about her, Tilly stood and looked for Harrison. She’d made sure he survived the camp, but he’d repaid her most unkindly.

“What the fuck were you thinking?”

“I told you before if you fell behind, we’d leave you,” Harrison said. He held a pistol in his hand, which Tilly assumed he’d used to force Nancy to get the boat underway. “I will not die out here. You understand? I’m going to finish this.”

Tilly looked around for a weapon, for a gun of her own. “You knew what was waiting here, didn’t you, you ass?”

A splash at the aft of the boat startled everyone. Rather than being attacked by another creature, they found Morrow and Clive climbing aboard, both battered and bloody.

CHAPTER NINETEEN

Morrow smiled as he stood on the deck smoking a cigarette he bummed from Nancy. "We do appreciate the ride. I thought we were certainly gone from this world for sure. For sure." He blew smoke that trailed the boat as it continued upriver. Clive nodded his agreement.

To Tilly, Morrow seemed as calm and collected as if he'd just finished a good meal. His grin was wide, his occasional chuckle genuine. His man, Clive, was not quite as at ease, though he played it like he was, handing the cigarette back and forth with hands that barely shook.

"What was the plan?" Ned asked. "What was your intent when you goaded those beasts into attacking?"

Rei glared at the men, his eyes gun barrel grey. "We could have all been killed."

"He's not wrong," Tilly said. "It could have gone either way for us. And I have to guess your men in the compound didn't fare too well back there. I don't want to speak for anyone else, but I'm itching to toss you over the side right about now."

Morrow laughed and waved his hands in surrender. "Whoa there, lass, easy. We are your humble servants here. We are unarmed and helpless, dear." He tossed the cigarette into the river and blew a cloud of smoke into the air. "No, we don't want to start anything here. All friends, all friends. But, ah, the plan didn't exactly go the way we'd intended, now did it?"

"It did not," Clive agreed.

"You got your boats all fueled up from our tanks, right?" Morrow asked. "Everything topped off and good?"

"We got about halfway through the refueling when things went sideways," Nancy said. "It'll get us moving for a while."

Clive dropped his wet jacket and shirt on the deck with a slap.

"That's good. We'll be fine. We can fill up the rest of the way at this Russian depot. Sort of tiny camp, but they have the petrol we need and likely some food. They'll not let us stay or anything, but hey, it's the Russians. They're damn boring, you know?"

Decator stomped across the deck toward Harrison, stopping short of stepping on the man's feet. "Are we okay with taking this pair with us further upriver?"

"What?" Harrison no longer paid attention to the conversation, if he had at all. He stared behind the boat, presumably watching for oncoming attackers or beasts that might trail the retreating craft.

"Why are we asking him?" Saburo held an axe at her side as she shifted from foot to foot, staring at their former boss. "He's not in charge here anymore."

"The fucking Scots screwed us over. The two standing right there. What do we do with them?" Decator asked again.

"Whoa, seriously. We didn't intend to bring harm to you and yours, honest. Those ox-beasties had been killing off our livestock and attackin' our people for nigh on three months. We couldn't let it go. Things escalated, you know? As they do. And we'd only seen the fucking bear bastards a few times, so who could have guessed they'd all show up today with friends, yeah?"

"We need all the help we can get." Harrison's voice was low and lost. "Trust me."

"What?" Saburo shouted.

"*Brilliant*," Ned added, dripping with sarcasm.

"Look, mates. I know we got off to a poor start. As first impressions go, we screwed the pooch here. But honestly, we're excellent soldiers. We know the area and will help any way we can." Morrow's face softened. He suddenly looked like a lost puppy with wide, sad eyes and upturned lip. "We're grateful to be alive."

Tilly looked to see if anyone was falling for the man's obvious manipulation and was happy to see the rest of the group looked as angry as when he'd climbed aboard.

"So. With that sorted, who has a gun for me and my mate here? Hmmm? Pistol will do. Anything." Morrow returned to smiling his wide, toothy grin.

Nancy leaned out of the wheelhouse and nodded to the soldiers they'd picked up at the U.N. camp. She waved them up toward the bow. "Let's keep our eyes on the path ahead, people. Who knows what the fuck awaits us around the next bend." The four remaining soldiers set up on the deck, two on each side to keep watch on the trees, bushes, and debris they passed on shore. The captain kept an eye on the group at the back, lingering on Harrison.

Tilly followed the U.N. soldiers' example and moved forward. She took a seat next to Nancy in the wheelhouse.

"Your boss looks off his nut." Captain Nancy guided the boat without taking her eyes off the river. "Those vacant eyes are hard to miss."

"I can't say you're wrong."

"What are you and the others going to do about it?"

Tilly thought for a moment. In the army, she'd dealt with leaders that were idiots, and some that were clueless. But she'd never been in the position of following someone in shock like Harrison was. "You're the captain of the boat," she said. "Shouldn't *you* do something?"

"I suppose if it comes to it, I might have to. But we're pointed further into the country right now, with all the known dangers between us and the U.N. base. We can head back and hope to avoid them, I suppose, or fight our way through."

"Or we can move forward into the unknown and hope the perils are not as life-threatening? Why do you assume I'd be in charge if things went to shit?" Not that Tilly had avoided leadership positions in the military. She was always worried promotions would take her out of the sky and reduce her flight time.

"No offense to your comrades, but have you taken a good look at them?" Nancy laughed. "Your current leader is a basket case right now. One of your military brethren is having trouble working the NaNi you loaned her. The other gangly son of a bitch is awkward as hell, and those other two-Harrison's soldiers-look like they were pulled out of a mailroom somewhere and dressed from a catalog."

Tilly sighed and thought back to the interview that started it all for her. "When they hired me, they asked if I'd killed anyone. I thought they were kidding." She focused on those words again. "Who asks that, right? I should have known this was a freak show right there and then."

"Have you?"

"See, that's the thing. I didn't give them an answer exactly. But I've never killed anyone. Not with a gun or a knife. I flew bombing missions, but only against unmanned targets. I've never been able to do it."

"I figured," Nancy said. "Sorry to have to tell you this, but it actually makes you the only level-headed badass on my boat."

Tilly shook her head, dismayed at the confirmation and the compliment. "Never been called that before."

"Get used to it."

Tilly studied Nancy. "*You* ever kill anyone?" She knew how triggering that question had been for her.

"That's kind of personal, don't you think?" Nance lit a cigarette and blew smoke into the cabin.

Tilly smiled and let it go. "I know it's different from an aircraft, but I'd be happy to take over the wheel if you need a break."

"I might take you up on that, badass. But… you may also want to check the hold to see if your cat friend is okay."

Once the madness erupted at the camp, Tilly had forgotten about Mingmei. She excused herself and stepped past the team members scattered around the deck. The rest of the crew slept, with a few soldiers rotating guard duty. They slept where they could, which meant sitting on the deck and leaning against the bulkhead. In the case of a woman from the U.N. camp, she even slept on the stairs to the hold below. It was tricky to step around her without waking the soldier, but Tilly managed.

As she crawled through the rows in the hold, Mingmei called out. "Are we safe?"

"Yes, Mingmei. It's me, Tilly."

"I know. I could smell your scent coming."

Another first. No one had ever told Tilly they could smell her. She didn't know whether to be proud or afraid to continue without a shower. "Okay. Good. Uh. We're on our way. These soldiers at the last camp were fighting with creatures somewhat like you. Did you know there were others out there?"

"What kind?"

"There were the bear creatures, and ox men, I think?"

In the low light, Mingmei clawed lightly at the hull. "I know them. The oxen are a community from Yuncheng your doctor lured here. The bears are from Beiguancun."

"What do you mean, they're from Beiguancun and Yuncheng? What does the doctor have to do with this?"

"I've tried to tell you. He's the one who made us. He and Kalidas lured us from cities and towns miles from the temple. That's where these animal beings are coming from, the people of those places. He's drawing them in like a… a magnet, and he's changing my fellows into… well, things like me."

Tilly felt a twitch in her temple as she tried to decrypt what Mingmei was saying. "Are you… Are you saying you and the others are the Chinese citizens who lived throughout this region?" The tiger-woman nodded slowly. In the whirlwind of the last few days, Tilly had forgotten the mystery she'd chased in the U.N. camp. "I can't see how that's possible. I can't believe he has the science to do what you're saying. He's a conservationist, not a geneticist or a surgeon. How would he create masses of… people like you?"

"It is *not* science," Mingmei said. "I knew science before he did this to me. No, he stumbled onto something only found in our folklore. And *that* something *convinced* him what they were doing was science, but it wasn't. It was darker. It was ugly."

As the possibility of Mingmei's truth hit her, Tilly thought back to the masses of ox-men and bear-bats slaughtered at the E.U. camp. The implication was they weren't some strange creatures emerging from the forests to attack the men and women who'd settled there. They were the people themselves, rising from the remains of their ravaged country to push the invaders from their land.

"If it wasn't the doctor alone, who then?" she asked.

"Your doctor has awakened Kalidas the Hundun. One of the Four Perils," Mingmei said. "And your doctor has no notion of what he has done. He has summoned a force he cannot hope to understand or fully control. You should go home now. Turn back."

"Mingmei, I can't."

"The war is over. Long over. So why are you here? That's the question. You're not Chinese, so you don't fight for us. You're not even Asian. So why are you here?"

"Honestly? I wanted a job where I could fly. I love to fly. And it brought here."

"So, go fly businesspeople from meeting to meeting in the big cities. Drop skiers on the tops of mountains, or some other bullshit. But why come here?"

"I don't..."

"Better than Disneyland, they tell me," Mingmei said. Even with the features of a tiger, a rueful smile on her face was unmistakable. "The others that come here like you. The excitement, the danger. You can't find it anywhere else. You can kill, fuck, burn, eat whatever you want here and, as long as you are in the right zone, no one gives a shit. Better than Disneyland."

"No," Tilly said. "I needed a job. We're looking for a scientist and then going home. That's all."

Mingmei sniffed at the air and looked around. "Yes. That's a good story. No one really goes home, though. They leave important parts of themselves here. I'm afraid your pale employer is going to find out as well. I can feel the presence of Kalidas in him already. You would do well not to learn the same lesson."

CHAPTER TWENTY

Saburo and Captain Nancy took turns piloting the craft into the night, cautious of debris near the shore, fearful of any sounds in the forests. While awake, they ate rations directly from the can or box. Tilly sat near the wheelhouse and thought about what they were getting into and whether anyone would take the time or effort to listen and understand. Whenever she tried to wrap her mind around how the doctor could have changed so many people, she shuddered.

"It's good we haven't stopped. I think it gave a nice boost in putting some distance between us and those hordes of beasts," Nancy said.

From the moment the sun had come up and lit the hazy horizon, Morrow slid up close and quietly stared at the passing shore. He smoked someone else's cigarettes and leaned against the outer railing near the door. The smoke wafted through the open portal and lingered in the cabin. He perked up after an hour and shouted to Tilly. "Not far now. Look." He pointed to a twisted mass of metal and tree branches wrapped around a series of concrete pylons. "That's where their old water treatment plant stood. Not far at all. A mile, maybe two."

Tilly focused on the water ahead, while Nancy signaled to the smaller boat behind them. Per Morrow's prediction, they came to a wider point in the river and a small dock on the shore to the east. The dock was attached to a small building surrounded by trees that seemed to hide more buildings beyond.

Morrow tossed his cigarette into the water and stepped onto the railing. He balanced himself using the roof of the wheelhouse. "Ay. Wake up, comrades. You have visitors," he shouted. "Up and at it, boyos. Our boat needs a wee bit of a drink."

"We can leave him here, yeah?" Nancy murmured.

Tilly wasn't even sure the fuel depot would be real. But now they'd encountered it, ditching the loathsome Scot sounded like a good idea. "I guess it depends on whether I'm in charge here. But I see no reason why not."

On the dock, a pudgy man in camo shorts and a green t-shirt appeared and waddled toward the end. Despite the shouts of greeting and love from Morrow, the Russian didn't appear happy. He threw a rope to Clive and another to the fast attack boat as it glided up alongside. Once they'd tied the boats off, the man finally waved to the Scots.

"Mister Morrow," the Russian said, nodding grimly. "Long time."

Morrow stepped off the boat and hugged the man. "So lovely to see you, Maksim. Bloody lovely. What's it been now, three weeks, perhaps?" He turned to the others in the boat and presented his friend. "Everybody, this is Max. He is the fucking shit here in Little Russia."

"I am the garrison master at arms for the Soviet Federation Huang He River outpost. I suppose one could call me the shit if they wanted. I would not dispute it." He did not crack a smile. "What is it you need here, mister Morrow? We agreed you would only visit us on the first of the month if you required a trade. Your presence today is against our terms."

It was evident to Tilly the Russians were as fed up with Morrow as she was. "We were on an expedition up the river," she said. "And while we stopped at the E.U.'s camp, we were attacked and had to flee without refueling fully. Morrow said we might get gasoline here."

"This is what he said to you?"

"Yes."

"Hey, we have an agreement for trade and bartering, don't we?" Morrow helped Clive and then Saburo up onto the deck. "We want to talk about it. Fuel is all we need. Maybe some ammunition. Possibly fresh drinking water. Alcohol, if you can spare it. But we mostly need fuel for these mighty fish here, and then we'll be out of your hair."

As Max looked the two Scotsmen over, Tilly realized what a sight they were. Both men had blood on their clothing and sported nasty cuts and scrapes across their bodies. She hadn't noticed in the heat of their escape, but the blood on their clothing must not have washed out as they swam to reach the departing boats. As she glanced around, their craft was just as frightful, with stains on its decks and torn canopies.

Morrow laughed at his appearance. "A wee bit dirty. Running a camp is filthy work, you know?" He pulled his clothes off clear down to his underwear and tossed them into the water. Standing there grinning in his underwear, he took a couple of steps and jumped into the water. He resurfaced and shouted, "Anyone have a bar of soap on them?"

With a mad laugh, Clive followed his lead. Then, with only slight hesitation, the four U.N. soldiers did the same. The men whooped and whistled when the female on the U.N. team stripped out of her clothing, but she appeared unfazed. She tossed her shirt and trousers onto the dock before cannonballing into the river. To Tilly, it seemed like an idiotic thing to do, with no idea of their surroundings and no indication of what awaited them in the water. Here and there, trash floated on the surface.

Despite the filth and occasional floating debris, the men swam in the river willingly and joyfully. Morrow floated on his back and sang a Scottish song that Tilly couldn't understand and was glad for it. The few words she made out had to do with lass's asses and other crude things that rhymed. He seemed incredibly proud of himself and of his off kilter singing voice. The remaining mercenaries and Scotsmen splashed and laughed, having stripped to at least their skivvies.

Captain Nancy stood at the railing and watched, slightly bemused. "You're probably swimming in mostly shit, you know."

The men hissed and splashed *The Myrtle*.

Mingmei showed her face at the bottom of the stairs before she retired to her nest in the hold. Ned followed and assured Tilly he was looking after the tiger-woman so no harm would befall her. Up close, the fueling station was still nothing to speak of. A couple of huge petrol tanks, a guard tower, a shitter, and a barracks behind the main building. Six Russian soldiers eventually came out and lounged on the deck, in no hurry to assist with anything. Drying towels and shirts on a nearby clothesline suggested more of the soldiers lurked nearby or slept in their quarters.

Harrison sat grimly on the boat, looking half-comatose as Rei and Decator asked him questions. Decator was still in his neat, uniform-long sleeves and all. The full gear made Tilly cringe. It had to be hot in the dark clothing, but the man wasn't sweating. The uniforms were no longer clean and new, though. They were brown from mud and water, torn in places. Both men had the look of contemplation, likely evaluating their employer. Rei fiddled with a tiny portable fan, blowing an ineffectual breeze in his own face. Harrison didn't speak and offered no help with the Russians. He stared at the river with a metal cup of water perched on the seat next to him. He occasionally sniffed or grunted at what he saw out on the water. Anyone looking for what had agitated him saw nothing.

"How much longer is this going to take?" Decator asked. He didn't really aim the question at anyone and didn't seem too concerned when no one replied.

Staying out of the way of those that knew what they were doing, Tilly strolled to *The Myrtle*'s bow. She stared at maps of the Huang He from before the war and laid clear plastic pages of updates on top of it, showing where they were in approximation to the cities before. The water today covered much of the areas where the city of Nantong once stood. If she was right, the town was now fifty feet below the water. This meant several of the tallest buildings in the town—the Nantong TV Tower and the Zhiyun Temple—still should have broken the surface. With neither visible, that meant both had likely toppled, and their debris now lurked dangerously close to the surface. She'd remembered from the warnings issued to pilots flying in the area and landing to take on injured soldiers or drop off fresh troops entering the region.

"Hey, captain," Tilly said. "Somewhere around here is a massive temple and tower. May want to watch for them when we head out."

It took a minute for Nancy to tear herself away from the men in the water. Her amused smirk gave way as she spoke. "Nah. Not a problem. The temple came down in the flooding. Snapped in half, like a goddamn matchstick from what I hear. They found relics and bits of it miles downstream."

"Really? What about the TV Tower?"

"Crumbled. Between the flooding and the war itself, it couldn't escape. Parts are still out there. Much further out, so it shouldn't be a problem. I'll stick to the shoreline until we're clear of camp," the captain said. "No big deal."

"Sounds like you have this figured."

Nancy shrugged. "I managed to get a few things out of the Russians while the rest of the crew goofed off. Turns out, if you act the opposite of how Morrow acts, people react favorably."

"I guess they would."

Morrow tromped up the dock in his underwear and boots with a look of satisfaction. "Shitter's free, if anyone is so inclined. I lit a match, but Lordy, it smells in there." He picked up speed and ran off the end of the wooden structure, hugging his knees as he leapt into the water. His plunge splashed green-yellow water over his fellow Scot and the others.

"Fucker," Clive shouted. When Morrow surfaced, Clive leapt on his countryman's head and shoved him back underwater. "I'll do ya for that." From there, it devolved into a crude shouting match, everyone throwing punches and shoving each other.

Saburo woke from her nap and stretched. "Miss anything?"

"Afraid not."

Saburo nodded and fished a plastic baggie from her shirt pocket. She climbed onto the dock, where she rolled what appeared to be a cigarette and lit it. "You want?" She held it out to Tilly and exhaled a cloud of smoke. Tilly stared at it harder than expected before rising and taking it. She brought it to her lips and inhaled deeply. I pleasantly surprised her to find it was a much better class of weed than she'd remembered. It lingered in her head, filling her nose and mouth. She felt a smile coming on as she handed the joint back to Saburo, who turned and headed toward the latrines.

"She shouldn't smoke so close to the fuel depot," one of the

Russians said. He slouched so far down on his bench, it looked like he might slide to the deck if he moved another inch. "There is no smoking permitted around the tanks." He pointed to a nearby blackened sign on the wall that reiterated his point.

"Is that why the sign is burnt to shit?" Tilly asked.

The Russian looked at the sign. "No."

"I'll be sure to let her know," Tilly said, stifling a giggle at the man's seriousness. "What do you do out here all day? Isn't this the most boring assignment? I mean…" She looked around for any sign of escape or enjoyment in the drab camp. "This seems like a really fucking boring post. What do you do out here? For real. I mean, I see living quarters, a guard tower, and what? An office? Is that what this building is?"

The Russian shrugged. "We play cards. Dice. Not so bad."

Tilly shook her head and climbed the ladder onto the dock. "If you say so." She passed Saburo on her way back from the lavatory. "Watch out. The guard is extremely concerned you'll blow us up if you smoke near the gas again."

"Well." Saburo blew a stream of blue smoke into the air. "You better take this with *you,* then." She held out the joint, passing it off to Tilly.

"Good idea." Tilly placed the joint between her lips where it dangled as she rounded the corner to the latrines. The smell immediately hit her, and she stopped. It certainly wasn't the smell of the toilets, though it was bad enough. There was another smell that overpowered them. She covered her nose and walked past the row of privies until the wooden walkway ended. There, thick reeds of some unknown type obscured the land and water. As she stood thinking and finishing her joint, the smell grew stronger.

"Fuck," Tilly said. She took a last drag and exhaled before seeking a place to toss the dying joint. When she pushed some weeds aside, looking for a sign of water, a shimmer caught her eye. As she stooped to drop the ember, Tilly found herself inches from the bloated face of an ox-man. She shrieked, the cannabis making her fear worse. She stumbled backward. She caught herself before falling over the other side of the walkway.

Saburo was the first to come to Tilly's aid. "What the hell happened? Are you okay?" She followed Tilly's gesture toward the weeds. Saburo, too, recoiled. More alert, thus prepared, she didn't scream. "It's dead," she said. "Decaying. It must have been here a while." She put her arm around Tilly, guiding her away.

"No, I'm okay." Tilly went back, determined to see it all. After the incident in the Scottish camp with the fireworks, seeing the creatures up close proved fascinating. Pushing the weeds aside, she discovered there were more than the one. They counted three bodies, all dead and decomposing. "Jesus. What the hell is wrong with these people? Why are they killing them and torturing them like this?"

Harrison's men came running. The anti-smoking Russian followed, seemingly unaffected. "I told you it is not boring out here. We find things to do." Disinterested, he turned and walked away.

The men shoved past and parted the weeds.

"What is it?" Decator asked.

"More of those ox things," Saburo said. "They've been dead for a while."

Rei covered his mouth and nose with his undershirt. "Explains the smell, I suppose."

"Hey, assholes," Morrow shouted. He and two others stood at the end of the dock in their dripping wet underwear. "Boats are fueled, and we got places to see. So, if you're done with your prayer circle or whatever you're doing, let's get the fuck out of here so we can find that missing cunt of yours." The trio turned away, shoving each other as they went. Morrow and Clive turned toward a supply shack at the last minute, while the third returned to the boat.

Harrison finally wandered up to the group and peered at the bodies without a word. He swallowed hard, like he was trying to keep something down.

"Why did you let them join us?" Saburo asked. "They don't really seem to have our best interests at heart."

"I didn't let them," Harrison said. "They didn't exactly ask." His reply was weak, but approached the bluster he'd had since the first meeting.

Pushing through the group, Tilly couldn't hold her tongue.

"Mingmei seems to think your doctor is responsible for all these creatures. Says the doctor is into something he can't comprehend."

Harrison ignored her and signaled for his men to head back to the boats. "Let's get the hell out of here while things are still going our way." Seeing the dead creatures had apparently sparked something in him. Even if he wasn't back to his old self, something at least gave him the strength to shrug off Decator's help and trudge forward on his own. Tilly thought about the things he'd said when they were trapped at the Scot's cabin. He'd mentioned dreams or revelations. Something he was going to tell them.

The two women followed behind the group. Tilly could tell from Saburo's expression she was equally concerned about the turns the trip had taken. It also seemed the plan to leave Morrow and Clive with the Russians had gone by the wayside, with Harrison's insistence on continuing upriver. Most of the group moved up the dock toward the boats, while Tilly waited for the rest of their people.

"Holy shit," Morrow shouted, his voice muffled, emanating from somewhere inside the fueling shack. "Is this what I think it is?"

Max, the Russian in the shorts, turned slowly.

After sounds of clattering and thumping came from inside the building, the front door swung open. Morrow emerged, dragging a pile of wire, tubes, metal, and foam padding. It was hard to tell where one end of the junk began and where it ended. What little metal Tilly saw appeared corroded and red, with pieces flaking onto the dock. Despite the state of disrepair, Morrow seemed genuinely excited to have found it.

"What the hell is it?" Ned asked.

"Are you fucking kidding me?"

Ned shrugged. "Looks like a pile of trash to me."

Morrow shook his head and walked over to the Russian. "Tell me this isn't a German Army-issue BlackCarver mark three exoskeleton. I've only seen one in action before, and you have one gathering dust in your fucking storage shed?"

The Russian grimaced. "Ack. That thing? It's only an arm unit, and we could only get the hand section to power up. It's useless. *Beyond* useless."

"Where did you get it? Where's the rest of it?" Morrow looked more excited, correct in his assessment. "Come on, man. Why did you never tell me this before?"

"What's to tell?" Max said. "Some of the men found it in a field one day. It's broken. No one can use it properly. Why would someone want one arm of an exoskeleton? It would be unbalanced. There's no support for it, so it would be much too heavy for someone to carry for any length of time. It's scrap. *Useless*."

"Where's the rest of it?"

"Who knows? Out in the fields somewhere. It probably crashed and broke up. Scattered every-damn-where across the landscape."

Morrow untangled the parts and the pieces as best he could. When a section clunked onto the deck, Tilly wondered how heavy it was and how a thin wiry man like Morrow would handle it. He looked like he weighed a hundred and fifty pounds, tops. The Scot's arms were muscular, but when she stared at the shirtless man, she had trouble seeing anything more than the ribs that poked through his torso.

"It's only sitting in the damn junk shed now." Clive moved to get a better look. "Taking up space and rusting."

The Russian leaned forward, interested in the conversation for the first time. "You want it?"

Clive shrugged. "I don't know. I mean, if only one of the arms works, it isn't much use."

"That one arm, though. You could punch through a damn tree with that one arm if you get it working."

Clive and Morrow exchanged a look, then Morrow shrugged. "A tree? Sounds strong. Sure. We'd be interested in taking it with us up the river. What do you want for it?"

The Russian leaned back in his chair and scratched at the stubble on his chin.

"It's pretty fucked up." Clive nudged the pile with his boot.

"It's *rare,*" Max said.

From the boat, Nancy shouted in a hoarse voice for them to hurry the hell up.

"Look, we have all kinds of supplies back at the camp. There are so many things I think you'd like to trade for this worthless pile of shit," Clive said.

"Such as?"

"Fireworks? We have so many different types of sparklers, bloomers, spinners. You name it, we have it."

"Fireworks?" Max said. "Nyet."

Clive nodded. "Of course, nyet. What the hell would you need those for? How about..." Clive looked around at the group. "How about helicopter parts? We've got those."

The Russian was slowly looking disinterested.

"Money? Gold?"

Judging by the camp Morrow was running, Tilly was pretty sure they had none of the things Clive was suggesting. And no matter what sort of scavengers they were, there was no evidence they had any money.

Finally, the Russian held up his hand. "We have had a good relationship in the past, Mr. Morrow, but I'm already letting you have gasoline on faith you will pay it back. If you want the suit so badly, bring something back to exchange for it when you reimburse me for the fuel. I will be happy to consider any fair trades then."

"Look, Max, I've been nothing but fair in our little dealings," Morrow said. "I think you could give me a little grace here and trust me to..."

The Russian stood, seemingly uninterested in being talked down to any longer. "Why did all of you look like the devil himself was chasing you when you pulled in?" he asked. "Where did all those wounds and blood come from on your bodies? And why do your vessels have scratches and gouges in them? And it seems as though you're planning on continuing up the river to look for this scientist. Why would I believe you're coming back?"

"Look..." Clive said.

Morrow stepped up and put his hand on the other Scot's shoulder. "He's right mate. We don't plan on coming back."

The sound of a nine-millimeter handgun surprised everyone, and Tilly threw herself flat on the dock for cover. When she looked up, Morrow was lowering his pistol. The Russian fell to the ground in front of her.

"What the hell?" Ned shouted from the boat. "What happened?" He climbed onto the dock and rushed over to the group.

Morrow lit a cigarette and stared down at the Russian on the deck, bleeding on his t-shirt and shorts.

Shouts in Russian emanated from other nearby buildings. Soon, the unmistakable sound of soldiers running in boots approached.

Tilly stood and ran for the boats. Behind her, Morrow and Clive laughed as they dragged the parts of the exoskeleton with them. It was nearly a minute before the sound of high-powered rifle fire erupted. She jumped onto the boat as the Scots jumped in behind her. The exoskeleton landed with a thud and a clatter. No sooner had everyone tumbled in than they were underway, flanked by the smaller boat. As the Russian troops shot at the retreating boats, the gunners on each vessel returned fire. Smoke issued from the side of the building where Morrow had found the exoskeleton.

"This is the second camp we've had to flee because of your insanity," Tilly said as she slid down seeking cover inside the boat. "You assholes are going to get us killed!"

"Not today," Clive said.

"At least get a gun and help us fight them off. They'll be on us soon."

Morrow waved her off. "Nah, the Russians don't have so much as a wee rowboat, let alone some sort of attack craft. Nor do they have aircraft or drones. Plus, I set their fuel dump on fire. They'll want to put it out before they do anything else. They'll not be following us any time soon."

They all gazed up to find Harrison standing over them, a dull expression on his face. "What's this shit?"

"Exosuit, sir."

Ned came over to look at the pile of metal and strings of wire.

"It doesn't actually work, *sir*," Tilly said.

"If it did," Harrison said, seeming half asleep by the tone of his voice and the shuffle in his movements, "what would it do?"

Morrow turned on his usual wide, greasy smile. "Why, it could help a single man lift a ton. They could run like a gazelle; they could punch through an elephant." He sang the words, almost like a commercial for the dismantled weapon. "It could do any, any, anything!"

"Any, any, ANYTHING!" Clive repeated with a guffaw.

Harrison shrugged. "So, what does it do now?"

"Noth, noth, *NOTHING*," Tilly grunted. "It's useless. He fucked us with the Russians for nothing." She turned and watched the smoke from the Russian outpost fade into the distance. True to Morrow's assessment, no boats, no aircraft, no soldiers followed.

Tilly and Nancy exchanged a glance, reminding her of their previous conversation. Tilly was the voice of reason, the true leader of the expedition. At least as far as most of the group were concerned. She debated what to do in the situation. Morrow was bad for the group, and led them deeper into trouble at every step. However, a confrontation at this point would throw them deeper into chaos. The surviving few on the boats were already jumpy and terrified by whatever might happen next. Creating a fight now would only make things worse.

Harrison walked away without another word.

Tilly eventually sat back and relaxed. She allowed herself to doze on the boat's deck, leaving the others to pace and stare into the trees, looking for creatures and enemies that may or may not be watching back. The crew mumbled back and forth at the sight of anything they couldn't immediately identify. Occasionally, one would confirm that a dark form in the trees was merely a crushed convection oven, a tree trunk, or a trashed home. The flooding had brought so much garbage downstream, taking entire homes, offices, and farms, unearthing landfills. All of it: garbage, personal effects, animal waste and animals alike, ended up somewhere between the dams and the ocean. It landed on the shores, the beaches, and, she guessed, the bottom of the river and its offshoots.

At least the smog clouds were thinner that far from the major cities. As Tilly put her feet up on the railing, she almost felt warm, like the sun's heat was reaching her. The air smelled better out there, too. Gone was the stench of burning rubber and dead fish. Gone was the smell of decaying food and rotting people. She took a deep breath and exhaled it slowly, ignoring the odor of the unshowered soldiers walking past her in a tizzy. Whenever the image of one of the ox-people or bear-bats, or any of the other things came to mind, she closed her eyes and thought of flying-transports, helicopters, kites, whatever-and waited until the monsters had gone away.

Harrison never came near her, and she never heard his voice. Before she'd moved forward, she saw him with his men at the front of the boat, staring at the water like he was trying to read the future. His face was stony, hiding any apprehension or emotion about their situation. This made trying to guess their next move a mystery. What he'd billed as a couple of days flying up the river was turning into nearly a week on a boat. They had lost members of their crew along the way, despite assurances she, Ned, and Saburo were only along for a precaution.

The mysterious tiger-woman, Mingmei, had vanished and hadn't emerged from the hold. Once she finished her round of guard duty, Tilly determined she should go find the woman. She needed to reassure her the crew would take care of her, that the corporation did not know what was going on in the woods of the Huang He River. Unfortunately, it wasn't exactly how Tilly felt. They had hired her to help the company men out, but no amount of money would make her feel good about the trip, no matter who was in control.

"Excuse me," Saburo said. "I don't mean to bother you, but the NaNi face you lent me keeps making noise and buzzing. I'm sorry I've kept it so long."

It had slipped Tilly's mind that she no longer had the device. She hadn't even missed it, really. But she took it with a nod and reattached it to the wrist unit. Her wrist twitched right away and NaNi's voice drifted on the breeze. "*It has been one hundred forty-seven days since you took... Dad... to his physical therapy appointment. Shall I schedule a physical therapy appointment with Doctor... Tahama*?" She felt another twinge, and NaNi repeated her message. "*It has been forty-seven days since you took... Dad... to his physical therapy appointment. Shall I schedule one with Doctor... Tahama*?"

Tilly swatted her wrist to stop the device from buzzing. "NaNi?"

"Yes… *Tilly*. What would you like me to do?"

Saburo watched on in fascination.

"NaNi. Remove all alarms and reminders regarding dad."

"Remove all alarms and reminders regarding... Dad," NaNi repeated. "*Please confirm.*"

"Yes. Confirmed."

The device paused. "*Are you certain? Command seems counterproductive… Dad needs…*"

"No. We've been over this. Dad is no longer with us. He is dead. Delete the appointments, please. And do not ask again. Remove them. These are old reminders."

"*These appointments stop the spread of the cancer and reverse its course. To summarily dismiss the doctor's orders would be detrimental to… Dad's… well-being.*"

"He's dead, NaNi. He's been dead for a while."

"*But the cancer will continue to spread if he does not make his full regimen. According to the schedule created by… Doctor Tahama…*"

"He's dead. The cancer can't continue to spread after he dies."

The machine vibrated, tickling her skin and sending a shiver up her arm. "*Attempting to download cancer protocols from Johns-Hopkins University.*" It buzzed again. "*Failed. Unable to connect to information source.*"

"NaNi, there's no connection around here. No one can get a source."

"*Attempting to download cancer protocols from The London Clinic.*"

"NaNi, shut down."

"*Failed. Unable to connect to information source.*"

"NaNi, please shut down."

The device was feeling warm against her skin and the gentle vibration it emitted felt stronger. "*Attempting to download cancer protocols from The Central Hospital of Vienna AKH.*"

"What's going on?" Saburo asked. "Did I mess something up?"

"No. It has a glitch and does this sometimes."

Tilly grabbed the device and felt along the side for the hard shutdown button. Her thumb rubbed against it and she held it down.

"*Failed. Unable to connect to*--" NaNi vibrated one last time and then ceased to move or speak.

She slipped the entire device, band included, off and stuffed it into the upper pocket of her flight suit. It brought up ghost appointments more often than she liked. They were always some unwanted reminders of her dad—some remnant of his treatments and appointments. They crept back in months or years after she erased them. She figured maybe the sensors were out, or the microphone wasn't working, so it couldn't hear her to stop trying to download the information. She wondered if its memory had somehow been corrupted.

"Well, thank you for letting me test it out," Saburo said. "It was pretty killer. I guess I didn't know what I was missing."

"Any time. Hell, if we can reset the owner identification, you can have the damn thing until you can find a better one."

Saburo nodded. "I would really like that."

"Here," Tilly said, offering the gadget back to Saburo. "Slip it into your pack, if you have room."

The woman took the NaNi as if it were an egg. She cradled it and slowly wrapped it in something inside her backpack before drawing the container shut again.

There was commotion on deck, sounding like more than a hallucination or someone's active imagination. The trio on the fast attack boat were shouting and pointing at the river ahead. Tilly suddenly found her view blocked by Harrison, his men, and Captain Nancy.

"What?" she asked, rising to look over their shoulders. "What the hell is it this time?"

The men fell silent, but following their gaze to the river ahead, Tilly saw what had them so transfixed. More of the same creatures they'd seen after their encounter with the Smog Hags lined both sides of the river. The bear-bats held rocks, tree limbs, and other makeshift weapons pulled from casted off trash. Ox-men were scattered among the winged beasts. They covered the shoreline by the dozens, some standing in the water up to their waists.

A half mile ahead, a vast structure rested half in and half out of the river. It was a dull green and white, partially covered by strands of dark brown ivy and the occasional orange of rust. It towered over nearly everything except for the massive trees nearby. Between the structure and the attack boats were lines of wooden docks stretching from one side of the river to the other. From the looks of the combination of creatures and long wooden pathways, there was no way to continue up the river, even if they wanted to.

The crew, the soldiers, the captain, all looked as tense as Tilly had seen them on the long journey. They pointed their rifles from target to target, mumbling to each other and kneeling for cover where they could.

In contrast, Harrison stood, smiling and holding his hands open expectantly. “It’s true. It’s all true.”

CHAPTER TWENTY-ONE

Upright creatures, like Mingmei, lined the docks and pathways across the water. They were hunched, as though they might leap the quarter mile to the approaching boats. In the center of these monstrosities stood a man who seemingly didn't belong in the primal picture of beast men and women. Tilly couldn't tell if he was overweight, or if he only seemed like it with the way the wind billowed his ragged white hazmat suit. The man didn't wave or offer any indication as to the intentions of the gathered creatures.

"Is this your missing scientist?" Tilly asked.

Harrison jerked as if he was waking from a dream. "What? Doctor Oscar? No. Certainly not. I have no idea who that man is."

"But that *is* your missing laboratory behind them, yes?" Morrow asked.

"It is."

The boats cut their engines and drifted toward the mass of wooden docks and awaiting lion people. Nancy nudged Harrison. "We can turn back right now. If we keep to the center of the river, they can't hurt us. Shit, they don't even have distance weapons. What're these fucks going to do to us?"

"If they're so harmless," Harrison said, "why do you want to turn around?"

Saburo addressed the captain. "Remember what those bear-bats did to our other boat? They don't really need weapons, now do they?"

"I don't know what's in there," the captain grumbled, pointing to the lab, "but things look kind of grim around here. Are you prepared to find your science team dead? Shit, you ask why I want to turn back? Look at these things. Maybe they ate your people and they're looking for their next meal. I'd rather not be an appetizer."

"You're not fascinated?" Harrison's wistful smile grew.

"Are you shitting me?" Captain Nancy asked. "Fascinated? I'm terrified."

"A good feeling. Stay with the feeling. You have good instincts," Mingmei said. She'd crept up behind them and knelt out of sight. "Doctor Oscar *has* eaten everyone. He has… chewed up the people and spit them out so they appear like me. He does not want for subjects, but he will change you all the same. You will be next. Running away would be the wisest course of action."

Tilly agreed with Captain Nancy and Mingmei. "Let's go. There is nothing we're going to learn here, and I'd like to leave with my life, at least. I have no stake in this lab."

"You do have a stake," Harrison said. "You were hired to—" The racket of machine guns cut him short. The crew of the escort boat unloaded with all the guns they had on a set of flying bears swooping overhead. After the recent confrontation with the bears, their reaction did not surprise Tilly, but the gunfire broke the silence and drew more of the beasts into action.

Ox-men threw rocks and sticks, impacting the boats with more force than Tilly would have thought possible. The projectiles mostly bounced off the hull, but a few thudded on the deck near the crew.

"Stop shooting," Tilly shouted at the other boat. "Stop."

Rei pulled her away from the railing. "Shut the hell up and get down before they turn on us." He tried to shove her back further and shield her, but Tilly wouldn't allow it. She gripped his arm and twisted at the wrist until he kneeled in pain. "Fuck," he shouted.

"Sorry, but this isn't a democracy," she said. "I'm in charge, not Harrison."

More bear-bats flew over *The Myrtle*, swooping in as they dove. A greying beast landed at the rear of the craft, shaking it and threatening to capsize the vessel. In one hand, the creature held a large rock the size of a car tire.

"No," the man on the docks shouted. "No. That's not necessary. Nobody needs to get hurt." He ran forward, waving his hands over his head. "Stop, please. Everyone? Hello?"

The bear-bat slammed the rock down, narrowly missing the

soldier at the helm, but destroying the controls. The pilot of the craft scrambled to his feet and pulled his pistol. He aimed it awkwardly as he tried to recover his footing. He fired two shots before the creature pivoted and smashed the huge rock into his torso, crushing his body and knocking him into the water. The creature then set its sights on the other crewmate.

"It's okay," the man in the plastic suit said as he moved more quickly toward *The Myrtle*, nearly shoving the creatures out of his way. "You can stop. All of you!"

The man's voice calmed many of the creatures, commanding their attention, distracting them, including the bear things hovering around the small boat. Similarly, Tilly's efforts kept more soldiers from joining the fray. But the bear-bat on the smaller escort boat looked beyond reach. It continued swinging the rock, chunks of it falling away. It further crushed the controls, knocked off a support for the Bimini that shaded the cockpit, and tore through the canvas. Only one crew member survived long enough to jump from the craft, diving headlong into the river to escape. The creature barely noticed. It continued smashing the boat until it sank around it. The creature took to the air and flew over the woods, shouting a savage victory howl as it disappeared.

"Stop! Hold your fire," Tilly shouted. "Wait for my signal."

"Look, I'm sorry about your man and the boat and everything. That's unfortunate, but you're in their domain now. Right?" the man said. "It's a shame, but look, he did things, you did things, so it all evens out, right? That's right. It's the law of the jungle or something. It's nature. It's nature at its darkest. But kill or be killed, I guess." He still waved his hands almost hypnotically to placate or distract the creatures swarming him. His plastic suit still swished as he quickly approached the end of the long docks. "Put it here. Come on, and guide that big old fucking thing right in here. No problems. Nothing to worry about." He reached out and helped guide the boat up against the dock. "So sorry for the confusion."

Captain Nancy glanced at Tilly, rather than Harrison, looking for instruction. It was the first time Tilly believed the captain was truly frightened on the voyage.

"Hey. This guy is a… a… lab assistant. I saw him in the files," Harrison shouted. "He's alive." Harrison's eyes welled with tears and he openly began weeping as he stumbled toward the bow of the boat. By the time he shoved Saburo and Ned aside, he was shaking. "It was true. The visions, the messenger, it was true. They're alive. All of them, and…" He couldn't continue talking, nearly choking as he cried.

In the wheelhouse, Tilly whispered to Nancy. "I don't know if we have much choice here but to dock."

"I think if we bolted, the rest of the crew would be behind us," Nancy said. "After what that thing did to our other boat, I think they're shitting their pants."

It was true, Tilly *knew*. But she also knew leaving would likely mean more carnage at this point. "If we try to run, they'll be all over us. We're better armed than the fast attack boat, but shit, look at all these things. I don't see how we'd make it a mile back downriver."

"Alright." Captain Nancy sighed and guided *The Myrtle* toward the man in the hazmat suit. "You're the boss."

"*Don't remind me*." Tilly laughed despite the situation. She wondered what had so incapacitated Harrison with joy and tears. What's more, she wondered if she wanted people calling her boss at this point. Someone had to lead the group if Harrison couldn't, but it didn't have to be *her*. In the field, she'd taken over recons and ops when communications went bad, but this was different. This was *all* different.

"Yep. Bring it here. Right here." The man reached out and grabbed the line from Decator at the bow and pulled it around a dock cleat. Ned and Rei stepped from the boat to help on the dock. As they landed, one of the ox-men stepped toward them and snorted. This one had wide horns curled around to thin points and a short, thick neck. It held no weapons of any kind, but stood about two feet taller than the men. Its body was as thick as a tree trunk.

"Stop. Hey. Back up. All of you. Get off the dock. Come on." The heavy man whistled and waved the creatures away. "Clear off the docks. These are guests. These are friends. We can't make them uncomfortable." He turned back to the boat with a smile. "See? No problems. They're good. They'll listen to me. No worries."

The pair tied off the line, then moved to the stern to do the same.

The man stood expectantly, waiting. "Come on up. I'm thrilled to see you all. We haven't had visitors for ages. Let me see you. Americans? Any of you Americans? I'm from Florida. Anyone else? Florida? Fucking Jacksonville. *Go Gators*! Anyone else? No football fans?"

The group reluctantly climbed out, this time with fewer members than the last time they had disembarked. They were down to *The Myrtle* carrying two of Harrison's men, Harrison, the captain and one of her soldiers, Morrow, Clive, Ned, Saburo and Tilly herself. The others had died along the way from bear-bats, ox-men, and everything else the Yellow River had thrown at them.

"Hell of a group. Look at you. Let's get up to camp, get you cleaned up, put some food in those stomachs." The man talked quickly and personally helped everyone off the boat. "I forgot to tell you, I'm Seely. Seely Green. This is awesome. *Great great*. I'll get your names when we get to the camp. You don't have to tell me now. I'll never remember if you tell me now. Keep them to yourselves."

"We're here to see Doctor Oscar," Harrison said, sniffling. "We're with the Hōfuna Corporation, and we need to see him."

The smile faded from Seely's face. "You're with the company? Really? We haven't seen anyone from the company in a long time. Hōfuna? Wow." He turned and walked up the long dock toward shore. "Wow." He continued without looking back.

The group stared after the man uneasily.

"He is one of them. That man was there." Behind the group, the tiger-woman, Mingmei, had emerged from the depths of *The Myrtle*. "He should be destroyed like the doctor."

Seely spun quickly at the low, scratchy voice. "Holy shit. You're from the company *and* you brought a cat with you. And she talks. I've never met one who still talks. Fucking outrageous. Where did you—"

"It sounds like she wants you and the doctor dead, so I'd suggest you move on," Tilly said. She put herself between the doctor and

Mingmei, in case the tiger-woman got ideas of attacking the man in the big, crinkly suit. If he was part of the experiment that altered Mingmei, Tilly had no problem with letting her have revenge, but not before they talked with the doctor and got a few more answers.

"Hey, yeah. No problem. Not a problem at all. Did you Americans just land here, or have you been on one of the U.N. patrols? Is it your first tour? Do you have cigarettes?" As Seely continued along the long dock, the creatures stepped aside, moving off the crisscross pattern of docks and walkways. "I don't smoke, but I kind of miss the smell of people smoking real cigarettes now and then. Been a long time. I have a lighter if someone has cigarettes." The man patted his hazmat suit, searching before giving up and staring at Morrow. "What do you have there? A big mechanical fist? It's really cool. Can I use it?" Morrow hugged his assortment of wires and scrap closer to his chest without replying.

As they passed the rows of creatures, Tilly took the chance to examine them close up. They were a strange amalgam of things, not unlike Mingmei, that didn't belong together. It was nearly impossible to tell where the beasts began and the people ended. The ox-men stood partially hunched with thick torsos and wide legs. Their heads and faces were nearly identical to the animals they imitated, only slimmer; a snout with wide nostrils and thin white whiskers. The eyes differed from the animal, though. The eyes were still round and thick, but there was something in them Tilly found reminiscent of their human counterparts. She couldn't determine if it was fear, or anger, or maybe sadness, but something about them held a glimmer of humanity.

Once they'd passed a large strip of leafy trees, an enormous temple carved into a cliff side revealed itself. A row of three primitive stone pillars, chipped, decaying, and covered in some sort of ivy and vines, framed the entrance. At one time, intricate carvings were likely chiseled into the supports, but now they were caked in dust and dirt. Steps up to the building appeared hand-cut from the dark natural stone of the outer shell of rock. The wide chamber beyond the pillars was lost in shadows.

"The fuck is that?" Ned asked.

"What?" Seely asked.

"The goddamn temple," Clive said. "What the fuck do you think he's talking about?"

Seely nodded. "That's what I thought. Well, as far as we could find out, it was the temple of something, or someone called a Hundun. Some people we encountered early on said the floods had washed it free. It was buried in mud and sand years ago, centuries ago. Maybe longer. But the floods chipped away at it and this is how we found it."

"What's inside?" Tilly remembered the word Hundun from Mingmei. "Hey, didn't you mention something about this temple to me?" She received only a long, low growl in response.

Surrounding them, the creatures followed *The Myrtle's* crew with their eyes. Planted firmly in place, they turned only slightly to follow the group's progress. None of them made a move to walk with.

Seely led the group along a path through the parting sea of beasts and stopped at an intersection with another trail that led toward the entrance to the WHEEL. A row of ox-men and a single creature with a horse's face blocked that path. Seely continued up the path to the top of the shallow hill. There, a long, shoddy building waited. It reminded Tilly of all the other disused barracks and storerooms they'd stayed in at camps along the way. Rickety, rusting.

"Seely?" Harrison shouted to the man. "We were hoping to talk to the doctor today. I mean, we've come all this way."

"Oh, I don't think that's possible today." For a moment, he looked as though he was considering it, but eventually came back with the same answer. "No. Not today. Impossible. He's pretty busy today."

"This is important. We've come to see him on behalf of the company. They're concerned for his safety and the safety of his people."

"I'm fine. *For one.* I'm fine. But he can't really… Look. Let me get you settled in, and then we'll talk about the doctor, good? Yeah?" Seely continued up the hill.

"So, Doctor Oscar is still here?" Harrison asked. His face had grown pale. Sweat blanketed his forehead. "He hasn't moved on or anything?"

"Still here? Mister, where else would he be? He has work to do. He has a symphony to finish. His opus is still in progress. He wouldn't leave before his work was done. He's saving the world, right? His work is saving the world, okay? You don't get to press pause."

Harrison dropped his bags and ran up the hill to Seely. "Once we get our things into the building, we can see him? Is that what you're saying?"

"You really want to see him?" Seely smiled and nodded. "Right. Of course, you want to see him. *Of course, you do*. People come from everywhere to see him. All over China. *Everyone* wants to see him. And he would like to see you. He would." Seely led them up a staircase that twisted away from the enormous lab. "But you don't drop out of the clear blue whatever unannounced and expect to... to... meet with a man like the doctor. He's got a process and he can't be interrupted. He works for three days straight. No more, no less. Nobody gets in. After three days, he eats and sleeps and sometimes he sees visitors." His smile faded. He pulled a thin stick from inside his plastic suit and began chewing on it. "Sometimes."

"And where is he in this process?" Harrison asked, growing impatient.

"He's working, and began only this morning."

"So, we can't see him for two more days?" Ned asked.

"Maybe more. He sleeps a lot after so much work," Seely said. "Look, tomorrow morning you can talk to one of the scientists on his team. They'd love to talk to you at length when they're not busy. Yeah. That's the right thing in this situation. Shit, yeah." His smile returned, and he shoved the stick in his mouth like a cigar before waving for them to follow him into the dense overgrowth, marked by simple, worn wood stairs.

Plants and tree limbs covered the trail. As they continued, Tilly could see it was slightly deeper than the surrounding area, worn down by past travel, she guessed. But beyond the trail, the forest was as dark as the nights had been under the smog-choked skies. They climbed the steep hill, sometimes needing to pull on branches and vines to get themselves up. Mingmei went off the trail, bounding nimbly through the brush and disappearing, only to emerge from behind a tree a few yards later.

Harrison was the only one who truly seemed to struggle with the terrain. He constantly bumped into trees and got thrown off balance. Growing annoyed, he charged ahead like a bull, plowing into the thick weeds, only to trip on a rock obscured by thick fronds. He appeared weak and disoriented at times, and his men had to prop him up lest he fall and tumble back down the hill.

When they reached the top, they discovered there was little more than the one building. A dripping water pump waited a few yards from the structure. A half a dozen small huts sat smashed and burned nearby, the remains little more than wood and leaves. The whole compound formed a vague 'U' shape.

"What happened here?" Tilly asked.

"Don't worry about it. You'll be in the main house," Seely said. "We'll keep an eye on the place and your stuff. No one will touch your boat down there, and everyone knows better than to lay their hands on you." The assurance didn't make Tilly feel any safer.

He opened the door to the larger building and ushered the group in. "There are three rooms you can use to sleep tonight. Nothing fancy, I'm afraid. Some bunks and bedrolls, but they're all clean, I assure you. I've slept here myself when things got a little weird." They stood in a large room with a few chairs and an old beat-up sofa to one side, a stove, sink, and beige fridge on the other. Under the front window, a large, wide television gathered dust. "Oh, hey. Feel free to make use of the TV. It's got a DVD player on the top—still works—and a stack of discs in the box on the side. Lots of good stuff, old shows, comedies, cop shows. Love those. I found the discs washed up on the beach one day. Good stuff, I swear. Mostly in Chinese, but some have subtitles if you're homesick for a little English." He moved through the building, chomping on his stick, pointing as he went. "Down the other hallway are the commode and showers. Sorry, not much privacy, but we haven't had the inclination to get too, uh, you know, precious out here in the… the…

glorious… what did the government call it during the war? The Other Zone? Place wasn't even important enough to give a number or a code. Only `Other'." He smiled and walked back to the door. "Zone one was held by the Chinese government. Zone two was disputed territory. Zone three was an active combat area throughout most of the war, and four and five changed hands every other week. Zone six, seven, and eight all had significance because the Americans said so. But here? It was worthless. No one cared. *Other*. Well, people care now, don't they? *You* all care, right?"

Morrow moved toward the kitchen area, and dumped his broken exoskeleton parts onto a table. "Hey. Mister?" He pointed to a small, flat, rectangular box on the wall by the old refrigerator. "Is this place run on that storage battery? Is it some sort of high-capacity thing?"

"Sure. It stores wind-generated power from turbines on the roof. Powers the whole place. We've even used it to keep the WHEEL going in a pinch. Why?"

Running his fingers over the edges of the box, Morrow said, "No reason, mate. No reason."

"Look, when can we talk to those scientists you mentioned?" Saburo asked.

"When I bring them to you. And not before," Seely said. "This area is pretty dense, and all manner of things would love to skin and eat you, so I suggest you stay here in the main house and don't open the doors."

Tilly nodded, sure she'd never heard sounder advice in her life. "Didn't you just tell us you'd watch after us?" she asked.

"Long as you stay inside. Have a good night. You'll find some potable water from the sink and some food in the cabinet. Not much, but something. Anyway, goodnight." Seely left, trodding carefully down the hill toward the WHEEL.

"You get the feeling he's a little off?" Ned asked. "He's a little *weird* or something?" He laughed nervously until one or two others joined in with chuckles of their own.

"Wouldn't stop talking," Rei said.

"You noticed?" Ned asked. "Hard to miss. Anyone else get a word in?"

"I'm going to check out these rooms." Tilly hoisted her pack onto her shoulder and stepped into the hall. "Make sure we're not getting locked in again."

"I'll join you," Saburo added. Mingmei fell in behind and followed.

"Hey," Decator said. "I thought about that. About getting locked in again. But I noticed the front door doesn't have a latch on the outside, only on the inside. And there's a brace here to bar the door from the *in*side."

Tilly checked the rest of the room and found similar conditions. "There're windows in here," she said. "And they're plenty big enough to climb out if we had to."

With Captain Nancy deciding to stay with the boat, the only women in the group, Tilly, Mingmei, and Saburo took the room together, leaving the men to divide up the other two rooms amongst themselves. There were three bunk beds in the women's room. As soon as Tilly began to make the bottom of one, Mingmei lithely climbed onto it. A sigh must have escaped Tilly's mouth, because Mingmei immediately shrunk back.

"It is okay I sleep here, yes?" the tiger-woman asked. "I don't want to be way over there." She pointed to the bunks on the other side of the room, a mere eight to ten feet away.

"It's fine," Tilly said. "I get it. Saburo? You good with sleeping *way over there*?"

"Fine." Saburo smiled at her new roommates and tossed her stuff on a bunk along the other wall.

Mingmei let out a cry of delight and spun in a circle. "I'll be quiet. I promise I will." She curled up and grinned.

"I'm not sure this place is nearly as clean as our host let on." Saburo sniffed a blanket and cringed. "Not nearly so."

The women lay on their bunks, letting the ceiling fan cool them as the night turned muggy. It could have been midnight, or it could have been morning. It was hard for Tilly to guess without having NaNi to look at.

"Why did you follow us?" Saburo asked Mingmei. "If you're afraid of this place."

"I didn't." The thin tiger-woman had all but curled up in a ball on the top of the bunk. "I was running away from this place. And hoped you would take me far away from here. I did not know you would be so mentally deficient as to come back to find the doctor. And I didn't realize what direction you were going until it was too late."

"Harrison seemed keen for you to come along," Saburo said.

"Right. He seemed surprised to see her at first, but was instrumental in getting her here." For Tilly, it was hard to tell if Harrison had been genuinely surprised at what Mingmei had become, or if he knew the group would find something unusual. His babbling suggested he had an inkling, but surely, he would have been better prepared for beasts like this, or worse, if he knew what he was walking into. He would've brought more soldiers, or better weapons.

"Once the doctor unlocked the secrets of the Four Perils," Mingmei siad, "he was well on his way to wiping out every enclave of people for miles around. The villages and towns fell, and they helped attack the cities still standing."

Intrigued by the allusion, Tilly joined the conversation. "We heard something similar from Seely when we first arrived here. He said something about the research or something already being here," she said. "Is that what he meant? There were some other tribesmen experimenting with genetics and DNA?"

Mingmei shied away. She pushed her body against the wall, appearing to shrink in the dim light.

"What is it?" Saburo asked. "Why are you so afraid? We're here. Nothing will happen to you."

Tilly nodded in agreement, though a stone was forming in her throat she couldn't quite swallow. She moved to the bunk with Saburo so she could more easily look at Mingmei and gauge her reactions.

"No," the tiger-woman whispered. "These small communities in the forests were not… I don't know… they were not… advanced? They worked the land in the same way their fathers and grandfathers had tended to it. Genetics? I'm sure most hadn't even heard that word until the doctor arrived."

"Then what did he find out there?" Tilly asked. A shadow broke the light from the crevice of the closed door. The hall light was partially blocked. Someone was standing out in the hall, listening.

"He and his people found the home of The Great God Long River in the temple when they were looking for creatures to save," Mingmei said. "They were looking for weird things to take back to their home. Some of the lab's team wanted trinkets or something of value to make up for the fact their mission was failing. They found something, all right. And it changed everything for them."

"How? What was it?"

Mingmei shuddered hard enough Tilly could see her body moving even in the darkness. "I don't know what started it. But soon, my family, my friends were all hearing voices in our heads. We had strange visions for weeks. They twisted our memories and brought our fears to the surface. We heard the name Kalidas the Hundun in our minds and in our dreams. He told us to come to him. To come to the simple temple in the rocks. We were powerless to resist. We did as he told us. It was at his altar we were remade as the things you see. He forced us into a pit and we emerged as these monsters."

"Do you know where this place is?" Saburo asked. "Is it close to the entrance? Can we go investigate?"

"I don't think it's a good idea," Tilly said. "I mean, shit, I'm not getting paid enough to wander out in the middle of the night with a bunch of jackass soldiers."

"*Fuck* 'em. Leave them." Saburo smiled. "They'd only slow us down."

Punctuating Saburo's point, a thud shook the building. Morrow and Clive cackled out in the common room. The lights in the hall flickered and buzzed before settling.

Mingmei looked less thrilled than Tilly felt. "No. The temple is not a place we should be. Certainly not the three of us. They'll stop us. That's what they'll do. They already want me to die for running away. You saw the surprise on the man's face when I spoke to him today. Most of the creatures Kalidas created lost their minds almost immediately, but some lost their faculties much more slowly."

"The man from the lab told us to stay inside at night," Tilly said. "I'm sure he had a reason." She returned to her bunk and pulled a blanket around her. "In the morning, we can talk to Ned and Harrison's men about this. If we still want to go, we all can."

It should have been the end of it. Whether on purpose or through innocent suggestion, Saburo stirred the pot. "How do you know they won't come for you here?" Her voice was hushed. "Hell, we're in a room with one door and a window. Where the hell will you go? Where will any of us go if you're right about the doctor being responsible for this Kalidas the Hundan? No. We can't stay here. We need to look into this place you're talking about."

Tilly waited for the tiger-woman's response. It looked as if Mingmei was terrified to return to the temple, but her fear could be heightened by the possibility of being caged up or killed. From out in the main area, the men chuckled, still enjoying the fact they had made it to their destination. She guessed they didn't care about how or why the doctor made Mingmei the way she was.

"I don't believe anyone will come here," Mingmei said. "It is forbidden."

"Unless someone says it's okay. Right?" Saburo said. "What if the doctor or researchers told the other beasts to come and get you?" Her tone changed, sounding slightly more confident, trying to find what fear she could play on to goad Mingmei into walking into the woods.

"No." The tiger-woman curled up, faced the wall, and fell silent.

The other two women stared at each other until Tilly shook her head. There was no way they were going to push hard enough to get Mingmei out into the dark night to investigate the temple.

"Mingmei, do you want a blanket?" Tilly noticed the tiger-woman hadn't taken a sheet or covering of any sort. She was lying on a bare mattress. By the time the silence got Tilly to stand up and check, their companion had already fallen asleep, snoring lightly. Or was she purring? Tilly couldn't tell, so she took a sheet and covered Mingmei with it.

After a quick visit to a bathroom facility smelling equally of pine cleaner and beer vomit, Tilly settled into the bed above Mingmei, fully realizing she could easily move to any other bed and the sleeping feline-human hybrid wouldn't realize it until morning. Saburo was still awake, tossing and rolling, trying to get comfortable.

CHAPTER TWENTY-TWO

Six Years Earlier

Tilly stood in the kite shop's lobby, sweeping. Her father and Hirata were working on a project in the back room, squabbling in Japanese over some detail or another. As she listened in, the mail carrier knocked at the door, startling her. Earlier than usual, he'd found the door still locked.

The mail carrier greeted her with a smile when she opened the door. "Hello, Tilly." He handed her a stack of letters. "All the way from the United States. Must be pretty important."

"Eh. Not everything from there is so special." She winked and said thanks.

There was an envelope from the States in the pile, straight from the office of military operations. She opened it and found a letter regarding her benefits options, her discharge stipulations, and a general good luck from the U.S. military.

"Could've emailed this shit," Tilly said. She turned to the trash can and tossed the junk mail.

"Anything for me?" her father shouted from the other room. "Did I get a package of supplies from the Irish gentleman with the bamboo?"

"No, pop. Bunch of crap." She folded her letter and shoved it in her back pocket before taking a seat behind the front desk.

"Getting actual pieces of mail should be special by now, don't you think?" Hirata said. "With life and business being electronic and virtual. Deliveries should be an art. They should be valuable. A man takes the time and effort to walk through your neighborhood and hand you something, it should be welcomed. Treasured."

"Yeah, Hirada," her father said. "There's a side business for the two of you. Special mail. Saving the great lost art of mail."

Her father coughed, burying a sudden peal of laughter. The spell went on for nearly a minute before he said, "Who would pay for that? It would have to be costly. The materials, the time, the training to figure out what someone would value enough to have handed to them by a stranger." He coughed once more. "Besides, we need to master our current craft first."

"You're right, pop."

"Have you been practicing today?" her father asked. "You have nothing else to do at the desk most of the day."

"I'll get to it." Tilly spent the next hour looking for any and every excuse to avoid picking up the materials and following her father's advice to improve her skills—sweeping, dusting, washing the enormous glass window in the storefront. Eventually, she ran out of excuses and checked in on the men in the back.

Her father sat slouched in his lounge chair next to the long table where he kept his materials. She could see how much he'd changed in the few weeks she'd been there. He'd shaved his head when his hair began to thin. It only served to show how thin he had become. Up til that point, he'd always kept his hair immaculate and well groomed. Seeing his bald head was strange for her-it was like seeing a stranger sitting there.

"You okay back here?" she asked. "It's nearly lunchtime. You two ought to take a break and eat something."

"We'll stop when the work is done," her father snapped.

"Henry." Hirada's voice was low and soft. "She wants to get you something to eat. You need to eat. She's looking out for you."

"If she'd learn the simplest of tasks, she could help us and we'd have time for lunch," her father said. "That would be looking out for me."

"*Henry*."

"It's okay," Tilly said. "He's right. I should help more." Tilly surveyed the work the men had completed and nodded. "Let me wash my hands and I'll do what I can." As she stepped into the restroom, she could hear Hirada and her dad talking quietly, but pointedly. Hirada even raised his voice a couple of times.

She returned to a silent room, the two men facing opposite directions and fiddling with the work before them. Tilly took a seat, picked up a project sheet, and reviewed the details of an order. The form requested kites of various types—octopus, birds, dragon, whale—each piece ordered in all black. Black paper, black tails, black string. Tilly opened the box to ensure each item was included and made to order. When she pulled aside the packing paper, she found a large pile of darkness inside. Not a neat stack, but a rounded mound of shiny ebony. When she poked it, the mound felt wet, smooth, and gave way under her touch. It bounced back when her fingers retreated.

"Pop?" she whispered over her shoulder. She meant to shout for him or scream, but decided it wasn't something to worry her ill father over. In fact, the way it gleamed in the harsh lighting was soothing in a way, satisfying to watch. She reached back in and once again placed her hands on the mound, planning to pull it out and get a better look. Instead, her fingers sunk into the object. She found herself unable to grip anything of substance, anything firm.

Worse, when she went to pull her hands back, the substance covered them. Her hands remained attached to the blob in the box. She yanked them back, trying to snap the connection, but the action only pulled the box off the table and knocked her to the floor.

She lay there, fumbling with the slimy material on her hands, when she noticed the box. It had come to rest upside down a few feet away. Long thick strands stretched black lines from the cardboard box to her hands. Her chest heaved in panic. If she didn't break free, something terrible was certain to happen. Tilly took deep breaths to clear her head and look for solutions.

"Wren?" her father called from the other room. "What's going on in there? What's all the noise?"

The box shook and rocked back and forth, scratching against the concrete floor. Two fine, writhing tendrils of the same shiny blackness slowly felt their way out from under the cardboard. They pushed themselves along the floor toward Tilly. Soon they dragged the box with them as they extended themselves and reached for her.

"Dad?" She couldn't yell it. Not this time. She couldn't bear to see him come in and see what enveloped her legs, her body. But as the viscous liquid encased her, she couldn't keep from screaming. Her cry was silenced by the darkness draining into her mouth and down her throat. She felt it spread across her smooth head. And as it covered her ears, she heard a last sound. It was like a whistle, a high melodic whistle, right before the world disappeared.

CHAPTER TWENTY-THREE

"Tilly?"

She rolled over slowly, her muscles rebelling at the unwanted movement. "What? Who's there? What time is it?" The false memory faded.

"Tilly, it is us," Mingmei whispered, her words a growl.

"What?"

Saburo hovered close, too. "Are you okay? You sounded like you were having a bad dream."

"No, it… well… It started out as a good memory, but it got twisted. It changed." Tilly wiped the sweat from her neck as she sat up. "It was a memory of my father, but there was this blackness, this strange beast intruding into my thoughts that shouldn't have been there, wasn't there originally."

"This is Kalidas the Hundun calling to you, as he called to my people and I," Mingmei said. "This is his will rewriting your history. Breaking you down to become one of his servants, like me."

"You don't appear to be under anyone's control," Saburo said. "You speak freely and openly."

"It will wear off, and I will be like the others you've met. Mindless, horrible beasts living only to do his bidding."

The thought set Tilly in motion. She picked up her rifle and checked it, then her pistol. "You're telling me my bad dreams are a sign I'm in line to be one of the doctor's next subjects?"

"Yes."

"Bullshit. Not chance. Let's go scout this temple. We'll see what we can see. Maybe even put a stop to it." She stood and pried the window open, then climbed atop nearby bunk.

"It is not so easy," Mingmei said. "There are many of his creatures in the forest. And there is nothing we can do there."

Saburo snatched up her own stuff and snapped on her belt and holster. "We need your help here. You don't want anyone else to…" she stopped short. Tilly knew what the end of the sentence was going to be. She also knew Saburo couldn't take back the beginning.

Mingmei scampered across the top bunks and sat down behind Tilly solemnly. "No. No one should become what I have. I will show you the temple, but we have no business there. There is nothing we can accomplish there to help."

"There's nothing we can accomplish in *here* that's going to do shit either," Tilly said. She stuck her head out the window and looked around. Seeing nothing, she pulled herself through and set herself lightly on the ground. Saburo handed out the weapons, then also dropped out of the building. Behind them, Mingmei poked her head out and nervously scanned the area.

"Come on," Saburo said. "You're the only one who can show us the way. We need you."

Mingmei sighed. "Do not patronize me. They turned me into a cat, not an idiot." She jumped out, landing with barely a sound. The tiger-woman ran a few yards ahead, disappearing behind a tree. "We should turn back," Mingmei said, when Tilly and Saburo had caught up. "I don't like being out here."

"We just left the building, for god's sake," Saburo said. "You're fine. There's nothing in these woods we can't handle." She scanned the area behind them with her rifle, while Tilly did the same with the path ahead. Between them, Mingmei fretted with each step.

The forest was dark enough in the daytime. The lack of direct sunlight combined with the cover of branches and leaves made sure each step was a chore. But nighttime was something different. Everything seemed coated in ink, saturated by a blackness that clung to each twig and weed. The two soldiers used lights affixed on the end of their rifles, set for low brightness. The glow allowed them to see their trail, but made their detection easier for anyone, or anything, that might roam the trees looking for a meal or a prisoner. Once she stopped fretting over every little sound, Mingmei scouted ahead, partially out of fear the lights would get her captured, partially because it was in her nature to explore.

After twenty minutes of hiking through the dense forest, the tiger-woman slunk back and whispered, "There are two ox-men coming this way. You must stand behind those trees over there."

"Why those?" Saburo asked.

"You'll be downwind, and they will not smell you so easily as I do."

The trio did as told and flattened themselves in the roots of an enormous tree where they wouldn't be seen from the trail. In less than a minute, two ox-men approached, tromping through the trees, crashing over leaves and branches. They didn't speak to each other, but snorted and sniffed as they went. Tilly imagined they were good in a fight because they were horrible at stealth. One of the ox-men stopped and looked around, eventually gazing in the trio's direction. The other continued on, oblivious to its companion's actions. After a moment, the straggler discovered he was being left behind and hurried to catch up.

Tilly grew concerned, not for the possibility of an attack, but for the very real possibility of getting lost. "You're sure this is the way?" she asked. "This trail branches off and gets buried in leaves and crap."

"I should have told nobody about this place," Mingmei said. "We should never have left the other place of safety."

"I need to know if we're going the right way."

"Yes," Mingmei said. "Forgive me for being weak and letting you talk me into doing this."

Saburo pulled out her pistol and held it out. "Do you need a weapon? If this place is as bad as you say, maybe you should take my gun. Or at least a knife."

"Really?" In the glow of Saburo's flashlight, Mingmei held up her bloated hands. "I can't even put food in my mouth. You think I can pull a trigger, or hold a knife?" She still had five fingers, but they had each expanded to nearly twice the normal size. They were thick, unarticulated, and more like the large cat they created her from. "If a villain gets too close, I'll shed on them or something."

Saburo shrugged and fell back into her position at the back of the line. "We'll watch out for you."

Ahead, a faint crackle caught Tilly's attention. It sounded like someone moving toward them quickly through the brush. "What was that?" she asked. Saburo remained silent, but shook her head.

"Fire." Mingmei retreated a step.

"I don't..." Saburo began.

"She's right," Tilly said, noticing something barely breaking over the hill ahead. "Look up there. In the distance a bit." A faint, orange glow brightened the night through the trees.

Mingmei slunk back down the trail a few steps. "No. We need to go back before they find us. We need to get the others. The light illuminates the entrance to the temple's pit."

"I want to see what this place is. We'll go after I get a look." Tilly looked to Saburo for confirmation and received a tentative nod. "As soon as I see what's going on here, okay?"

"You do not need to see. I have told you what it is."

With a wave of her hand, Tilly moved ahead, keeping closer to the trees and off the main path. She had heard Mingmei's story so many times, she needed to see for herself. The brush was thin. She was confident she could keep hidden if need be. Saburo followed a few feet behind, crouched, weapon ready. Mingmei, however, had vanished from the line, escaping unseen into the forest of darkness from which they came.

The pair crested the hill, following the light. Ahead of them, the glow intensified. A large group of torches lit the way up a crude staircase into a small doorway built into the Temple's side.

"What is going on?" Saburo asked. "Mingmei made it sound like there was some sort of elaborate lab out here or something where they turned her into... whatever she is."

"She never said there was a lab. Only a place where she was changed. She mentioned the temple and a pit, though. And my guess is this is where it all went down." It was too dark to see what awaited beyond the doorway or how far in it went, but Tilly was determined to get a look. She moved closer to the parallel lines of torches stuck in the ground on posts. Saburo's hand held her back.

"Whoa, whoa, whoa. We were going to look really fast and run like fuck, right? Well, we've seen it. Let's go tell Harrison and the others."

It wasn't enough for Tilly. Something inside the temple's darkness beckoned to her. "There aren't any doors," she said. "None that I can see. There's a sizeable gap in the thatching near the front, though. This thing has to be it, this pit she's mentioned. Come on, Saburo. We need to go in there. *I* need to go in there. Stay here, if you want. You can cover me." She slung her rifle over her back and pulled out her pistol. "A quick look, that's all."

"Other than the front," Saburo said, "with all the creatures milling about, this is the only entrance I see. If you go in, your exits will be limited."

"I'll stay sharp." Tilly shrugged off Saburo's hand and broke cover. She crept out of her hiding place on her stomach and crawled toward the crumbling temple. She was careful to keep in between two torches, in hopes it would keep her from being fully illuminated and visible.

She paused as she neared the gap in front and looked inside the structure. It was not a temple as she would have typically envisioned one. Instead, it was merely a single room, one of many, she assumed. How it fit into the rest of the structure, she did not know, but it seemed to be one vast chamber with a deep pit carved in the center. A ramp went down one side and back up the other. On either side of the pit stood more torches and little else. Tilly scanned the darkness for a guard, some defenses around or inside the pit, but she was alone. Only the sound of her boots scraping the crude dirt and rock floor broke the quiet. The floor wasn't made of concrete or wood, but appeared to have been dug into the ground and left as mud and rock.

She made her way further and looked down into the pit. Rather than a hole in the ground, the pit was more of a strip of earth dug straight down; a trench with walls on the north and south sides. She guessed it was fifty feet or more from the top of the wall to the bottom floor. She walked cautiously a few steps down the ramp, stopping only when another sound joined in. It was so light and soft, she took it for the trees swaying and leaves brushing together outside. Then the sound formed words. She couldn't discern what the words were, what language they were in, or where exactly they came from. When they faded, she continued until she was off the ramp and onto the flat floor of the gouge in the ground. On either side, the pit's walls had been dug back, creating cavernous rooms framed by thick wooden bars. Tilly strained to see what was beyond the wood, and was startled when a hand reached out.

An airy voice similar to Mingmei's also reached out from the darkness. "Get away from here, girl." While Tilly's Chinese was poor, she'd heard words like "*Táolí*" and "*Táopǎo*" in combat situations many times. They all amounted to the same thing - "Get away."

More voices echoed the sentiment. "Flee this place." *"Run."*

She took a few more steps toward the voice, then in English, asked the woman behind the barrier, "Who are you?"

"Go," the voice said, slipping easily into English. "They're starting."

Beyond the bars, Tilly could just make out the speaker's face. The woman appeared to be Chinese. The first Tilly had seen since arriving in China. Further back, rows of people huddled together. Not animals, not the mixtures of human and creature, but actual people.

"Who are you?" Tilly asked. "Why are you here?"

The woman's hand released the bar and pointed to the ground. "You know why we are here; he has called to you as well. We merely followed his voice, as you have." The old woman stepped backward. "Leave now. It is beginning." At their feet, the pit's dark dirt began to shake and crack, throwing Tilly off balance. Chunks of earth fell from the walls as the tremors intensified. From all sides, the moan of hidden people rose to a terrified chorus.

"What?" Tilly asked. "Is this a tremor? Some sort of earthquake?"

"Run," the woman said. Her voice was calm, ethereal, as if resigned to what was happening to her and the others.

"I can get you out." Tilly ran further into the hole in search of a door or gate to release the people. She heard a splashing sound with each step she took. The ground seeped some sort of liquid. She knelt for a closer look. The liquid looked much like motor oil - black and brown, shiny and thick. Tilly reached to touch it.

"No!" and "*Méiyǒu*!" came the shouts from a group behind the bars.

Tilly froze.

"Do not touch it," the first woman she'd spoken to earlier said. "Get out of this cursed chasm. It is too late for us. Go."

On all sides, the frightened voices rose in several languages; some Tilly understood, some she didn't. Those she understood were split between admonishing her to run and begging for her help. She wondered if the sounds were in her head, or actual shouts filling the trench. Tilly raised hands to quiet them, concerned their cries would alert whoever put them in the cages.

The puddles of darkness beneath her feet increased in size, bubbling as it rose from the ground. As Tilly stared into the cage nearest her, she was stunned by how many people reached through the bars trying to grab her.

The liquid nearly covered the entire pit floor. When Tilly lifted her foot, the substance clung to her boot, sticking her to the ground like paste. She did her best to run for the wooden bars and bash into them with her shoulder. They were only wood, some so thin she believed she could break them if she tried hard enough. When her initial charge failed to work, she stood back and kicked at the bars.

A snort from the other side of the trench made her stop. Tilly grabbed for her gun out of pure reflex. There was another set of crude bars on that side, and something was moving inside.

"What was that?"

The woman spoke. "The ones we are to be bound to. You must go. Kalidas is rising again."

At the bars on the other side of the pit, a large tiger appeared. It wandered forward with awkward steps, careful not to get too close to the people, and stopping as it drew within inches of the large wooden barriers. It sniffed the air and stared at Tilly with glassy black eyes.

A deep snarl drew Tilly's attention back up the ramp to the temple above. A shadow fell across the entrance. A muscular ox-beast stood at the top of the slope. Unfortunately, that was Tilly's closest route back out to Saburo. If she ran the other way, she'd struggle through half a football field's worth of black goo. She took a step with some difficulty, as the inky matter nearly reached her ankles. It was rising more quickly than she'd anticipated.

The ox-beast snarled, creeping down into the pit. It was one of the larger ones she'd seen. It easily stood twelve feet tall. Its set of massive horns spiraled up from its head another two feet into the air. The beast carried what looked like a tree trunk in one hand and a rock in the other. The sound of more creatures approached from the nearby forest behind it.

Tilly moved herself toward the thing, hoping to get herself free of the muck before meeting her opponent. Lifting her feet became a struggle. She had to yank herself free with each step, while the ox-beast descended with ease, unencumbered by the muck that held her back. Figuring there was no way she'd make it out in time, she reached back and unslung her rifle. Keeping her balance proved increasingly difficult, as she couldn't easily move her feet. The last thing she wanted was to fall face-first into the gunk below.

When they stood only yards apart, the sound of a single rifle shot startled Tilly. The ox-beast staggered. It struggled to keep its balance as a spot of blood suddenly appeared on its naked shoulder. The monster shook its head and angrily continued toward her. It seemed surprised when a second shot tore through the upper part of his chest. It heaved in a deep breath, struggling for air, and wobbled to the inclined wall for support. Tilly turned to find Saburo at the lip of the pit, kneeling next to one of the torches. Tilly raised her hand in thanks.

The ox-beast wheezed and dropped the enormous branch to the ground.

Behind Tilly, the black oil rose fast. It had nearly caught up with her again. She forced herself forward, still struggling as the thick liquid sucked at her boots. The sound of more shots drowned out the cries of the people in the pit below. This time, Saburo was not so selective as to fire single shots. She'd opened her rifle to fully automatic and strafed the far side of the pit. There, more of the ox-beasts charged from the main entrance. Tilly moved as fast as she could, only to be stopped by the injured ox-man. It grabbed her arm and weakly held on.

With little time to battle the injured creature, Tilly pulled her knife free of the sheath at her side. As the beast continued to hold on, she sliced its leg. She then cut the hand that held her fast. The ox-beast bellowed and released her, allowing her to flee up the incline. The injured thing teetered, trying to keep its balance, but the fresh leg wound betrayed it, giving way. A second later, it fell face down into the growing dark pool. It yanked its arm free and flailed to get out. Stuck face first, it could neither claw itself up for air nor pull itself out.

Tilly climbed the slope, at one point falling on all fours. As she pushed herself forward, she came face to face with a line of three ox-beasts. These seemed to come from the same small entrance as she had. She held onto her knife and waved it in front of her threateningly. The ox-beasts continued, undaunted. One swung its arms, attempting to corral her. The others bore thick logs and advanced behind the first.

Tilly charged the creature without a weapon, hoping to get past it quickly. She dodged a clumsy strike from her opponent and stabbed it in the abdomen. As she turned her attention to the other two, a sudden movement caught both her and the ox-men off guard. Mingmei leapt onto the back of one creature, raking her claws across its neck, then used it as a springboard to launch herself at the other.

In the momentary confusion, Tilly brought her knife up into the chin of her opponent. Standing nearly two feet taller than her, the chin was the only part of its head she could hit. It convulsed, dropped the rusty bar, and sank to its knees before dropping with a wet thud on the ground. By the time Tilly had pried the knife out, Mingmei had killed the other two assailants.

"Now, we should leave," Mingmei said. "If you did not believe me before, surely you understand now."

Behind them, the shouts and cries of the trapped people grew more desperate.

"We can't leave them," Tilly insisted. "They need our help, or they'll die."

"They will not die. Not most anyway." Before Mingmei could offer further explanation, Saburo fired again, downing a stray ox-man that had charged in from the trees. More gathered at the nearby tree line.

Tilly saw the wisdom of wanting to get far away, but she still couldn't bring herself to leave the others. She'd taken only one step before the screams stopped. The black substance had risen high enough to cover the ceilings of the barred rooms, and therefore, the people's heads.

Mingmei was in front of Tilly before she could take another step. "Some will die, yes," the tiger-woman said. "But others will share the same fate as me, or worse—they could end up like these monsters." She indicated the dead ox-beasts. "Nearly mindless, doing only as they're told. I'm not sure which I would choose."

"But," Tilly glanced again at the pit.

"I've been in there, I know. Let us go now, so we may live for the next fight." The muscular tigress pulled hard on Tilly's arm and dragged her into the brush. "Many more beasts of all types will be here soon. They will pull the peasants from the muck once it recedes."

Tilly didn't resist. She allowed herself to be dragged for a few paces. Then, after a quick glance back, she moved on her own, eager to get away from that hole in the earth. Once she had some distance from it, she felt as if she were waking from a dream, or some sort of trance brought on by the blackness. She noticed an absence of the smell of it. Her senses had taken it in and adapted to it so quickly, it didn't hit her until it was gone. The scent was that of the creek behind her house when she was young; stagnant water and dead frogs. And now it was missing, for better or worse.

"I think a tactical retreat is in order," Saburo said as the other two regrouped around her. "An immediate one. All the way back to our quarters."

"I agree." Tilly tried not to think about the people they left behind and asked Mingmei to lead them back to the camp. The tiger-woman didn't wait to confirm she would help. Instead, she ran ahead on the trail, bounding back and forth with feline grace and speed.

"I hope we can keep up," Tilly said. She motioned for Saburo to follow their swift companion, then waited a couple of beats before bringing up the rear of their little patrol. She remained cautious of any sudden motions or shadows behind them. She tuned her ears for the sounds of growls, snaps, and crunches—anything that might indicate they were being followed.

The trio moved so quickly, Tilly occasionally lost the others at turns on the trail. Thick trees and the darkness of night caused her to panic more than once when the women had rounded a tree, making them impossible to spot in the forest ahead. She also tired quickly. Even in the military, long runs weren't her forte. She'd spent most of her time in the helicopter, watching the fun and excitement from above. All she'd ever wanted to do was fly, and that made her careless about keeping herself in shape. She could tell from all the free weeks at home that she was going soft.

When Saburo stopped after ten minutes, Tilly joined her at the base of a tree. "You okay?" Tilly asked. A nod was the only reply she got. Saburo's heavy breathing made it clear she hadn't kept up with a calisthenic regimen, either.

"It can't be much further, can it?" she asked. "We didn't hike that far in, right?"

Tilly wasn't sure, but she feared it was. Assuming their feline companion knew where she was going, it could still be ten or fifteen minutes. She took comfort in noticing she no longer saw the light of the torches from the pit. Unfortunately, she couldn't see the lights of the camp, either.

"Where did Mingmei go?" Tilly asked. "Did you see her?"

"Shit. She was in sight a few minutes ago," Saburo said. "But she skipped on and off the trail so much, I doubt I could even find her tracks now."

"Let's keep moving," Tilly said. "We know the trail leads back to the camp. Let's follow it and keep an eye out for those *things*." She knew it wasn't the most reliable way to go, but it was all they had. She also hadn't paid attention enough to notice if the trail forked at some point when they made their way in.

A familiar brogue cut through the darkness. "What things? What are we talking about now, my wee lasses?" They expected Morrow to emerge from the shadows, but were startled when Clive stepped from behind a tree instead. His arrival triggered Tilly's defenses.

"What are you doing out here?" Tilly asked.

"Me?" the Scot said. "It's late. *You* lot shouldn't be out alone in these big, nasty woods."

Saburo backed away from the group. Tilly suspected they trained her to keep some distance between her and her squad mates, so as not to bunch up and make it easier for an enemy to hurt more soldiers at once. "Maybe you didn't notice, but we aren't alone."

"Yeah, and where's your little kitten? She wasn't in the room, either." Clive squinted into the dark and silent woods. "Here kitty, kitty."

Saburo scowled. "You were looking for us? Why? Late night team meeting? Looking for someone to braid your hair and gossip with?"

The smile Clive shot back made Tilly shiver. A pale and failing flashlight pinned to his vest illuminated his teeth. They were shiny and yellow, appearing larger than they should in his long, narrow face. "Wouldn't mind a go at a pillow fight if you ladies are up for it."

Though Tilly could think of a few choice words to shoot his way, the pair instead walked past Clive and continued down the path without responding. It wasn't worth getting into an altercation with the Scot—verbal or otherwise. Between the possibility he had some of the other men nearby, and the very real thought that the ox-men could still approach, she didn't want to risk being caught out there.

"Where are you going? I asked ye both a question."

The women continued, maintaining their spacing, while Tilly slipped her hand to the pistol at her waist.

"Out here, I might as well be yer goddamned superior officer," Clive said. "And I say you two shits need to stop right there." His voice grew louder with each syllable, becoming more distinct and deeper as he spoke. He ran around them and once again stopped in their path. "Understand?"

"Look, we're all in this together out here," Tilly said. "We need to cut the crap and work as a team." They had little time to argue out in the open, and Clive's rising voice only served as a beacon for anyone or anything looking for them. "So, I'm going to let you in on a little intel. There are God-knows-how-many of those ox-things headed our way right now. We took a quick tour of their temple and guess what? It's basically a factory for cranking out more of those beasts."

"Do tell."

"Yeah," Saburo said, "and we think it's a good idea to get indoors. Now." Saburo drove her shoulder into Clive as she pressed on.

"You with us?" Tilly moved past the man, avoiding contact, but visually sizing him up. He smelled like the tail end of a bender, appeared to be armed with nothing more than a bottle of rum, and was dressed in only his underwear and t-shirt. She suddenly felt confident he posed little threat.

"Fuck the both of you," he shouted as they ran off for the now-visible lights of their building. "You… You better keep running."

Mingmei crept out of the shadows and helped Saburo climb into their window. "You two are brave or stupid, I think, to talk that way. He gives me a chill up my spine."

"You?" Tilly asked. "You know you could probably kill him in a heartbeat, right?"

"Oh, I could not."

Once Tilly had climbed inside, she and Saburo both helped the tiger-woman get through the window, even though she needed no one's assistance.

Saburo looked back out the open window. "Clive?" She kept her voice low. "Clive, get in here." When her voice faltered a little, Tilly guessed it had more to do with fear of death than concern for Clive. "Should we look for him? Should we wake up the others and go find him?"

"We risked our shit to get ourselves back here," Tilly said. "We warned him." It was the right thing to say, to keep the others from risking their lives. She still felt a pang of guilt. The Scot had seemed drunk and unlikely able to defend himself. "For all we know, he already went around to his own window. Or the front door. He could be sound asleep on the floor out in the main room."

"I don't know." Saburo leaned through the window and gazed into the night before shutting it.

CHAPTER TWENTY-FOUR

In the morning, Tilly could hear the men arguing with Seely in the common room.

"See here," Morrow said. "I'm missing one of my people. We need to get into that lab to see if he's in there. The Brit can inspect the WHEEL for himself at another time. I also understand the good doctor is still occupied. I only want to find my man, you understand?"

"There's no way he got in there." Seely sounded exhausted.

"You don't know that," Morrow said. "The man is a hustler and a bit of a magician. He can worm his way into anything."

"Not this place. The doctor will open the doors when he is ready."

Tilly grabbed her pants and slipped them on, followed by a shirt that she buttoned over her t-shirt. She slid her boots on last, doing her best not to wake the others in the room.

The argument stopped with Harrison's nearly slurred words. "Don't be ridiculous. This is an enormously expensive piece of property belonging to the Hōfuna Corporation. Not to the doctor, not to you. To the *Hōfuna Corporation*. I have the express permission of the company to take possession of it. Now, we've played this your way and now a man is missing."

It was obvious Harrison was impaired, though Tilly wasn't sure it was alcohol. Red faced and with a slight shake to his hands, she wondered if it was some sort of drug, or if his quick confession back at the Scot's camp had something to do with it. Was something calling out to him? Controlling him?

Harrison shoved Seely out of the way and walked out the door. Morrow allowed Rei, Decator, and Ned to leave as well, but stood between Seely and the door. Morrow now wore an old backpack with wires protruding from it. The lines led to the mechanical fist he'd been dragging around since the Russian camp. The huge glove-like device looked cleaned up. Less chaos and fewer bits and pieces hung from it. Morrow cradled the glove to his chest. Red and blue lights flickered and blinked across the wrist of the device. Whether the thing was operational, Tilly couldn't discern, but it was apparent that Morrow saw some sort of value in it.

Once the men were gone, Seely followed. Tilly trailed behind by a half-dozen steps. The group headed directly for the ramp that led up to the front entrance to the WHEEL. The doors remained shut, same as when the group arrived. "Did I hear something about Clive going missing?" Tilly shouted after the group. She hoped she didn't sound as half -hearted as she thought.

"Clive, missing?" Saburo suddenly appeared at Tilly's side. "What happened?"

It was startling how quickly the woman had gone along with Tilly's lie. Had she known Saburo was there, Tilly might not have had the wherewithal to even say it. There were three people that knew they'd left him, and it was hard to keep that many people from spilling the truth. What's more, it was an awkward lie that benefited nobody.

The others moved ahead without acknowledging Saburo's question.

"Open this." Harrison pointed to the enormous metal door.

"I can't." Seely stopped a few yards short from the men.

"Can't?" Morrow asked. "*Can't?* I have a few ways to change can't to can in a hurry." He smiled, showing off a prominently chipped tooth. "It's my mate that's missing, and believe me, I'll not rest till I find him."

"Clive will turn up, right?" Saburo said. She briefly met Tilly's glance before each turned away.

"Sure," Ned said. "I can't believe he'd wonder off on his own like this."

Harrison ventured up the ramp to an extended control panel. "I gave you the chance. You could have worked with us as a gentleman, but you refused. If you won't open this, I will." He pulled a data pad from his pocket and scrolled through some information. His brow dripped sweat. "These are *our* laboratories, and we have override codes for all our property in the event someone tries to get cute and lock us out. Or there's a data wipe situation." He referred to the data pad and tapped some information into the control deck. "Precisely like this." Harrison poked a key and stepped back with a smug expression.

The group looked on, but nothing happened.

"What's going on?" Saburo asked. "Is this like a time lock? Do we have to wait for it?"

Harrison wiped his brow, then held up his hand. "Hold on. I must have fucked the combination." He leaned in and punched the keys again, consulting the pad for the digits. "Probably transposed some numbers." This time, when he was finished, a screen above the panel crackled to life. The screen flickered and ran through a blue screen. Rebooting information scrolled up the monitor.

"Now we're getting somewhere," Harrison said.

The blue screen disappeared, replaced by an animated version of the Hōfuna logo. The monitor's speakers popped and a soothing tune that Tilly immediately recognized began. She knew the first image before it came up. She successfully predicted the words that came next.

Welcome to Hōfuna Asia Conservancy. We are happy to have you join us on our journey of preservation and love for all creatures throughout Asia.

It was the same presentation she had watched over and over before her interview. Word for word. The only addition was the company's logo at the beginning, and that was likely a part of the boot program.

The mission of Hōfuna is to save endangered and on-the-brink creatures of all genus and species. A large part of our efforts...

The door didn't open.

"Look. Doctor Oscar changed everything," Seely said. "He got really paranoid there for a while. He thought people were going to come in and disturb his work, steal his shit, you know? A brilliant man like that, surely everyone would be after his research, right? He's not wrong, you know? The stuff he was doing, *is doing,* the stuff he *is doing* is life-altering, mind expanding. Anyone would want to steal that. That's why you people are here, right? Am I right?"

"First off," Harrison said, smacking the keypad, "this is our bloody research lab. He works for us."

...by collecting a sampling of those animals to house in zoos and private sanctuaries for the express purpose of breeding and repopulation.

Tilly observed the two men closely, considering the situation. The doctor wasn't the only one who lived and worked in the WHEEL. "Second," Tilly said. "You seem to come and go pretty easily. There's security and other employees in there, right?"

"Yeah, mate. You must know the password, or the code, or the magic handshake, right?" Morrow nudged Seely with his rifle butt. "Don't make us get all bitchy and bent out of shape about it."

When the video ended, the speaker buzzed and hummed before beginning again with the same music and images.

Reluctantly, Seely answered the question. "Look, the security guys are trained to lock the place down if something threatening happens. You know? Terrorists, murderers, militias, soldiers. The list goes on and on."

"So, they aren't going to open the doors for us?" Harrison asked.

"Look, I've been nothing but nice to you guys," Seely said. "I gave you a place to sleep, clean blankets. I kept the things out in the woods away. Nothing came for you in the night. You had fresh water and fruit, right? I thought we were all friends here, man. Obviously, judging from the guns poking me in the back, I was wrong. You're savages. Exactly like all the beasts in the forest."

"Tell them to open it." Morrow pushed Seely again, harder this time.

"Seriously? That's your reaction? You didn't hear what he said?" Tilly asked. "What the hell did you just say about the things in the night? You control them?"

"No. I don't control the beasts; they *listen* to me because they equate me with the doctor. I'm his man, so they pay attention. They certainly don't *have* to do what I say."

"But they have to listen to the doctor? Is that what you're saying?" Ned asked.

Seely shook his head. "The doctor is… The doctor oversees the WHEEL. That's it."

"Where are all these creatures now?" Harrison asked. "Where do they go?"

Saburo came up from the building. "We figured that out. We went up to the temple and cranked up their little monster factory."

"What do you mean?" Seely asked.

Tilly had hoped to keep that piece of information a secret for a while longer, but knew the cat would eventually be out of the bag. "We went late last night. Mingmei showed us how to find the trench in the temple and everything. A group of people were being drowned in some black muck. Is that how you turn people into these beasts, Seely? Is that it?"

"I do nothing of the sort," Seely said. "I don't have that kind of knowledge. I'm not a visionary like the doctor. Right? Who can do that? Not me. I sweep the cabin and do what he tells me. You don't even know what he's seen, what he's done. He's not… he's not like you and me. Our brains can't pull the same signals out of the sky. You get what I'm saying? It's not even close how much smarter he is. There aren't words for it."

The man talked so quickly, Tilly had a hard time keeping up with him, but she got the gist. "I understand," she said. "He's smart, we're dumb."

"*No*. That's not even it. It's not about brains, or who's more intelligent or who might be brain deficient. It's about ideas and… and thoughts and his unique connection to the universe," Seely said. "You look into his mind and the work he does, and you see the broader universe. You can see distant planets, where life began, here and everywhere else. You know? If God exists, where did he come from? What was before God? If life started from a big bang or a spark or some shit like that, what came before that? Who lit that spark? He knows. Everything has a beginning. Everything starts somewhere. You look in the doctor's eyes, you'll see that. You'll see where you came from." Seely paused, winded from talking so fast.

Tilly gave Ned a side glance, wondering if he had any idea what Seely was on about. Was the man under the influence of some hallucinogen or some drug that made him babble on so? Could it be that Harrison was in the grip of the same thing?

"You really shouldn't have gone out there," Seely said.

"To the temple?" Tilly asked. "Why is that?"

Seely didn't answer.

"Let's go then. Where is it?" Ned pushed forward.

"It's out in the woods," Saburo answered. "Mingmei took us."

"Where is she now?" Harrison asked.

"I don't know," Tilly said. "Still asleep?"

"She wasn't in the room when I woke up," Saburo said.

"Do any of the other doctors or assistants go out there?" Harrison asked.

The man's bushy brow furrowed. "The others?"

"The people you work with. Did any of them go out there?"

"Yes."

"Will they take us out there?" Morrow asked. "Can you get them to come show us? Maybe Clive wandered out there in the middle of the night. I suppose if the ladies can do it, so can he. Contact one of your people." Morrow intensified his glare at Seely.

"They can't do that. The doctor won't let them."

"Surely your security people can open the door. Where are the cameras? We'll get their attention, and I can hold up my Hōfuna identification." Harrison began patting his pockets in search of something.

"They can't do that."

Whatever was going on, the lab assistant didn't want any of their group to go inside. Seely immediately dismissed anything they suggested. They were hitting a brick wall.

Tilly stepped around the curved side of the WHEEL and followed it around to the water, searching for another entrance. The WHEEL seemed to be stuck high on the shore. Weeds and grass stood tall. Reeds sprouted from the water and surrounded the base. She looked the structure up and down, ignoring the conversation that continued by the door. There was a wide vent halfway up the side, toward what she guessed was the second floor, but it was far too thin to climb through. Add to the fact it was likely thirty feet off the ground with no easy handholds to aid in the climb. She wondered if the other side was any better, but since that side currently floated in the river, she didn't see how it would be of any use to them. She walked back from the water's edge.

"Look, mate," Morrow said. "We've been attacked by yer weird-ass companions out in the forest, and ta be honest with you, it was not as much fun as we'd hoped. So, enough of this bullshit. Open the doors, or we'll kill you and dig yer heart out with a god damn soup spoon. Then we'll find our own fucking way inside."

"Whoa." Saburo found the Scot's language humorous.

Tilly laughed a little, too. "We were all thinking it. He just had the guts to say it."

"Easy. Calm down." Harrison put his hand on Morrow's shoulder. "We're all a little on edge here. Let's calm down..."

"I'm not on edge and nothing is funny here, so shut the fuck up the lot of you." Morrow unslung his rifle and repeatedly began smashing the butt against the panel. "Open the damn doors!" he shouted.

"Hey, come on. Stop that. You'll screw the whole thing up." Seely pushed his way through the crowd and made his way toward Morrow. "You're going to break it, and we'll never get it open."

Seely's plea didn't deter Morrow in the slightest. He continued smashing the gun against the metal control box. "Shut up." His face turned red, and his jaw clenched tight. "All of you shut the hell up." One of the metal sections broke off and rattled to the ground. It only encouraged Morrow to further violence. With a wicked smile, he howled as he continued to pound in the same spot until his rifle stock cracked.

"Look, seriously. You need to stop before something happens." Seely sounded stern but didn't advance beyond where Harrison stood. "It's not like we can really fix stuff out here. Without spare parts, we're kind of screwed. Like, royally. So, stop."

The screen flickered and popped.

Your support makes it happen. Hōfuna. Hōfuna. Hōfuna....Hōfuna. Giving Life A Fighting A Fighting A Fighting Chance.

A different female voice, this one more mechanical and distanced, followed the speech that Tilly knew so well. *"Please stand clear of the outer lab doors. Please stand clear of the outer lab doors."* The exposed area of the controls buzzed and popped, sending a spark of light into the air and a puff of smoke wafting up.

"That's right, ya piece of shit circuit pile," Morrow said. "Smash a computer hard enough, it'll start speaking your language."

"No, Dumbass. Someone inside opened it. I heard the lock go," Rei said. He had remained silent through the entire thing, apparently content to stand back and watch.

"Nobody opened it. Who would have opened it?" Morrow asked.

"I honestly do not know," Seely said. "Maybe you accidentally hit on a correct code?" Seely pressed forward, pushing everyone away until he blocked the enormous bay doors. "Stay out of here. You don't belong in here."

This didn't make Morrow happy after pounding so hard on the controls. Sweat stained his shirt, and he breathed heavily. "Are you shitting me? Get out of the sodding way and let us talk to yer team."

"*They're dead*," Seely shouted. "They're all dead. Been dead for years. Are you happy now? Is that something that satisfies you?" He paused and eyed everyone as he caught his breath.

"What the hell are you saying?" Rei cautiously stepped forward to look around the man. "What happened to everyone?"

"Did you kill them?" Saburo asked. She gripped her rifle tighter and dug her feet into the ground.

Harrison's face paled in the cold lights of the WHEEL's inner hall. Tilly suspected that if he had to wait much longer to meet with the doctor, he might break. But now, if Seely was telling the truth, there was no doctor or crew to talk to.

"Did you kill the doctor?" Tilly asked.

Seely looked surprised, almost hurt by the question. "What? What do you mean? I couldn't kill the doctor. He's fine. I said that already. I said that he was here, right? I didn't kill anyone. Why would you ask that?" He looked behind himself into the building's rounded halls. "No. *Shit.* I mean. Is that what you think of me? The doctor is saving all the world's creatures. To kill him would be a crime. An act of sheer ignorance."

In small increments, the men were stepping toward Seely. Morrow's lip curled into a slight smile as he drew closer to the lab assistant. He held his pistol behind his back, finger on the trigger.

"Who killed them then?" Harrison asked. "Just... Just let's go inside and talk about this. You can tell us what happened, and we can get it sorted. No need for games, no need for secrets. We're not angry or anything. I have to know what to tell the company about his research." Harrison held his hands up to let Seely know it was alright and that he would not harm the man. "I need to see for myself."

Seely nervously glanced behind him again.

"It's ok," Harrison said. His hands shook and his smile was twisted and forced.

Morrow slid forward another couple of inches.

It looked as if Seely might say no. He appeared angry for a moment as his brow furrowed. His nostrils flared. "Fine. But I didn't do any of it. None of this is my fault. *None of it.*"

The floors inside were filthy and showed tire tracks. They appeared to be from some sort of wagon or cart. The trails of dirt led down the hall to the right before disappearing around the corner. Muddy boot prints veered in both directions, some of the mud dry, some still wet. The walls had scuffs and dents at multiple points along the way. To the right, a leak from the ceiling created a puddle of water. It was unlike anything Tilly had seen, and certainly not like any lab or medical facility she'd seen, either in military life or civilian.

Harrison brushed past Seeley and took a long look in both directions. "What is this?"

"Ah, I'm the only one that cleans up here," Seely said, "and it's so hard to keep up with the dirt and mud and the sheer volume of muck that I track in. I have to use a dolly to transport supplies from the main house into our commissary, and fresh fruit from the boats, and whatever else the doctor asks his children to bring in."

"Children?" Tilly asked. "You mean creations. Fucking experiments. So, you admit that he's the one doing all of this? Making these abominations we've seen along the river? Those things that blocked the river when we arrived? Did you help?"

The crackle and buzz of the ceiling speakers startled the group as it ticked and thudded to life. "*What is this? Seely? You have not been cleared to have anyone enter the facility. You don't have the authority.*" The voice was indiscernible as male or female, distorted by the speakers and the howl of feedback. It all made Tilly's temple ache. "You must not go any further. Exit immediately through the forward doors."

While the voice may have startled everyone, it terrified Seely. "Shit. Shit, he's here. He's awake. Let's do what he wants, okay? He can be a reasonable man, you know? He's fair," Seeley mumbled. "Everyone else said that he was fair."

"Before they were killed?" Tilly asked as the lab assistant trembled and slowly retreated toward the open doors. "Is that when they thought he was fair?"

"No, no. You're misunderstanding. You don't get what he's doing out here. He can save all the endangered species, and everything else that will be endangered one day. He figured that out. The company sent him out to save the world, and now you're going to question how he does it? You're going to look at the eggs he had to break and tell him his omelet is too big? That's not how it works, no, sir."

"How do we get to this doctor?" Morrow asked. "Where is he? Let's talk about his eggs and his omelet face-to-face, what say?" He took another glance around, then ventured down the hall to the left.

"Man, don't do that," Seely implored. "He wants us to leave. Don't do that."

As a 'fuck you' to the lab assistant, the others followed right along behind the Scot. Harrison and his men, Saburo, Ned, all walked quickly, as if they had some place to be, an appointment to keep.

Seely was almost out the door, but stopped when he reached Tilly. "Look, he's been talking to you, right?" he asked. "He said he's been talking to you in your mind, in your dreams? He's going to kill me for *not* killing all of your friends. That's funny, I think. *Kill me for not killing them.* Catch twenty-two. Is that what that's called? I don't want to kill them, but I don't want to die. Catch twenty-two. Or maybe… maybe 'Damned if you do, damned if you don't' sort of thing. Something."

"The fuck are you talking about?" Tilly asked. "He hasn't been talking to me. I don't even know the doctor. I'd have to check my NaNi to remember what he looks like." She pointed in the opposite direction of the group, who had vanished around a corner. "What's this way?"

"It all leads to the same place, miss. I think that's what he was trying to tell you. Everything leads to the same conclusion." Seely stepped outside and gazed up at what passed for sunshine in the smog-colored skies. "You're not going to kill him, are you? I sincerely hope that's not why you're here."

She feared turning her back on Seely, so Tilly kept one eye on him while exploring.

"Your dreams haven't been right, have they?" Seely continued. "That's him. That's him messing with you. He drew you here. Can't save the world if all he has are Chinese people, right? He needs you and the others. Americans, whites, Anglo Saxons, whatever. He needs a wider sample if he's going to save the world."

That he knew about her dreams concerned Tilly. "I want to go home, and I can't do that until we get to your scientist. No one asked me to kill him."

"I'm right. He did a number on my dreams, too," Seely said. "You could've gone home whenever you wanted, you know? You didn't have to come this far." Seely exited through the front door where, in the bushes and trees beyond, a scattering of creatures gathered.

This hall was just as muddy as Tilly continued to explore on her own. She encountered a handful of locked doors marked "lab" or "specimen storage." The hall curved, and she was sure it would wrap around to meet her companions. But then she came to a wall of debris that blocked her way. It looked like something had punched the WHEEL, cleanly shoving the outer bulkhead inward. There was no door to pass through, no way around it. Tilly slung her gun over her shoulder and pushed the wall as hard as she could. She'd hoped the section blocking the way would budge easily, but it didn't. Where the wall met the floor, she could see jagged areas where everything was smashed together.

Tilly had to turn around, but this time, she followed the mud on the floor more closely. The footprints didn't come this far. Following them, they led her to one of the locked lab doors. The muddy shoe prints told of someone going in and out of the lab with frequency. It also appeared to be the same foot print each time. No other prints were visible in the muck.

She fiddled with the door's controls and had little luck opening it. When Tilly grabbed the handle to yank it open, she felt something like electricity course through her. She fell backward, stumbling until she hit the opposite wall. She ended up on the muddy floor. Her hands still tingled and vibrated as an energy coursed through them. Bringing them up for a closer look, Tilly's fingertips twitched, her fingernails turned black.

Your support makes it happen.
Hōfuna. Giving Life A Fighting Chance.
Hōfuna. Giving Life....Giving Life...

CHAPTER TWENTY-FIVE

Six Years Earlier

They walked for a bit, basking in the sunlight and company of hundreds of people doing the same. Hirada had dragged her outside to get some fresh air while her father was getting his treatment. It would be hours before they could take him home. They didn't talk about him, nor what his odds were. They simply walked as Hirada gave her the grand tour of the area. He pointed to the Atomic Bomb Dome and Hiroshima Castle, giving his quick take on both.

"When you were in China, did you see much combat?" Hirada asked. "Were you dragged into the fighting yourself?"

It was something she hadn't talked about with her father. Or anyone else, for that matter. The war was the war, and she hadn't spent all of her time flying in it. "I was on the ground some. Didn't do much shooting, though. Mostly logistics and transportation."

Hirada nodded with a slight grunt and pointed to a shopping center ahead. "Let's go in here. I'll buy you a treat. You're always so good about what you eat. You really should splurge sometimes. Have a little fun."

And just like that, Hirada dropped the subject of war. He guided Tilly into the crowded shopping center with a smile, weaving through families and lone shoppers alike. They made their way to the line of food vendors, where Hirata pulled her further on. He laughed like a schoolboy.

"Come, this will cheer you up. Make you feel at home." He waved to an area ahead with a black arch over their store. "You'll love it." The red letters showed it to be Manhattan Roll Ice Cream. A small version of the Statue of Liberty joined their logo. "Right? It's like back in the United States. We should bring your father here.

Manhattan!" He pointed to the Statue of Liberty and laughed.

Back home in South Carolina, she frequented an ice cream shop up the street from their apartment. It was called The Big Freezy, and featured larger-than-standard homemade cones with ice cream dipped in rainbow sprinkles or coated in chocolate that turned crunchy. Manhattan Roll appeared to be a bit different, but she appreciated the effort.

"Look," Harada said, standing in front of a glass case, perusing huge buckets of pastel-colored treats. "They have all these flavors, but instead of giving you a scoop, they use this tool to sort of peel it off until it becomes a swirl. They mix it with your favorite confections, the best toppings. And they do this many times, many times until you have three or four…?" Hirada looked at Tilly as if expecting her to complete his sentence, but she drew a blank.

"Rolls." Hirada smiled again. "Like the name? Manhattan *Roll* Ice Cream?"

Tilly smiled and nodded as Hirada continued his perusal of all the available flavors. Maybe the trip was as much for him as for her. He'd been taking care of her father long before she arrived, and it couldn't have been easy. Maybe he needed a day out to clear his head, to not think about Henry Coleman, to not think about death or dying. Maybe he just needed ice cream.

His order was as full of childish delight as he seemed to be. "I'll have the Choco Banana with strawberries and almonds. Whipped cream for sure."

"Tea & Sweet potato?" Tilly scrunched up her nose as she read the menu.

"It's very good," a young lady behind the counter said. "It is my sister's favorite."

Tilly nodded, though she wasn't sure the sour look had left her face. "I might try the strawberry and lime. It looks like something I'd enjoy. Perhaps I'll get more daring on my next trip." The young lady behind the counter nodded and disappeared to make the concoction.

They ate as they strolled back through the park toward the shop. Hirada's smile had widened as he devoured his cup of ice cream.

"Choco Banana is a long-time favorite."

"I'd never heard of this, but you're right. It's really wonderful."

Hirada looked over at her cup for the first time and didn't seem pleased. "What did you get? What is all that?"

"It's mostly fresh berries."

"Are those strawberries on top? The big ones?"

"Yes, they're delicious."

Hirada reached over, and before Tilly knew what was happening, picked two large, red berries off her ice cream with his fingers and shoved them into his mouth. She was stunned, couldn't believe such a normally prim and proper man would break so far with etiquette and do such a thing. He continued walking, unfazed, unapologetic for the action. Not even a devilish laugh to let her know he was being silly.

"You need to try everything in life," he said. "You can't live forever with berries and nuts or whatever." Hirada looked out over the park, eating as they walked. Only instead of using his spoon, he was dipping his hands into the cup and bringing the food to his mouth. "Like I said, you have to splurge a little. Who gets ice cream with fruit?" He looked over at her cup again. "In fact, here. You have nothing in that cup that could be construed as fun." He dipped his hand into his ice cream again and brought his hand toward hers. He dripped chocolate syrup over his container, across the ground, and splattered onto the white rolls of ice cream still in her little bowl. "Look, it's better the more you can cram into it. In fact," Hirada reached into his bowl again and brought out a chunk of banana, "here. Add this. It will be so much more fulfilling."

"No," Tilly said. She pushed Hirada's arm away, splattering herself with chocolate and melted ice cream. "What is wrong with you? I don't want all this. I didn't ask for it." She shook the dripping chocolate sauce off her fingers, glancing around to see if anyone else had noticed Hirada's strange behavior.

To her horror, the twenty nearby people were all staring at them. She'd expected one or two, but every one of them had stopped what they were doing. Some sat in the grass picnicking, some walked with their children, others strolled alone. Each one of them had stopped and turned to watch Hirada and Tilly.

"Hirada? Maybe we should go."

One man who stopped stood only a few feet away. He shuffled up and grabbed Tilly by the arm. He proceeded to pull a cookie from his coat pocket and crumbled it into her bowl, covering the ice cream in chocolate chip crumbs. A woman who had been feeding the birds from a nearby bench stood and dug her hands into her bag of breadcrumbs.

Tilly backed away from them all, Hirada included. She held up her syrup-covered hand in front of herself, keeping everyone at bay.

CHAPTER TWENTY-SIX

"Tilly?"

The voice pulled her attention from her fingertips. Mingmei stood a few feet away.

"Tilly, is he calling to you?" the tiger-woman asked. "I told you. You shouldn't come here. He'll kill you. Or worse."

"What?" Tilly asked, still disoriented by the voice. The memory of Hirada was still fresh in her mind, the ice cream still cold on her skin. She glanced back at her hands. Her black fingertips were back to normal, neither covered nor stained in the way she'd feared a few minutes ago. "What the hell?"

"It's him. It's your doctor friend. He has called forth Kalidas the Hundun from the temple, and the Hundun is enslaving everyone he can find. That's his plan for saving everyone. By combining them with beasts. Leave now. Go home. You still can."

The door that Tilly had been working on opened with a hiss, and Saburo poked her head out into the hall. "Tilly, where have you been?" she asked. "We've been searching for you."

"I was right here. I think I got an electrical shock from that door, so be careful."

Saburo looked confused. "Uh, Tilly? I searched this area myself. I even sent your NaNi off to search ahead of me. You weren't here."

Tilly's muscles ached as she sat up. "Look, I don't know what's happening here, but I haven't moved."

"I found her," Saburo shouted over her shoulder. "I don't know what happened, but you need to come and see this." She stared at Mingmei, surprised, yet not surprised, to see her.

Tilly needed help to stand. Her legs were more than a little sore. It was like they'd fallen asleep. Her feet tingled as if she was walking on pins and needles. She followed Saburo through the door into an enormous laboratory in the center of the structure. It was wide open to the ceiling, the second and third stories clearly visible on both sides. These weren't what caught Tilly's attention, though. The enormous gap in the far wall drew her focus. Extending from floor to ceiling, the hole was wide enough to fly two Cyclones through at once.

She walked toward the hole in the WHEEL, while everyone else checked out the rest of the room. Tilly felt Mingmei behind her, clinging to her flight suit.

"You've been in here before?" Tilly asked.

"No," Mingmei said.

They approached the hole and confirmed that it wasn't some feature of the lab, some door that slid open to observe the outside. In that area, the structure was crushed and crumbling. Exposed wires hung from the ceiling. Tubes were cut crudely and unevenly. To Tilly, it appeared as if something had taken a huge bite out of the WHEEL, or had smashed that section with a massive object. It didn't appear to have been blown up by an explosion or missile. There were no burn marks or signs of scalding.

"What do you think of this?" Ned shouted. "We found the doctor."

On the other side of the room, Harrison and Ned huddled over a long container that resembled a freezer with a glass window at one end. Rei and Decator stood back from the object, arms folded, eyes still taking in the rest of the lab. Tilly and Mingmei had to navigate crumbled workstations, containers, fallen tiles, and more garbage to cross the room. Harrison and Ned stared into the small rectangular window on its top. Through the clear surface, Doctor Oscar's face stared back.

"What the fuck?" Tilly stepped back. "Is he dead?"

"We don't know," Ned said. "We can't find any sort of control to open the thing, or monitor that reports his condition. It's like a big slick freezer."

The two women searched the large, white container, but found nothing but smooth sides. "Is it… I don't know… is it plugged in?" Tilly asked. "How is it powered?"

Ned shoved the thing. With difficulty, he managed to move it along the floor far enough to reveal there were no connections from below. "Your guess is as good as mine."

The speakers in the vast room crackled. The few working lights flickered. "You have made a grave mistake. Kalidas the Hundun does not take kindly to trespasses."

Still standing next to the doctor's plastic resting place, Ned said, "His lips didn't move. If that means anything to you."

Tilly leaned close to the tiger-woman. "Mingmei?" she asked. "You've mentioned Kalidas. Does the doctor think he's this god from Chinese mythology?"

"I don't know what he thinks, but that man is not Kalidas."

"You've seen the doctor before?"

"No, never."

"But—"

"You have seen me, creature," the voice came through the speaker. "You saw me at the temple when you were first matched with the animal you were to save. I watched over you to make sure the ceremony went as planned." The speakers continued to buzz around them even after he finished speaking.

"No, there were no other humans there," Tilly said. "Only the Hundun."

In the river outside the building, something splashed. The group turned toward the water, on edge for anything that might come. Tilly feared the ox-men were on their way in through the gap. When after a moment nothing had appeared, she sighed with relief.

"No, little bird, the Ox-faces and Horse-heads are not coming for you. Not now." The voice sounded lighter. "You have *his* attention. Though you'll wish you didn't."

Another splash drew Tilly closer to the gouge in the wall, closer to the water and nearer the source of the noise. This time, it startled her when the tip of an appendage slid out of the water and slithered over the edge of the cracked floor.

"The hell is this now?" Morrow shouted. He pointed his gun toward the movement and stepped around to get a better shot if need be.

The slimy gray appendage continued to advance; a single tentacle with round pink suckers on one side. Its other end remained in the water and out of sight. The exposed end was joined by another, then another. The trio squirmed across the floor toward Tilly. While their ends were thin and delicate, the tentacles widened the further back they went, looking as fat as a cow at the other end.

"He is here. *This* is Kalidas." Mingmei moved to the white container that held Doctor Oscar's body and hid behind it.

"This monster of yours is an octopus?" Ned shouted.

The sound system in the WHEEL crackled again. "You'll wish it was a common Cephalopod. For there is nothing common about this test subject. This is the answer to continuing life on our planet. My partner in saving the world, Kalidas the Hundun."

Now numbering at least a dozen, the tentacles, dripping wet and constantly undulating, gripped where they could on the floor and the nearby walls. When each appendage found a hold, the thing heaved the rest of itself onto the lab floor. Its breathes came labored and heavy. It struggled to pull itself further inside. The lab shook and leaned slightly in the creature's general direction, allowing water to flood into the low end. The great thing lunged forward, revealing shiny forward flippers which it used to drag itself along. Its enormity revealed itself slowly in increments too small for Tilly to bear, but she couldn't look away. Its thick torso resembled a whale's hide—smooth, shiny, and grey, though it wasn't half of a whale's mass. The rest of the body didn't match. Its bulbous head melded into its neck with rolls of blubberous fat. The slimy tentacles disappeared into an area right above those neck rolls where, Tilly assumed, its mouth lived. Large, feathered wings clung to the monster's back; multiple sets embedded in a random fashion. They weren't huge, powerful wings that could ever lift the thing aloft.

The eyes, though. It was the eyes that stopped Tilly from running right there and then. The long ovals seemed to stare in every direction at once. They enthralled her with how they shined crimson in the dim morning light. Even from the far side of the room, she could see herself in them. But there was more there. Not only her own image, but she could see the others in those eyes—Mingmei,

Saburo, Harrison, and the soldiers.

The thing slobbered, spilling saliva and detritus out onto the floor, bringing Tilly back to the present. She stepped back and glanced at the others, who were all staring just as intensely. All except the lab assistant, Seely, who watched the group's reactions while clenching and unclenching his fists.

"What the fuck..." Tilly said, nausea washing over her. She briefly closed her eyes, trying to regain her sense of where she was and what she knew to be real.

"What do you mean?" Seely asked. "That's him. How could you look upon the great Hundun and not be awed by his presence?"

"Him?" Tilly asked. "Doctor Oscar?"

"He once went by that name, but look upon him now. Is there any poetry in all of human history that could've prepared you for the coming of such a wonderful master?"

The wave of sickness enveloped Tilly as she glanced back at the form resting before them. Her first look had been purely clinical, an analysis of an enemy, taking in its form and capabilities. The next observation created a chaos of those conclusions. The twitching and searching tentacles slapped against the floor, just out of reach of the group across the room. It moved like a beached sea turtle—unable to gain traction in the sand and too dense to go back to the sea. She forced herself to look away and grabbed Saburo's arm for support. Saburo still stared at the thing on the wet floor, seemingly dropped there by a nightmare. Tilly shook the woman and turned her so that they met each other's gaze. After a full minute, where Tilly was sure her companion hadn't taken a breath, Saburo wheezed and coughed. It was Tilly's turn to support her teammate.

"What the hell?" Saburo looked around as though she'd just arrived.

Harrison fell to his knees and vomited, sobbing as he struggled to fight his nausea.

"You said *that* was the doctor." Tilly nodded toward the chamber where the old man's body lay. The figure inside hadn't moved.

Seely waved his arms, presenting the creature to the group. "Do you see? Do you understand what I told you? The doctor is one, and one is the other. They're a single mind, and they're all minds. He's my mind, he's your mind. He is on a level that none of us can even comprehend. Look at him. You understand how we are all lesser beings, and he is great and powerful now."

The creature continued to drag itself out of the muck along the river bank. It slid a tentacle forward as yet another emerged from the water. The body continued to slither and roll, its skin shimmering and slimy. Tilly looked again into the wide, dark eyes that were immediately focused on her. Their black hue refused to reflect the lights in the room in the same manner as the body. It was those eyes that made her head swim, thoughts that made her anxious and weak.

It was also in those eyes that she saw an outline form. A shadow of a person broke through the blackness. She recognized her father's face long before the details filled in. Only the image wasn't the thin, failing man she'd taken care of in the last months of his life. It was the younger version; the office worker, the one that played piano in their tiny first house in Chicago, the one that married Tilly's mother.

CHAPTER TWENTY-SEVEN

Six Years Earlier

"Look, we put this thing together," Henry Coleman said. "We should test it out in the park."

"Pop, you can't fly that thing." Tilly laughed and handed the kite back to her father. "You'll never get up enough speed to get it in the air from your wheelchair,"

"Do I look like I need a wheelchair?" Her father stood with the kite, reminding her that he was young again. He appeared spry and fun. A man she barely knew.

"I guess you don't."

"You guess?" He wore a black suit with a gray shirt and tie underneath.

CHAPTER TWENTY-EIGHT

"Little one," Mingmei shouted. "You have to move."

The Hundun slithered forward, its tentacles a mere few feet from Tilly.

"What?" Tilly asked, her voice sounding far off and dreamy.

CHAPTER TWENTY-NINE

Six Years Earlier

"You're still faster than me, Wren," her father said. "Would you mind running with the kite to get it in the air? I'll do what I can, but you have to run."

The kite was back in Tilly's hands, all black like she remembered. She felt the tail of the dragon they'd created already starting to wrap around her ankle.

CHAPTER THIRTY

You have to run."

As her father faded from view, Tilly found she couldn't shout, and her legs wouldn't let her give chase. She felt a sudden pain in her side and fell to the floor. She fought to get up, to pursue her father, but Mingmei was on top of her, trying desperately to separate Tilly from a tentacle that gripped her leg.

"What happened?" Tilly asked.

Mingmei crouched and stayed close to the walls as she scrambled away. "He is hard to resist." She pointed, and Tilly turned toward the behemoth. Growing larger with every passing moment, it had grabbed Harrison in writhing, dripping tentacles and now raised him into the air. The man hung limp in the thing's grip, neither struggling nor shouting, though he seemed quite awake; eyes open and wrapped in a wide smile.

Morrow approached the coffin-like tube that held Doctor Oscar's physical body and stood behind it. "Stop," he shouted. If the monster heard, it failed to comply and instead stretched two tendrils toward the Scot.

A group of speakers near the door whistled. "I set out to collect life, but now I have done so much more than document it, or house it. I *am* life. After the rest of the world has burned to ashes, I and I alone will allow it to live on." The creature twitched, and a ripple rolled down its back like a wave in the ocean. A grunt of discomfort roiled from inside it. "These things inside me claw and howl to live again, driven by their instincts to roam free. I will grant them that wish one day." With that, the thing rolled to the side, splashing in the puddles of water gathered on the dinghy deck. It brought several tentacles down into the river, then raised them again. Water dripped over its back. "Everything…" The beast heaved and sighed as the doctor tried to speak. "Everything lives on through me. And I through them. Millennia of..." Doctor Oscar's voice trailed off, and Tilly couldn't tell if it was a momentary loss in what the man was trying to say, or if the speakers had clipped off his next words.

Tilly glanced around. The group appeared in a daze, content to hang back and watch to see what Kalidas would do next. Everyone except Mingmei. She nervously stalked back and forth, studying the monster from the shadows near the door. Tilly took up Morrow's strategy and moved toward the coffin-like container that held the doctor's body.

Harrison, still trapped in the monster's tentacles, began to scream.

"Get away from that vessel," the doctor's voice echoed. "Or I'll kill this one."

The scream turned to a gasp as Harrison struggled to breathe.

"You were going to kill us all anyway, right?" Tilly pointed her rifle at the glass. "If he's you and you're him, what happens if *you* die, doctor?" The thought of shooting a defenseless man brought on a wave of revulsion, but the situation called for a split-second decision, and that was all she had.

The creature's sudden intense focus on Tilly and Harrison seemed to break the spell on Morrow. The Scot fell to the ground as his knees buckled. "Ack, my head," he moaned. "What happened to me?"

"Kalidas happened to you," Tilly said. "He was hypnotizing us, playing with our minds."

"I'll kill the bastard for that."

"Did you get a good look at him? I'm not sure how the hell you'd do that."

"Do you have a plan?" Morrow was still on the floor, looking up at Tilly.

"My plan is to run. You grab Decator, Mingmei will get Saburo, and I'll take Rei. Grab them, drag them, slap them, whatever it takes to get them to snap out of it and run."

Morrow peered around the coffin and looked at Kalidas. "Jesus fucking hell."

"Probably best not to look at it very long."

"Amen."

Tilly spotted Mingmei behind them, still pacing. "You hear any of that?"

"I heard. I can do it." Her voice shook, but she clenched her fists. Tilly took that as a good sign.

Seely hovered in their escape route, blocking the room's only open door. He looked nervous, sweating. "What are you going to do? You're not taking the doctor away, are you?"

Tilly and Morrow exchanged a look that told her he was willing to do it. That killing the doctor was something that might help them in this situation. The Scot nodded and pulled out his pistol. She didn't have time to consider the ramifications, or whether she'd be able to do it or not. The thought of killing a helpless man wasn't something she'd found herself in a position of considering before. But now, she only had to decide if she'd allow someone else to do it. And at the moment, she couldn't find a reason to say no.

She ran for Rei and grabbed him by the collar, yanking him harder than she'd intended. Behind her, the sound of Morrow's pistol echoed in the WHEEL's interior; one shot, then another, then a third. Tilly grabbed Rei's arm, pulling him along as she charged at a clearly confused Seely. Nearby, Mingmei carried Saburo over her shoulder, pack and all. Morrow continued to shoot into Oscar's container, a look of grim satisfaction playing across his face.

"Morrow, get Decator and let's go," Tilly shouted. When the dazed Rei collapsed to the floor, she had to drag him the last ten feet, stalling her charge at Seely.

"It's not doing anything," Morrow mumbled. "The bullets aren't doing anything to the doctor's pod."

Nearly at the door, Tilly stopped and turned back. The sullen Scot stood over the unharmed doctor.

"What about that robot fist thing of yours?" she asked. "Could that do something?"

"I could tear the container apart, I guess. At least get us in." Morrow lifted the mechanical hand off the floor and fired up its power source. Surprisingly, perhaps only to Tilly, it tore through the metal like paper. After ripping the top off the pod, Morrow hesitated. In that split second, Kalidas' thick tentacle swatted him aside.

Gunfire erupted in the outer hall. Saburo and Rei shouted obscenities loud enough to be heard over the din. The grunts and howls of beasts charging in from outside soon joined the noise as rifle fire mowed them down.

A splash from the open side of the lab drew everyone's focus to the half dozen ox-men pulling themselves out of the water and clawing their way onto the torn metal floor.

Morrow groaned and tried to stand. "If you think this is going to work, you better do it quickly," he shouted. "Kill him now!"

Gunfire once again shattered Tilly's thought process when two of the charging ox-men were gunned down by a barely mobile Decator.

"Do it now," Decator shouted. "We're running out of ammunition and time!"

"Not running out," Rei said, coming around the corner from the hall. "We *are* officially *out* of bullets."

"Tilly!" Saburo shouted. The soldier knelt and slid a long machete across the slick floor. The weapon spun to a stop mere feet from the doctor's pod. "We're down to these. Good luck!"

Amid the surrounding chaos and combat, Tilly did her best to shake the images of her father and the guilt she'd carried since the day he died in the hospital; the continued angst as his business failed around her; the feeling of sorrow as his meager savings disappeared. All while trying to recover from his loss and find some meaning in her life.

She looked down at the doctor.

The same feelings seeped into Tilly's consciousness now, as the group looked to her to kill a man, instead of save him. She couldn't do it in the war. Nor was prepared to start with someone defenseless. But she had no choice. She waved the machete around, gauging its heft. The weapon felt weightless in her hand.

"Damn it, Tilly," Ned said. When the gunfire stopped, everyone had a knife or club in their hands, prepared to defend themselves. Though he staggered to move about with its weight, Morrow still wore the metallic glove and used it to punch creatures as they charged.

In the corner, Decator fell to two ox-men in a brutal charge.

CHAPTER THIRTY-ONE

Six Years Earlier

From the cold, leather hospital chairs beside his bed, Tilly and Hirada gazed upon her father. He hadn't moved since Tilly got there. The orchestra of mechanical beeps and pings had grown maddening after an hour of waiting.

"He has a living will directive on file," Hirada said. "He doesn't want any extraordinary measures taken to resuscitate him."

"What does that mean, extraordinary measures? What are *extraordinary* in a case like this?" Tilly asked. "Saving someone's life should be ordinary, normal, shouldn't it?"

"We're both named as proxies for his end-of-life care. I guess he added you when you came to Japan," Hirada said. "He left me on there as well."

"But do we have to follow his wishes? I mean, can we just ignore it and make the doctors take care of him?" Tilly felt terrible the moment she'd said it, but she wasn't ready to let him go.

Doctor Mouri waited for the right moment to interject. "The decisions here are yours, and I won't point you in one direction or the other. But the stroke was severe enough that permanent brain damage is almost a certainty no matter what you do. Should you choose to put him on a ventilator, his quality of life will likely not improve."

"But he'll live a little longer, right? He'll still be alive."

"If you choose to put him on a ventilator," the doctor said, "yes, he'll be alive. If you do nothing, he will likely die this evening, or early tomorrow morning."

"Hirada, I don't know that I can make this…" Tilly locked her jaw tight to keep from sobbing.

Her father's friend patted her hand and nodded. "I know it is difficult, but it must be done. Your father cannot continue like this. He knew this day would come, and he left instructions."

"I can't do it. You're right, but I can't do it."

"Tilly," Hirada said.

"You do it." Tilly took a deep breath and sighed it back out. "You knew him better. Tell them what he wanted." Tilly stood, feeling more cowardly than she'd ever felt. To mourn her father was one thing, but to leave his life in someone else's hands was another. She escaped to the hall and found the nearest restroom.

A wave of nausea wracked her body. Shuddering, she grabbed the sink. She stared at the dark, circular drain as her fingers gripped the cold, white porcelain. Small drops of water exploded as they dripped from the faucet into the bottom of the basin. The song of the hospital equipment echoed in her bones. As she thought about her father lying in the bed and Hirata sitting next to him, her chest tightened. Despite her best efforts to hold it back, a tear rolled down her cheek and splattered against the edge of the sink.

As she fought the next one, the dark dot of the sink's drain quivered like it was struggling to come into a camera lens's focus. It soon became more than a dot. It elongated, and the darkness became a tendril that danced and swayed out from the drain. As much as Tilly wanted to flee, she couldn't. The thin, murky appendage reached for her, wrapping itself around her neck.

CHAPTER THIRTY-TWO

More and more beasts threw themselves at Kalidas. While they slowed the Hundun's progress, they didn't stop the monster from grabbing Tilly and encircling her neck. She fell to the ground, attempting to pull herself free before realizing she still had a firm grip on the machete. Unable to gain a solid foothold, she swung the long weapon, barely grazing the tentacle's slimy outer skin.

"Tilly!" Rei shouted. "Hang on." No longer the smartest dressed of the party, he dripped water, blood, and the slime from the monster's flailing grip from head to toe. He ran toward Tilly, firing his pistol at the appendage's thick base.

Tilly felt a twinge in her captor's limb. It loosened its grip. She seized the opportunity, steadied herself, and sank the machete's heavy blade as hard as she could. The machete carved a gash into the Hundun's flesh nearly a foot deep. It severed tendons and called forth a stream of dark purple ichor that spilled out across the lab's floor.

"Either kill the doctor or we need to get the fuck out of here before Kalidas thrashes us," Morrow shouted. He and the others were doing their best against the monster with whatever weapons still functioned. Rei tossed his pistol aside and rushed toward Tilly, determined to save her from the appendage that now twitched at her feet.

From the lab's shadows, Mingmei emerged, and within seconds, drew up next to Tilly. "The doctor did not understand what he was unleashing. He did not comprehend what the Hundun could do. Perhaps it is only fitting that this is all ended by one who does comprehend it." In a handful of fluid movements, the tiger-woman gripped the handle of the machete, wrested it from Tilly, then pounced over to Doctor Oscar's shattered enclosure.

"Mingmei," Tilly shouted. "We can't. He's helpless."

"Courage, my friend. It must be done." Without further hesitation, Mingmei brought the long blade down on the doctor with a thud. The machete cleanly and easily separated the man's head from his body. Tilly looked away, unwilling to gaze upon the aftermath of what the tiger-woman had done.

Behind them, the speakers cracked and popped, but no voice came through. Only what sounded like a low rumble; a deep, mournful moan whose depth shook the floor. The Hundun quickly became agitated, slamming its tentacles against the lab's inner confines. It smashed the safety glass and workstations on the second floor, dented the walls.

Whatever spell had kept Harrison transfixed and silent while in the creature's grasp was suddenly snapped. The man screamed and flailed. He begged for help, though most of his words came garbled and lost in his cries.

Somewhere in the back of Tilly's mind, a dim possibility arose: she had to save Harrison. Or at least try. He was unpleasant to her, she knew, but he didn't deserve to die that way.

"Go! Get out of here. I'll catch up," she shouted. "I want to try to help Harrison." She tore herself from the others before they could stop her.

"Are you fucking kidding me, lassie?" Morrow already stood in the hallway beyond the door. "That rat bastard?"

The group exited through the doorway, still helping their confused and incapacitated members along. Seely was the only one still hanging around. The assistant sat on the floor next to the doctor's coffin, sifting through broken pieces of machinery as though he could fix it.

"I can take his place," Seely said. "You need a body, a human body, to commune with. Take me."

Unwilling to wait to see if the assistant's pleas had any effect on the Hundun, Tilly retrieved an abandoned machete off the floor and began waving it around and shouting. She hoped to distract Kalidas, get him to focus on something other than the pathetic man in his grasp.

The beast's eyes shifted away from Seely. As his attention zeroed in on Tilly, he smashed Harrison against the wet deck with a jarring crunch. Then the tentacle retreated, leaving the battered body behind on the glistening floor. Tilly stared at Harrison's bloody pile of remains, absorbing the fact the man had to be dead. She'd had no chance to save him. As she struggled to keep from vomiting at the sight, a thought struck her: if Kalidas could be in her head, anticipating her moves, toying with her memories, and causing her to black out, could he also read her thoughts?

"Tilly!" Saburo shouted.

As the Hundun rose from the water, a rumble in the hallway signaled more of his minions had arrived. As they came around the corner, Tilly waved the machete in her hand.

It surprised everyone when the beasts sidestepped Tilly, Saburo, and Morrow. They skirted each member of the search team and pounded their way toward Kalidas himself. The massive Hundun reached out with its tentacles. It swatted the first arrivals aside, slamming them into the walls of the WHEEL.

"They're free of his control now that the doctor is dead." Seely sounded exuberant in his observation. As he stood from where he'd been groveling to Kalidas, an enormous tendril whipped in his direction. The tentacle sent the assistant flying across the room and into the wall with a wet crack.

CHAPTER THIRTY-THREE

The roar of a thousand beasts shook the WHEEL. It rattled doors, shattered plastiglass frames, and set the entire structure to motion worse than any earthquake. Kalidas the Hundun lashed out wildly with its tentacles, denting the lab's metal walls and smashing the floors. Its mouth remained open, screaming, howling.

"Okay, is he dyin' now?" Morrow asked. "Please tell me he's dyin' now."

"I… don't think so?" Tilly said, shaking her head. The creature didn't appear in the throes of death or a change in its state of being. Not an expert on Chinese mythology or philosophy, she had no idea what a dying Hundun would look like. She doubted anyone else did, either. Rei, Morrow, and Saburo gathered around Tilly as the enormous beast's tantrum threatened to bring the walls down.

"Ye gotta be shitting me."

"We've severed his connection to our world by killing the doctor," Mingmei said. "Now we must convince Kalidas to return to the temple." The tiger-woman sprinted for the door, machete still in hand.

"You didn't say this was a multi-step plan," Rei shouted. "*Kill the doctor* is all I heard."

The roar of Kalidas the Hundun shook the ragged interior of the WHEEL as the great beast bristled with anger. The building tilted slightly toward the river.

"We should leave now, right?" Saburo asked. She gripped her rifle like a baseball bat, ready to swing if need be.

"That's… that's a fine idea." Morrow's jury-rigged mechanical fist rested on the ground beside him. The weapon remained wired to the thin backpack still harnessed to the Scot. His face was awash with sweat from the exertion required to carry the heavy contraption.

Kalidas swung his tentacles, shattering metal and plastiglass on both levels of the WHEEL. It brought down cages, computers, and carts from the top, sending them crashing toward the group. They scattered and ran for the doors to the outer hall.

"Tilly?" Mingmei shouted from just outside the WHEEL. "Tilly, you should come here and see."

Everyone exited with Tilly, wanting to get a glimpse of whatever had Mingmei so excited. No one had to ask what it was. The object of her excitement became evident the moment they stepped out of the structure.

The beast-things had regrouped outside. They formed small circles down the banks of the river, up in the hills, and on either side of the crumbling temple entrance. The largest of the beasts—the ox-men, the horse people, and other variations and combinations that Tilly could only guess about—made up the gatherings. Some trailed colorful makeshift flags that rippled in the light afternoon breeze, distinguishing one circle from another, one clan from the next. Inside each ring of six or seven creatures stood a single tiger-beast like Mingmei. There was no way of deciding if the ones in the center were all males or all females, or a mix of the two. Various fur patterns covered the feline hybrids, making identification difficult. All appeared as muscular as Mingmei. Those in the outer ring stood tensed for battle, crude weapons raised. Had the groups been advancing, it would have been a terrifying sight.

The tiger-beasts in each ring held only a coil of string in their paws. Each string led to a massive kite that flew overhead. Each gently floating object differed slightly from the next. All had rudimentary artwork depicting dragons or birds or nonsensical streaks that represented the best of the beasts' abilities.

"*The fuck*?" Ned asked.

Tilly nodded. "The Chinese believe kites have the power to chase away evil spirits." Memories of her father climbed up from the cellar of her mind and pushed away everything else. That maybe he truly thought kites could save him still seemed ludicrous. Could it be that maybe he was trying to help others stay safe? Were his kites special? Was the process special? He'd given no sign, and none of his customers conveyed anything about his kites having healing properties.

"How the hell did they make those so fast?" Saburo asked.

Ned shrugged. "Maybe they had them lying about for special occasions."

"And maybe it's easy if you've had practice," Tilly said. "Some people are dogged by trouble all their lives, and are always in need." The kites waved in the breeze, dipping and swerving almost in unison. Tilly hadn't seen a kite since her days on the beach with her father and Hirada, and she'd never seen such a sight as the brood that rode the air around her now.

Behind them, the WHEEL groaned and creaked as Kalidas continued to pound the walls and thrash about inside. Metal tiles rattled and fell from the structure's outer wall, splashing into the water. Tentacles emerged from the front door, two at first, then more. They gripped the doorframe and tore outward, crumpling the surrounding walls. High-pitched groans and squeals reverberated from the inside.

"What do we do?" Ned asked. "We're out of ammunition, low on personnel, and surrounded by creatures that want us dead. There aren't many ways out of here, are there?"

"Calm down," Tilly said. It was getting harder for her to think. That fog was clouding her thoughts again. Her head ached. "Seely said they were free of the Hundun now. That they were back in control of themselves."

"Seely was an idiot. *F.Y.I.*" Saburo said.

"We can get to the boat," Ned said. "That's our best bet. There are guns and transportation out of here."

Almost as one, the group turned toward the end of the docks. The boat wasn't there. The bamboo docks remained in position, creating a barrier to any craft attempting to make their way further, but they were alone. No boats, no equipment, no guns. Captain Nancy was gone, and the team's only mode of escape by water had disappeared with her.

"She fucked us," Morrow said. "She went and fucked us good."

Tilly couldn't argue. As fond as she was of Captain Nancy, she couldn't think of a good reason why *The Myrtle* would be gone.

"These are my people now," Mingmei said. "They've broken free of Kalidas and his mind fog, his tricks of the mind and memory." She pointed up the hill at even more crowds of beast people standing at the entrance to the temple. "They will fight to stop him now. Otherwise, he will continue unabated. I must help. Make your way to the temple and we will make our stand there." Mingmei bounded off into the brush, dodging trees and rocks as she disappeared.

The WHEEL's main doorway gave out, unable to contain Kalidas' hulking body. The great beast shoved forward, destroying the door and the walls surrounding it. He pushed through like a bird emerging from an enormous cracked egg. The metal panels fell away and tore open, contributing to the Hundun's emergence, his back a mass of flapping wings and fluttering eyelids.

Before Tilly could herd her group toward somewhere safe, and before the monster could extend its reach for them, a black and red object swooped low. It raked across the Hundun's back. One of the tiger-people yanked hard on their string, causing their kite to rise high above Kalidas and the demolished WHEEL.

The Hundun's reaction surprised Tilly. While it wasn't clear if the kite had done damage to Kalidas, the beast shrunk back as if it had been cut by a razor. Its body turned upward. Wide whale's eyes searched the sky for its attacker.

"What in the name of Christ?" Morrow asked.

The time to flee was slipping away. Tilly wasn't sure if she could drag the rest of the group away as she plotted a course up the hill, headed toward the temple. The thick forest grew along the ridgeline and continued westward away from the temple and off into the distance. She hoped to break somewhere along the way to forge their way through it all.

Another larger kite dropped out of the sky. It nosedived toward Kalidas, and this time, there was little doubt whether it made contact. Its downward arc allowed it to sweep across the beast's flank. The kite sliced a small wing clean off, sending blue and white feathers spinning in its wake. The Hundun howled in pain as puss-yellow fluid sprayed from the wound where the wing had been. The kite zipped back skyward, as though tied to rockets.

Kalidas the Hundun became enraged. Its roar shook the kites in the air. It threw its body on the ground in a tantrum.

"Time to go!" Tilly grabbed Saburo's arm and pulled, then shoved Morrow, interrupting his locked gaze on the Hundun. "Come on. Up the hill."

Ned needed no such coaxing; he was already crunching through the undergrowth at the trailhead. The ever elusive Mingmei was nowhere to be found, and Tilly realized she hadn't seen her since everyone came charging out of the WHEEL.

The group climbed amid shouts of anger and pain from the beast. When they reached the foot of the temple steps, they turned to observe what was happening below.

"They're still cutting the fucker," Morrow said, a hint of satisfaction in his weary voice.

Ned nodded, still catching his breath. "Looks like a whole bloody tentacle laying behind him. That'll hurt some."

"But he's still coming." Rei sat to rest on a thick, dusty step. "Why won't it die? This is bad. Mega bad."

Indeed, it seemed to Tilly that despite the near constant attacks by the kites, and the dozens of bleeding wounds on its body, the Hundun still approached. In fact, it seemed to gain speed. That they might need to resort to rocks and thick tree branches as weapons was not a good thought. Tilly looked around the ragtag group and tried to assess what they had going for them other than an oversized mechanical fist and a machete. Behind them, smoke from Kalidas' temple poured into the dark clouds, making it the worst possible shelter imaginable.

"Do you not travel with kites of your own?" Mingmei emerged from the shadows of nearby trees, followed by a horse-faced man and ox-woman, both semi-clothed in muddy tatters. The three carried one kite each, save for Mingmei, who held two. "They are quite a handy tool in this fight." Mingmei held one kite out to Tilly, the one with a blank face to it.

"I thought you'd gone. I was sure..." Tilly didn't take the time to explain to Mingmei why she was surprised the tiger-woman was still around. It seemed disappearing was the smartest thing for any of them to do in the situation. In fact, Tilly found it hard to begrudge Captain Nancy for running out on the group. She wanted to say that running was smart because it wasn't their fight, but the doctor had made it a war everyone had to wage. If they didn't, all would be lost for civilizations.

Tilly held the primitively constructed kite and thought back to the times her father had handed her a canvas and told to create something for practice. As she scanned the messy, stained cloth Mingmei had handed her, a design came to mind.

As if reading Tilly's thoughts, Mingmei said, "I was afraid of the doctor and the things he could do. The damage he could bring upon us by tampering with things he knew nothing about. I know the legends of the Hundun. I do not fear Kalidas. Nor do my friends Gozu and Mezu." She indicated the largest among the ox-headed and horse-faced people with her. "They are prepared to take their place among the mythologies our countries have told for a thousand lifetimes. The others will follow them."

"I'm not a part of your history," Tilly said. "I'm someone who wandered up a river."

"And yet here you are." Mingmei pointed to the kite. "You have little time to finish that, so stop looking foolish and get to work."

"I won't need much time." Tilly knelt on the ground and grabbed an ashen piece of wood that had fallen from the temple. It should have scalded her fingers but was cool to the touch. There was no time for her to ponder that fact, so she leaned over and made a line on the kite. It became a sweeping eye-like arch across the center and jagged points for the teeth. She drew a jawline, then wide angry eyes. She worked in a frenzy like never before. It took a minute at most to create a dragon she was pleased with.

"What do we do?" Saburo asked.

"Stay out of the way for now." Tilly pointed to the bushes from which Mingmei and her companions had recently emerged. "Hopefully, you'll know when it's time to either get involved or run for your lives."

"Wait." Mingmei raised her paw before Morrow could run for cover. "That mechanical hand you drag with you. It makes you strong, yes?"

"Stronger," the Scot said. "Absolutely."

"When we get Kalidas inside…" Mingmei pointed toward the temple. "Could you destroy that center column? The other supports have decayed enough that it is doubtful they can support the rock that forms the ceiling on their own."

"But…"

"When we get it inside, you must bring the roof down and trap it inside."

Tilly heard the conversation and didn't like the gist of it, but she understood that the resulting action would bring about the end of Kalidas' reign for now. "You heard her. Once we're inside, start pounding on that support column. With any luck, we can crush him in his own temple."

"But you'll be…"

"We'll be fine, mister Morrow," Tilly said. "We'll escape out the side door. We've used it before." She pushed the man hard enough to show she meant what she said. "Now go. Hide until it's time, then go all crazy Scot on its ass."

Once everyone else was out of the way, the quartet of Tilly, Mingmei, Gozu, and Mezu spread out, and one-by-one, tossed their kites into the air. Each gained altitude with little effort on the part of the three holding the strings. They then turned to Tilly and nodded for her to do the same. In all the years she had tested kites for her father, none had jumped into the air the way this one did. Before she could even release it, the thing felt like it was trying to take off of its own volition, practically vibrating in her hands. When she finally released it, it took a mere tug on the string to get the dragon-adorned kite to take flight. A breeze pulled the kite higher and higher, and while hers didn't quite hold as steady as the others, it flew as high in the sky.

They were waiting as Kalidas crested the hill not one hundred feet in front of them. Its bloated and sliced body was bloody from the gauntlet of vengeful beasts. Kalidas opened its largest mouth to roar its angry declaration, exposing more than just the one. Lining Kalidas' throat, more mouths gnashed their teeth, growled, and added to the singularly terrifying pitch of the local god's shriek.

All four standing at the temple entrance stumbled from the bombast of the creature's declaration. Tilly's kite wavered, dipping in the air and trembling in the wind. Even as it changed direction, she manipulated the string with expert fingers, aware of what it needed, what it desired to stay aloft. As she righted her own kite, another one faltered. The horse-faced man's kite drifted off to the right, threatening to tangle its string in the others.

Nearby, Mezu fell to his knees, staring up at Kalidas.

"No," Mingmei said. "Fight the beast. Do not be hypnotized by his horror and his lies."

Mezu's lips moved, but no sound came. A moment later, he tumbled over on his side, eyes still focused on Kalidas. When his hand opened, the string slid through his fingers. Mezu's kite soared high in the air over Kalidas, pulled by the wind and unanchored by its champion.

Gozu shouted "èmó." It was a word Tilly knew as demon or devil. The ox-woman used her thick arms to yank her string backward. Her kite dove at Kalidas. Instead of cutting it or slicing at an appendage, the kite landed with a thunk, embedding itself in the Hundun's skin behind the monster's left eye. The ox-woman snorted in satisfaction and yanked harder on the string.

"No shit?" Tilly couldn't help but smile. She had doubted simple kites could ward off evil, let alone be used as physical weapons to combat that evil face to face.

To reinforce the notion, Mingmei manipulated her kite as well. She made it dip and twirl above Kalidas, building up speed, whipping it into a frenzy. It cut at the beast's fluttering wings and tore away dull feathers. Then, she made her instrument dive as Gozu's had. The kite buried itself deep in the Hundun's back. "*Pāishǒu,*" Mingmei mumbled. She tugged hard on her line, ensuring the weapon's security, then looked expectantly to Tilly.

"I don't know..." Tilly said, shaking her head. "This isn't something I know how to do. I've never—"

"You can make a kite dive, surely." Grimacing with the effort of keeping her line taut, Mingmei revealed long teeth. As the Hundun twisted and thrashed in an attempt at removing the kites from its back, her feet slid through the dirt. "Please, the two of us cannot do this alone. We need you."

Not allowing herself to dwell on the weight of the situation, Tilly imitated her two companions. She yanked hard on the string. The kite climbed before she dropped it back down like an anvil. The point of the diamond-shaped object cut through grey flesh. It embedded itself in Kalidas' back, sending a cloud of pink mist into the air.

"You've done it," Mingmei shouted. "That should hold. Now comes the hard part."

Dread over what could possibly come next replaced Tilly's brief moment of pride. "That wasn't hard enough?"

"Now we drag him back to his home and bury him there."

"Ya'll must be kidding," Tilly said. "Can't we just kill him?"

"Pull," Mingmei shouted. "Pull like the devil himself is on your heels."

Tilly did as the tiger-woman said. As the three of them put their muscle into it, Kalidas bellowed. The simple kites with their bamboo frames and paper-thin cloth somehow held. When Tilly turned to check their progress, not only were the kites still firmly anchored to the beast, but they were digging further into the monster's flesh. The kites burrowed even deeper the harder they pulled. Soon half of Tilly's crude dragon had sunk into Kalidas.

Gozu shouted something in Chinese. The words escaped Tilly's understanding, but their meaning soon made sense. Gozu and Mingmei climbed the first step to the temple. They quickly did their best to move on to the next. Mingmei slung her string over her shoulder and pulled with all she had. The strain rippled through her feline features.

Kalidas seemed determined to not go quietly. Its remaining tentacles flailed and grasped at trees and rocks to anchor itself, to stop the slide forward. With every tug of the lines, the monster spasmed and cried. Some of its mouths gurgled with fluid. Its discordant wings became lethargic and lazy, both signs that encouraged Tilly to keep fighting and pulling.

Saburo and Rei charged out from the trees, determined to take some sort of action.

"Get back," Mingmei shouted. "You can't help here."

The pair ignored her and dropped to Mezu's side. Each took hold of the horse-faced man's shabby clothing and worked to pull him into the brush. Tilly worried about them, but their actions were too selfless for her to chide them for running headlong into danger.

The three continued to strain as hard as their bodies allowed. Mingmei finally spoke up. "We're stuck," she said. They were halfway up the stairs but making no further progress. "He's tethered himself to something. I don't know what to do." Whether or not Gozu understood, she chuffed air from her nose, then sneezed in reply.

The air suddenly hissed overhead a moment before two small explosions rocked Kalidas to the side. The bursts appeared as red and orange flowers blooming slowly on the Hundun's side. Fire spilled over its hind end. Seconds later, two large drones zipped over the temple, their engines rattling and smoking.

"Low-fis? Here? I thought they wouldn't travel this far upriver?" Tilly scanned the skies. More Low-fis emerged, but before she could count them, her string went slack. Mingmei admonished her, urging Tilly to renew her efforts in dragging Kalidas back. The fire from the Smog Hags' attack spread quickly, spurred on by feathers and flesh. The smell reached Tilly quickly. "*Fucking hell*! He smells like all get out."

The trio yanked and coerced Kalidas up the steps inch by precious inch. They were aided by another Low-fi that strafed the monster with a machine gun, gifting them with a less energetic opponent to work with. Within minutes, they'd wrestled the angry beast up the steps, past the front pillars and into the temple's enormous main room. The fires still raged, though a lack of flammable materials, and that solid rock surrounded it kept the flames from moving beyond the great shrine to Kalidas.

"Good. Now we drop it into the pit," Mingmei said. "And we

shall be rid of this scourge." Mingmei and Gozu dug for purchase on the rough rock-hewn floor and pulled again.

"We have to drag him further?" Tilly's arms and legs trembled from the exertion they'd already endured. Her hands burned from gripping the string and twisting it around them for a better hold. The fibers dug into her fingers. The string burned a trail down her palms every time it slipped. It was the most intense pain Tilly had ever endured… until it wasn't. The taut string suddenly went slack in Tilly's hands.

Behind Kalidas, the smoky-dark sky grew dimmer with the rise of a wall of kites. They formed a barrier behind the Hundun that spurred him faster, forcing him toward Tilly and the group. Unprepared for the beast's sudden rush toward her, Gozu fell to the floor. The battered and weary Hundun must have sensed an opportunity or felt a sudden fear, because as Gozu fell, Kalidas charged forward. It slammed into the temple's walls and dusty adornments, sending sparks and ashes flying from the burning vines and undergrowth.

"Hold fast," Mingmei shouted, taking the string in her mouth. The tiger-woman then bounded forward; her kite string clenched between vise-tight jaws. She deftly avoided fallen timbers and glowing embers as she rushed to the pit's edge. Gozu did not fare so well. Unable to rise fast enough, she was dragged under the immense beast with a sharp shriek of pain.

Tilly ran and pulled, staying out of the reach of swiping tentacles, but wasn't sure what would happen once they reached the pit's edge. It was far too wide to leap over. It was too late to go around it.

As Mingmei and Tilly reached the pit's rim, a bubbling, roiling blackness stared back at them. It was the same material that had transformed Mingmei and others but had left Tilly unharmed. This time, however, the inky substance was on fire. To Tilly, it looked like the oil fire she'd seen during the war. A tanker had been attacked and sunk out in the gulf, setting the sea ablaze for miles around.

Upon seeing the flaming pit, Kalidas attempted to stop its

charge. It proved a few feet too late. The Hundun slammed into Tilly and Mingmei. The force sent all three over the edge, plunging them into the thick fluid.

CHAPTER THIRTY-FOUR

"Wren?" A whispered voice emerged from the darkness. Tilly thought falling into the pit would turn into a fight for her life against Kalidas, but there was no struggle. She felt suspended in concrete, unable to move, unable to speak. The blackness solidified around her. A metallic crunch shook her stiff coffin.

"Wren?" Was it her father's voice far away, or was Mingmei whispering in her ear? The blackness began to fade. It grew lighter, like sunshine breaking through a cloud. "You will not become an ox or a cow," the voice said. "You will not be a horse or cat. You will be what you desire, not what Kalidas wants." The blackness became orange and warm on her skin. Flames fell on her through the dark substance. She could only watch as the fire consumed her from head to toe. It fluttered above her skin, rising from her hands and arms. Tilly could see it, but not feel it beyond a sensation similar to alcohol spreading through her body.

In the distance, somewhere by the entrance, people shouted for her and the others. The sharp thud of metal on stone suggested someone was smashing the pillar. Morrow, most likely. The sounds were a wake up call for Tilly, urging her to move again, despite the strange feelings coursing through her body. The atmosphere inside the pit changed. The dark and hard sticky goo melted, becoming more like a swimming pool, deep with what felt like warm water. She swam for the side and used a nearby jutting rock to pull herself out of the pit and onto the room's dirt floor.

Her legs were unsteady at first, but she managed to build speed, anyway. She raced toward the collapsing entrance. Halfway there, she leapt and spread her arms. It felt like a natural thing to do in the moment, but as she stumbled and fell, it proved a shaky attempt to fly like a bird. Tilly tried to stand but was startled to find thin red feathers jutting from her arms. She fell back to the floor, cautiously touching the feathers on her forearms and biceps. The black goo had thinned, dripping like honey from her arms. More shouts and clangs convinced her to stand again, her mind reeling from the discovery.

She ran and leapt again. This time, and with little effort, she glided for a few feet before landing back on her feet and running further. She could see Morrow pounding on the column up ahead, raising his iron fist, then slamming it into the rock. Beside him, Mezu struck the pillar with small boulders in each hand.

Tilly launched herself skyward again, managing to keep herself moving through the air and out the entrance. Then she lost control. She landed face-first in the weeds and trees at the bottom of the temple's steps. Other than wrenching her shoulder, she was fine. The dry leaves and grass around her, however, were on fire. Tilly gazed down at her still-fiery body, discovering that simply standing there had caused the dry foliage to burst into flames.

Saburo approached from a nearby trail. "Tilly?" The young woman's face showed a mix of awe and concern. "Are you… are you okay?"

"I don't really know." It was an honest self-assessment. She was on fire, but it didn't hurt in the least. And though feathers and large wings protruded from her back, they felt somehow natural. "Honestly."

Low-fis dipped low from overhead and fired at the temple, strafing the pillar. Lifting the huge metal fist over his head, Morrow brought it crashing into the massive support. The steps to the house of Kalidas buckled and cracked. A group of animal-people crested the ridge and darted up the perilous steps. With their shoulders down and hands raised, they slammed themselves against the pillar's crumbling stone. As more gathered, they formed a semicircle around Morrow, careful to give him plenty of room to strike without interference.

With NaNi flying overhead, Saburo monitored its video feed, watched for Kalidas, and called out the structural soft spots. As more ox-men and random beasts piled on, bits of the stone facade fell off in large chunks. Cracks on the sides widened and extended down the length of the principal support.

Tilly pulled her gaze from the flaming aura encasing her, turned away from the feathers that sprouted from her arms. She flapped her wings as hard as she could and launched herself into the sky. Her ascent slowed a hundred, maybe two hundred feet above the temple. The Low-fis zipped beneath her, firing at the temple, and circling back with a strange grace that Tilly couldn't understand when attacking the Cyclone. She witnessed great herds of animal people forming groups and charging up the hill. They were not mindless monsters, but battalions working together for a larger purpose. They worked as one with a common goal, a common enemy.

With a deep breath, Tilly dropped head-first toward the temple and the conflict below. She picked up speed quickly, immediately flying faster than any craft she'd ever piloted. Her arms fell to her sides, streamlining her, making her move at even greater speed. Below, the creatures swarmed the pillar like ants across ice cream. Except for Morrow and his massive fist, she could barely make out her friends.

An actual idea or plan never actually formed in Tilly's head. There wasn't a calculation, no educated guess as to what she should do to end the standoff against the mythological beast, the Hundun, the Great God Long River. It was an instinct, a natural, obvious mechanism that was suddenly wired in her brain. It was as if her body suddenly knew what to do on its own.

With no thought to the possibilities of pain or death, Tilly aimed herself for the pillar and plunged into its center. The impact shook her to her core. For a moment, she saw only spark, fire, and darkness. The roar of ancient spirits quickly replaced the rattle and snap of crumbling rock as they cried out in lost tongues. Ox-men and their ilk shouted battle cries to their enemies across fields of flowers and reeds. The powder of disintegrating rock smelled like ash. Her fiery body came to a stop, leaving Tilly disappointed that the sensation of flight was over. With the pent-up energy inside her having nowhere to go, she sparkled like a star behind her eyes.

She emerged from the temple's support, nearly blinded by the light inside her mind. Lacking control, her body wobbled like a twin-engine troop shuttle with a faulty collective. Tilly dropped to the ground only a few feet from Ned and Saburo.

Her fellow soldiers kept their distance as howls and shouts emerged from the nearby pillar. Animal people ran from the crumbling support. The overhang above it sagged, raining down rocks and debris. Morrow did his best to run with his comically large metal fist cradled to his chest. Gozu followed, mixed with the crowd of creatures. The stampede parted as it approached Tilly the way a river avoids a boulder.

Behind the masses, Kalidas bellowed in anger as the temple collapsed upon it. The god's indignant voice crumpled several of the animal-people to the ground with its sheer power. Though, his voice wasn't enough to stop the rocks from crumbling upon him. As a single tentacle snaked from the temple, an age-old section of mountain crushed the Hundun and killed groups of unfortunate ox and horse people who couldn't move away fast enough. The Hundun's appendage desperately flopped and swiped at the air, crushing sections of the stairs and the remains of a pillar. Each swipe crushed stone to dust until the flailing arm dropped and moved no more.

The group stood watch as the hillside reclaimed the temple of Kalidas. Dust from the ancient throne room and chambers filled the sky with dark smoke, like that from a tire fire. And as Tilly emerged from her fog, her crew seemed conflicted whether to watch the structure fall, or stare at her. Both options appeared to freak them out equally.

"Are you some sort of phoenix?" Saburo asked, her stare less frightened than curious.

"No, she is some sort of *jiāoliáo*," Mezu said. "They call them--"

"Wrens," Tilly said, still stunned by her sudden transformation. "They're some sort of fiery wren." Unlike when she'd first seen the Hundun's other creations, she didn't feel confused or ill. She felt no terror at what she'd become. Her mind was completely clear and focused. Her own transformation was somehow comforting and natural to her. It was a new stage of her existence, like a butterfly from a larva. She held out her arms and waved them, admiring the movement of the feathers.

But even as Tilly marveled at what she'd become, the flames that engulfed her died out with a flicker and a puff of blue smoke. "Hey," she said with disappointment. "I was getting used to that."

"It will come back one day." Gozu put her hand on Tilly's back and patted her roughly.

"What about Mingmei?" Tilly looked back at the temple's remains, concerned her friend might be trapped inside. "Is she… dead?"

"No. She lives inside you. Quite literally. I am sure you will hear her voice when you need the council of a good friend." Gozu smiled, baring her blocky, oxen teeth. It was hard to miss the blood that soaked her fur and the dark patches where she'd been burnt in the fiery temple. "You fell into the pit, did you not?"

"Yes."

"And so did Mingmei?"

"Yes. But…"

Gozu closed her eyes and said, "The two of you merged in there, became one entity. I can feel it."

"But…" Tilly shook her head. "How do you know?"

Behind her, Morrow laughed. "The bird lady is asking the huge horse man how the weird black pit thing affected her and her cat woman friend?" He shrugged. "Maybe nod and smile and agree with him?"

It was advice that Tilly took to heart. How could these things be explained? A legend had emerged from the past and made a bid to convert the world into human-animal hybrids simply because someone wanted to save the world. It would take years to unpack every part of that scenario.

"Do we go home now?" Rei asked. "Do we *ever* go home again?" He stared at Tilly, as he had when they'd talked in the warehouse. One of his eyes appeared to be his natural black color. He'd lost a contact somewhere in the fight. The other eye still had the glint from the contact, indicating some sort of romantic interest on his part. Tilly was confused. How on Earth could he be attracted to her in the shape she was in? Perhaps it wasn't love, but admiration? She'd never taken the time to really learn the meanings of all the colors.

"I'm not sure polite society is prepared for a flaming bird woman and her half animal friends," Tilly said. She wiped blood from her face with the remnants of her shirt and felt a fluffy texture on her cheeks she hadn't expected. How much did she look like a bird to everyone else? "I'd bet you dollars to donuts they'd have trouble letting me on a transport back to America."

"The two of us must stay here," Mezu said, gesturing toward Gozu. "We will make it our duty to guard the temple and watch for the return of Kalidas."

"Fuck me," Morrow said, eloquent as always. "He's coming back?"

"It could be centuries, my friend," Gozu said. "It could be a millennium."

"So, none of us will have to deal with him?" The fact seemed to ease Morrow's stress.

"Gozu and I must keep these tribes together." Mezu pointed to the riverbank below. Thousands of animal-people had gathered around the smoking temple, looking up at Tilly and her group. On the plateau, those that had survived the collapse looked to them as well. "These people must be allowed to contend with their curse in a land unburdened by the outside world's judgment or greed."

Regardless of who eventually found the victims of Doctor Oscar's experiments and his misguided use of Kalidas the Hundun's terrible powers, Tilly knew the world would never be the same. Not when enormous ox-men and tiger-ladies existed. Word was sure to get out. If they'd sent Harrison and his expedition up the river to find Oscar, then the Hōfuna corporation had a good idea of what was there. If they sent more than one team before, they'd surely send another. What the next team would find would be a much more prepared group of animal people. Ones that understood what they were and were aware of their place in the world. The next expedition would find a people no longer living in fear of the Great God Long River, no longer controlled by his will. They'd find a people who had learned never to trust the intentions of an outsider.

"That sounds like a cue to leave if I ever heard one." Saburo watched a trio of Low-fis rattle overhead and vanish to the east, where they had first encountered them.

"Maybe a quick nap first?" Exhausted, Rei sat down, and for all the world, looked as if he was already out cold.

CHAPTER THIRTY-FIVE

Tilly slid and cursed her sore muscles as she climbed the muddy hill toward the village. It had been only a few days since the ordeal at the WHEEL, and her whole body ached from the transformation it had gone through. She lost her feathers soon after they'd entombed Kalidas in the temple. It was for the best, she supposed. After all, she couldn't ride in the boat with the others out of fear she'd catch the boat on fire. Walking home would risk setting the forests ablaze should her flaming aura return. Though everything else had gone, her skin retained a reddish-rust tint.

She looked to the east, scanning as far as she could see. In the back of her mind, she felt a voice rising to guide her actions, and wondered if it could be Mingmei talking to her. The feline vibe made her entire body shiver with the need to communicate. Or maybe it was the bit of cat within her purring in contentment.

In the refugee village's main street, Tilly searched for the little blonde boy she'd noticed the first time she was there.

"Hey," Tilly shouted after finally locating him. "Where's your kite?"

"What?" The kid looked around to see who else the stranger might be talking to.

"Didn't I see you pulling a kite along the other day?" Tilly asked as she approached. "What happened to it?"

"It wouldn't fly, so I tossed it in the bin." The boy pointed to a nearby dumpster.

"I can help you make it work," Tilly said. "I know a few things about how to make kites." She went to the trash and rooted around, pulling out a couple of things she thought might help before reaching the broken and discarded kite. "Look, we could probably use some thin leaves in place of paper. That might work. And this wire. If we strip this wire down, we can use it in place of string."

"It's okay, I don't want it."

"No, it'll be easy," she said. "You'll be the envy of all your friends. And if you watch closely, you can teach them how to do it."

The boy looked skeptical as he watched her gather all the bits she needed for the kite. "I should really go inside," he said. "Maybe you can teach somebody else how to do that?"

"I don't know, kid. I'm not sure if there is anyone else that wants to learn it."

"*Good morning, Saburo. You have missed your last ten swimming lessons. Would you like to catch up*?"

Tilly turned to find Saburo standing a few yards away, watching her interact with the child. Further back, Ned leaned against a post.

"This NaNi you gave me keeps telling me I need to learn something," Saburo said. "So far, it has suggested backgammon, skydiving, lemonade mixing, and now swimming. You know what it's talking about?"

Tilly nodded. "Sure, dismiss the notices. I could teach you something, but I doubt you really want to learn how to make traditional Japanese kites."

"What? You don't think we can learn?" Ned limped over to join them. "I mean, we've got time, haven't we?"

"Yeah," Saburo said. "We don't exactly have a plan for getting back to Japan quite yet. We can't take the boats down river into Chinese-held territory. I don't think they'll let us pass without a few questions. And I doubt another helicopter is going to drop in anytime soon."

"Well, we have boots. We could always walk home."

"I think that would be a long journey." Tilly watched them both standing there with uneasy smiles on their face, and wondered if she even remembered enough about kite making to explain it to them.

She gazed down at the pathetic excuse for supplies scattered on the ground at her feet. It took a moment of thought, but she picked up the bits and pieces and began to make something of them.

Big Weird Thank You List

This is a weird book. It took a lot of people to convince me that it was weird in a good way and keep me working on it.

Thanks to fellow writers Heidi Ruby Miller, Mercedes Yardley, and Lee Murray for being willing to talk me down from the weird imposter syndrome ledge on numerous occasions while I was writing and submitting this book. Thank you, a million times.

Thanks to my publishers, past and present, for their encouragement and enthusiasm for my weird ass stories.

Thanks to my family for constantly supporting me, and for their ability to get weird with me at the drop of a hat. Love you all.

About the Author

Ohio native Matt Betts is a pop culture junkie—sometimes to levels that are considered unhealthy by the Surgeon General. He grew up on a steady diet of giant monsters, comic books, and horror novels, all of which creep into his own work. Matt's speculative poetry and short fiction have appeared in a number of anthologies and journals. *Red Gear 9* is a sequel to his first novel, the steampunk / zombie / alternate history adventure, *Odd Men Out*. His other books include *White Anvil, Sasquatch Onslaught,* and *The Boogeyman's Intern*. Matt's novel, *Carson of Venus: The Edge of All Worlds,* and the prequel comics, *Carson of Venus: The Eye of Amtor,* are continuations of a series created by science fiction legend, Edgar Rice Burroughs.